PUSH
BACK

By James Marx

Burning Chair Limited, Trading As Burning Chair Publishing
61 Bridge Street, Kington HR5 3DJ

www.burningchairpublishing.com

By James Marx
Edited by Simon Finnie and Peter Oxley
Cover by Burning Chair Publishing

First published by James Marx, 2020
This edition published by Burning Chair Publishing, 2021

ISBN: 978-1-912946-21-1

PUSH BACK

JAMES MARX

ONE

Smoke curled from the barrel of my gun and my ears were ringing. In the enclosed space of my kitchen the gunshots had been deafening.

Two cops lay sprawled on the floor, both dead.

The older cop had been called Gibbs, the younger guy Harris. That was about as much as I knew.

I had met them only five minutes earlier and right until a few seconds ago had no idea of the violence ahead.

The refrigerator behind where Gibbs had been standing was splattered with blood, bone fragments and brain matter. His body had fallen back against the silver metal door leaving a gory smear as he collapsed. It was a single shot and he had died instantly, which is what happens when you shoot a man in the face at close range with a .357 Magnum revolver.

Harris had taken two hits. The first a body shot that his ballistic vest gave him some protection from, but it had still punched the wind out of him. The second was another head shot. He'd knocked over a kitchen chair as he dropped to the wooden floor. His blood now crept slowly over the boards leaving dark stained lines in the joints. Forensics would like finding that.

Three bullets, three seconds. Not slow but not particularly fast either. It didn't matter. The end result was the same. Two dead cops shot with my gun and in my home.

Now the barrel of the .357 – my own gun – was pointed straight at me.

I hadn't been the one to pull the trigger and kill Gibbs and

Harris. I had no reason to. My gun was in the gloved hand of the real killer who now had it aimed at my head.

I remained kneeling on the hard floor with my hands behind my head and adrenaline hammering hard through my arteries.

The killer should have pulled the trigger right then and there and finished me off, but he didn't.

That was his second mistake.

His first was shooting the two cops. In my book he was now as good as dead. Despite the fact he was a cop himself.

I had first met Detective Peter Killick after he joined the Portland Police Department as a rookie detective. It must have been a dozen years ago when I was still a serving Detective Sergeant. He was a slimy little shit then and he was still a slimy little shit now. He had always been the kind of snide backstabber and political climber that made my fists itch. I had never trusted him but hadn't been partnered with him at any point; fortunately for me, doubly fortunate for him.

Killick grinned at me. He had been blessed with a good set of teeth, evenly spaced and well proportioned, the sort that movie stars pay thousands to get. But judging by the coffee stains and plaque Killick didn't care much for dental hygiene.

His narrow features were accentuated by high cheekbones under sharp grey eyes and greasy blonde hair untidily slicked back. It occurred to me that he could have been a good-looking guy if he'd given some thought to it and made an effort. I don't know, maybe what's inside a man always ends up showing through. As it was he looked like a vicious pimp.

"What now?" I asked, managing to keep my voice steadier than I expected.

"You'll find out," he said, nudging Harris's leg with the toe of his scuffed shoe. There was no response. I didn't know why Killick even checked. The guy was dead. Having your brains blown out tends to do that.

Many folks from the Southern states have an accent that can sound rich and musical. Their speech is a pleasure to listen to.

Killick came from Alabama, however his voice had an annoying nasal whine that made me think of a petulant child.

"The angle's all wrong," I told him.

"What?"

"I should be standing. For ballistics."

"I know," he sneered. He hadn't known.

"Want me to get up?"

Killick nodded. "Easy now. Nice and slow."

I rose carefully to my feet, hands still behind my head.

That was his third mistake. Letting me stand.

I guessed he just saw a middle-aged guy with graying hair, someone who wouldn't be a problem to handle. Okay, he knew I'd been a cop, a Detective Sergeant, but now I was retired. I'd been out of the game for nearly a year. Out of practice. Not much of a threat.

I wanted him to keep thinking that way.

What he didn't know, or didn't care about, was that before joining the Portland Police Department I'd been in the army.

Specifically I'd been a sergeant in the US Rangers for more years than I care to remember. I was used to adapting to rapidly changing high pressure situations and improvising solutions within a variety of environments. Do that for most of your life and the habits stay with you.

Then there were those years spent in the Portland PD. Being a detective wasn't a desk job as far as I was concerned. You had to be fit physically but any cop's greatest asset is their mind and being able to think quickly on their feet.

Even now, in my mid-fifties, it still made me a dangerous adversary.

Killick was about to find that out.

"What about the gun?" I asked Killick.

He looked puzzled. Evidently he was making this up as he went along, and he wasn't the sharpest tool in the box.

"It's my gun," I explained to him. "Why would I be shot from that distance with my own gun? Doesn't make sense."

"I know," Killick repeated. He switched the .357 to his left hand and reached inside his jacket, fumbling for his own gun.

Fourth and final mistake.

Before he had time to react, I closed the gap between us, shoving my revolver aside and pinning the hand that had closed around his own gun as I followed up, head-butting him hard in the face.

It was enough to stun but not enough force to put him down. I head-butted again – harder. Killick reeled back and I wrestled the revolver out of his grip. He may have been skinny but he had a wiry strength, and I could feel him tugging his gun out of its holster. I brought the revolver up, used it like a hammer and smashed the hard metal butt on the bridge of his nose. He gave a wet yelp as blood burst from his nostrils and flowed over his mouth. The grip on his own gun loosened. I hit him a second time on the top of the head with the revolver, like I was splitting a log, and he dropped unconscious to the floor, his scalp bleeding freely.

I crouched down and checked his holster. He had a police-issue Glock 17 automatic. I removed it, stood back up and looked around at the carnage.

My head hurt and I was about as confused as I was likely to be about what had just gone down over the last five minutes.

I only had the vaguest of ideas why Killick had shot Harris and Gibbs, and why he had been about to shoot me, but couldn't make much sense of it.

There was also the big question of what to do next.

Sure, I should call the cops, but a gut feeling told me Killick wasn't working alone, so that could mean I was back to square one and would end up at the wrong end of a gun again.

There was also the undeniable fact that the shots that had murdered Harris and Gibbs had come from my revolver. There was no point disposing of it. I'd been dutiful and logged it along with a ballistics profile while I'd still been on the force. Forensics would know the bullets that had killed the two cops had come from my revolver. Having the weapon itself was a formality.

Even if I was given the chance to say what had actually

happened, who would believe me?

Although I'd retired from the force after many years of service, I couldn't say I had an untarnished reputation. I got the job done the best and most efficient way I saw fit. And if that meant physically motivating perps to sign their confessions then so be it. Not something I look back on with pride.

Killick was still a serving detective. It would be his word against mine and I could see which way that would go. I'd be spending serious time in jail – assuming I made it there alive in the first place.

Options played out before me. Nothing looked good.

On the plus side, at least I wasn't dead.

Fourteen hours earlier my biggest problem was deciding on what brand of beer to take when meeting my nephew.

TWO

"Uncle Dean?"

"Sean? That you?" I held the cell phone to my ear. I'd only just switched off the circular saw in my workshop and still felt slightly deafened. I found it hard to believe how grown up the boy was. Correction – at twenty he was very much a man now. It made me feel real old.

"Yeah," said my nephew. "Can we talk?"

"Sure." It had been a month or so since I last spoke to him, and longer since speaking to my sister, his mother. "How are you, how's your mom?"

"All good thanks." There was a short pause. "Just wondering if you're free tonight?"

"Tonight?" That was a short order. I wondered what was up.

"Yeah." Sean paused. "Only if you're not doing anything."

This was out of the blue. Was there trouble at home? Unlikely. I had nothing planned that night other than a couple of beers and an old Bruce Willis movie I'd recorded. Anyway, what sort of uncle refuses to meet with his nephew.

"Tonight's good," I told him. "Everything all right?"

"Yeah, all good." The delay this time was barely perceptible, but I knew something was troubling him. Maybe a girl? Certainly something he couldn't, or wouldn't, talk to his mom or stepdad about. "Just fancy catching up and getting a bit of advice is all."

Yeah, probably girl trouble I reckoned.

"Sure," I said. "Want to swing around here?"

"I was thinking we could do some fishing, somewhere quiet.

Maybe down by Barton Bridge like we used to?" said Sean.

I smiled. I knew the place well. I used to take him there even before they'd built the new asphalt parking lot. He loved seeing the outline of the arched metal bridge at night and trying to catch fish in the moonlight. Not that we caught many, but it was still fun. I'd tell him stories of my time in the US Rangers – exaggerated of course – but like any young boy he wanted to hear about excitement and danger and action. We had a good time.

His dad, a guy called Mike Carter, was a close friend of mine and sometimes he'd join us and pull me up on my Ranger tales.

He had every right to. He was also a Ranger – a medic in the same squad as me – and had patched me up on more than one occasion. I repaid the favor by introducing him to my sister, Claire, one Thanksgiving. The rest, as they say, is history.

"Yeah, it's been a while. I'd like that." I told Sean. "Meet you about 7pm in the park?"

"Sounds good."

"Want me to bring a couple of beers?" I could say that now he was *almost* twenty-one.

"That'd be great. Thanks Uncle D."

"No problem – see you then."

"Cool, see you later," finished Sean, ending the call.

I remained standing looking at the phone for a moment, feeling a measure of worry that there was something wrong but happy about seeing my nephew again.

It also brought back memories of Mike, Sean's dad. I missed the guy like a brother. He'd been taken before his time but there was no one to blame.

They said the heart attack was unexpected and sudden and he wouldn't have known much as it struck so quickly. I don't know about that, but I hoped it was true.

That was ten years ago and since then Claire had remarried and Sean had gained a new stepfather in the shape of a desk jockey accountant called Richard Cresswell.

To be fair, he was okay. He ran his own investment company

and there was no denying he provided well for both Claire and Sean, but it was the sort of family relationship that was balanced in favor of money rather than time.

I still found him hard to get used to after the loss of Mike.

I went back to the cutting table, enjoying the comforting smell of sawn timber, and got back to work.

*

After a day spent in the workshop, I showered the smell of machined wood off myself, cooked a lean steak, grabbed a peppery salad and let the TV news wash over me as I ate. I checked my watch. I was in good time: it was only 6pm.

I found a four-pack of Canadian Moosehead beer in the refrigerator, picked up a fishing rod, net and bait box from the garage and went out to the pick-up.

As I got nearer I knew something was wrong. The old Dodge sat canted oddly on the cement flags of the drive. I placed the beer, net and rod down and circled around the truck. Straight away I saw the problem.

The tires on the far side were flat.

I got closer. The sidewalls had been slashed. Deep cuts, straight through the tough rubber. It would have taken some doing. Plenty of effort to stab a blade in that hard and pull.

I looked around. I don't know who or what I expected to see, but there was no one around. The growing suburban dusk was silent and unmoving.

I thought about giving Sean a call, to let him know I'd be running late, but it was getting too dark to start changing wheels and tires; and besides, I had another option.

Ten minutes later I was on the road, the soft rumble from the pipes of my Triumph Thunderbird Storm motorbike surrounding me as the warm September air tugged at the sleeves of my leather jacket. The panniers on the big bike were just large enough to fit the beers in and that was about all. To be honest I wasn't too bothered about the fishing, and I guessed Sean wouldn't be that troubled either.

My route took me out along Eagle Creek Road. It's a smooth and little-used road and it was nice to have an excuse to be out on the bike for once.

There is a relaxing freedom to riding a good bike on a quiet road. You still have a keen focus on your surroundings and piloting the machine, but another part of your brain becomes calm and allows you to solve problems you never thought you had.

As it was I was thinking about what Sean and I might be chatting about, wondering about giving some of my old Ranger buddies a call or at least dropping them a line, and maybe getting a security camera on my driveway.

I rode swiftly and made good time. Even after the delay with the tires I was going to be early.

A couple of miles before the Barton Park Road turn, I saw flashing lights and a patrolman flagging me down. It was either a speed trap or a spot check. I guessed the latter as I'd only been cruising. Even so, the Triumph was a powerful bike and it was easy to break the limit without realizing it, so perhaps it was even money.

I slowed and pulled in to the side of the road.

The guys were only doing their job; I'd been there and done that. But I didn't think an older guy on a bike posed much of a problem. If it was me out there, I'd have been pulling over some of those Jap cars with bean can exhausts that were a favorite with many of the dope heads of the region. Maybe things had changed since my day.

I dropped the kickstand and shut off the Triumph as one of the patrolmen approached. He carried more weight than he should have and looked soft. Too much time sat in a car and not enough time on foot patrol or in the gym. Or too much fast food. Most likely a combination of the two.

"License," he demanded, clicking on his flashlight and shining it at me. His partner stayed by the patrol car keeping his eyes on me.

I unzipped the jacket and pulled out my wallet and license, flipping it open so he could see my photo. He took my wallet and examined the picture. He shone the torch back into my face. I wear an open helmet and had tugged the bandana down off my face so there should have been no problems identifying me.

"Wait here," he said. He turned and went back to the car. I saw him slump into the seat and guessed he was on the radio. The other patrolman glanced at what he was doing but kept looking back at me.

A family sedan swooshed by, lights on, the shape hard to make out in the dusk. Dark and anonymous. They weren't pulled in. Other than that, the road remained quiet.

I relaxed back on the bike's saddle and waited.

The overweight cop took far longer than I expected. I checked my watch. Now I was going to be late.

I heard the distant howl of a car being driven fast. It got closer and even through the helmet it sounded like something loud, tuned and Japanese. It wasn't any wholesome American V8, that was for sure.

I saw it approach, slowing as it got nearer. The police cruiser's lights were still on, so the driver had plenty of warning. I heard them change down and the corresponding rasp from the exhaust. I was right. It was low and Japanese and showy purple neon lights glowed underneath like it was some kind of spaceship.

I looked back at the cops sat in the patrol car. They barely seemed to notice Starship Obvious as it roared by. I heard it accelerate away and shook my head.

That they choose to stop me and let something like that pass by without more than a glance irked me.

Another half a minute passed, and I was about to get off the bike when the fat patrolman opened the door and heaved himself back out of the cruiser. He took a moment to adjust his belt then ambled over to me. He took his time and was in no rush. He handed back my wallet and license.

"Sorry to have kept you Mr. Riley. Have a good evening, sir."

"No problem." My smile was tighter and less genuine than it should have been, but then again I guess I don't tend to smile a lot anyway.

The Triumph growled into life as I thumbed the starter. I heeled up the kickstand, gave the cops a nod and rejoined the road.

Once out of sight I opened the throttle. The bike snarled and I rode as fast as the beam from the twin lamps let me. I reached the turn off for Barton Park Road and powered the bike onto it, riding down towards the river and the parking lot at the end of the lane. On the way a dark Chevrolet sedan passed me going the other way. I thought nothing of it at the time.

The parking lot was deserted apart from one car, an old model Ford Focus hatchback in white that I was sure was Sean's. I parked the Triumph in the bay next to it.

I took off my helmet and gloves, left them on the bike and checked out the white car. There was no one inside. I left it and walked over towards the far end of the parking lot to the bank by the water's edge.

The Clackamas River flows under Barton Bridge, which can be seen from the riverside at the end of Barton Park Road. I've always liked the place even if the fishing is mediocre at best. I once caught a trout, but it was not big enough to claim as any sort of a victory, so I put it right back in the river again. Sometimes it's just about the surroundings and the company.

There was no sign of Sean. I pulled out my cell phone and tried his number. It went straight onto the messaging service. I frowned. That wasn't good. I walked back to the small Ford hatchback and tried the number again, listening for any ringtone coming from inside the car.

I heard nothing. The messaging service picked up again. This time I left a brief message asking him to call me.

I thought long and hard and then called Claire, Sean's mom. My sister. I'd not spoken to her for some time, and I think she had started to prefer it that way.

11

The phone rang four times before a voice answered.

It was Richard, Claire's husband; or 'Dick' as I thought of him though I never said that to his face.

"Hi Richard, it's Dean," I said, trying to be nice. "Is Claire there?"

Dick told me to hold on. At least he didn't tell me to go to hell and hang up. The sound over the line became muffled and I guessed he was checking if Claire wanted to speak to me. There was a delay and I half suspected she would be the one to hang up the phone. I wouldn't really have blamed her if she couldn't be bothered to speak to me.

The last time I'd been over to their place for dinner it had not ended well.

I'd had a bad day, maybe a beer or two more than I should have, and I'd pulled Dick up on his lack of involvement with Sean. In my view when you're in a relationship with someone you love the complete package – and that includes any kids, even if they're grown up.

The discussion had escalated, and I might have said some things that I shouldn't have. We hadn't spoken since then.

Thankfully Sean had not been there at the time.

"What is it Dean?" Straight to it. The tone of Claire's voice clearly told me my call was an unwelcome interruption.

"Hey Claire, you okay?" Formalities. Not that I don't care, but it has to be asked.

"Yeah, fine." She sounded tired. I also noted that she didn't ask me how I was.

I cut to it.

"Is Sean there? He called me earlier."

"No. He said he was meeting some friends for a movie and wouldn't be back until late. Why?"

"No reason," I lied. "Just wanted to have a quick catch up. It's been a while."

"Haven't you got his cell?" she asked.

I lied again and told her I hadn't. She took a moment and gave me the number. It was the one I already had.

"Thank you. I'll try that, but will you let him know I called."

"Yeah," she said. "Okay Dean, is that all?"

Maybe it wasn't the right time to mend bridges, but as she was on the phone I had to try.

"Hey, I'm sorry about last time," I started but Claire cut me off.

"That's really for you and Richard to discuss. Maybe best face to face. When you can find time to manage it." Her implication was that it was something she thought I wouldn't be doing anytime soon. Maybe she was right.

"Okay. Will do."

The line went dead before I had the chance to say anything else. I closed the phone and slipped it back in my jacket pocket.

So either Sean had decided to blow me off and go out with some friends – possible but unlikely without leaving me a message – or he'd lied to his parents, which was more believable. It was troubling, whichever way you cut it.

I looked at the white hatchback. Maybe the car wasn't Sean's after all, but if it wasn't his then where was the owner? There was no sign of anyone else around.

I kept coming back to the fact that, if he wasn't able to make it tonight or had been held up, I knew he would have called and left a message if he could. He was that sort of kid; or man, as he was now.

I was concerned, though part of me thought that maybe I was just worrying unnecessarily.

I walked back over to the bike, took one of the beers from the pannier and headed towards the river, figuring I'd have a drink sitting on the bank while I waited.

There was no surprise it felt a lot cooler by the water. I was glad of my jacket. Leather that can shield you from a hundred miles an hour on a bike has no problem with a chilly night. The breeze had dropped and what clouds there were moved reluctantly across the night sky. I took my time with the beer, looking out at the slow waters and across at the trees on the far shore. The shadowy metal arch of Barton Bridge loomed to my right, silhouetted black against the growing night.

I checked my watch. 7:43pm.

There was no way Sean would have been this late, I was sure of it. I took out my phone and tried his number again. Again it went straight to the messaging service.

Either his phone had been switched off or it was out of battery. For someone of his age group that was almost unheard of. I got up and returned to the parking lot. The white hatchback was still there.

I frowned. I couldn't shake the feeling that Sean was in trouble. I knew what I had to do, and my phone was still in my hand. I pulled up the previous numbers, selected the one I wanted and hit dial.

On the third ring Dick answered again.

"Sorry to call again Richard, I need to check something with you."

I could tell he was tempted to hang up or tell me where to go, but I guess something in my voice stopped him. Instead, he just sounded exasperated.

"What is it now, Dean?"

"Sean drives a white Ford Focus, doesn't he?"

"Yes, why?" I heard the unease plain enough in his voice.

"What's the license plate?"

"Okay, tell me why you want to know." I could sense his annoyance rising.

In retrospect, maybe I could have approached it better, but acting has never been one of my strong points. Even so, I tried to make it sound innocent enough.

"I thought I might have seen him earlier, but I couldn't be sure it was him." Lame.

"Bullshit," said Dick. He didn't believe me for a moment. "What's going on? Is he okay?"

"I don't know. It's probably nothing. Let me have the license and I'll know either way."

Dick reeled off the number. I was looking at the back of the white car as he did. The car was Sean's.

"Well?" he asked.

"Let me get back to you."

"Look, Dean, do you know where Sean is?" Dick's voice held more than an edge of tension. Maybe I'd got it wrong. Maybe he worried more about his stepson than I gave him credit for.

"No, leave it with me and I'll get back to you as soon as I can."

"Come on Dean, what's going on?"

"It's probably nothing. Let me make a couple of calls. I promise I'll get back to you. I'm sure there's nothing to worry about."

I walked slowly around the little white car as we'd been talking but now I stopped. Richard said okay. Again I told him not to worry and ended the call.

But I was most definitely worried.

I'd seen the blood on the driver's doorframe.

THREE

It was only a small amount, and if it hadn't been on the white paint above the black window surround, I'd never have spotted it.

I looked closer at the glass of the side window. There were dark specks of blood there as well.

It was plausible that Sean could have caught his head on the edge of the door frame if he'd been clumsy or unlucky, perhaps when turning and reaching back into the car for something, but that was a long shot and, in my mind, very unlikely.

I took a handkerchief from my pocket. It was fresh and clean, and I used it around one of my fingers to pull the door handle.

The door was locked.

I went around the passenger side and repeated the exercise. The car had central locking, so I'd have been more surprised if it had opened but I had to be thorough.

I'd always been there for Sean in one way or another; after all, his mother was my sister and his father had been one of my most trusted friends. There was no surprise we'd ended up being close. Especially after his father, Mike, had died.

I couldn't be a replacement for his dad, nor was I young enough to be like an older brother. But he was blood and I loved him, so I guess being his uncle suited us both just fine.

I took a breath and tried to think straight.

The facts were that Sean had wanted to meet with me that night. His car was here which meant he had been here at some point.

Okay, I'd been a bit late arriving – but not by much – plus Sean hadn't called me to see where I was, so he would have thought I would be turning up soon in any case.

Why he'd asked to meet up here was still a mystery. It was more than nostalgia. He wanted to talk about something that he couldn't discuss with his mom or dad or any friends. Specifically it was me he needed to talk to.

Then we had the blood on the car. Not much but enough to be of concern.

All my instincts told me he'd been taken, abducted by someone. But I had no idea who or why.

I called the State Police Department directly. One of the advantages of being an ex-cop. You can avoid the switchboard and get straight to those that can act.

I spoke to a lady with the surname Callender who sounded efficient. I briefly introduced myself and got to the point. She made a note of the main details then went through the necessary formalities while I contained my impatience.

She assured me there was someone on the way. I was more grateful than she knew.

*

The first responder was a state patrol car.

As I leant against my bike I'd half expected to see the guys who'd stopped me earlier. Instead, a tall slim black woman with sergeant's stripes stepped out the passenger door and came over to me. Her partner, an equally tall Hispanic guy, got out a couple of seconds later and began checking around the area with a flashlight.

"You Dean Riley?" asked the sergeant.

I nodded.

"Vicky Collins," she said, introducing herself, "and this is Officer Hernandez". It was evident she had been made aware I'd been a cop as there was no bullshit and she got straight to the point. "We're here about your nephew. I understand you have concerns about his whereabouts?"

I told her most of what I knew. I said nothing about Sean coming across as troubled when we'd spoken earlier. At this stage she didn't need to know. We were just going to meet, have a couple of beers, catch up and talk about anything and nothing. That was all.

I didn't want any ideas forming of a young man seeming troubled and leading to thoughts turning to any possible suicide. I knew that wasn't Sean's way.

I could imagine him getting drunk and commiserating with pals because of girl trouble but nothing more than that.

I mentioned the Chevrolet I'd seen leaving along the road, but there were literally thousands of late model Impala sedans in the area and, as I didn't know the plate, I knew that was already a dead end.

Could it be that he'd met some friends and decided to go off with them and it had been their car? But then why no call to me, who he'd specifically asked to come out to meet him? Even if his phone had died, he could have borrowed one of his friends' to make the call.

Besides, would that sort of car really be used by an early twenty-something? It didn't seem their style. Then again maybe it belonged to a friend's parents and had been borrowed for the evening?

I could keep on second guessing myself.

If the driver of the Chevrolet was just a passer-by, would they have seen anything of any use in any case? If they had seen someone falling into the river, they'd have already called 9-1-1 or been burning rubber going to get help.

My conversation with Collins was interrupted as Hernandez called out.

"Hey, Vicky," he said. "Under here."

He was shining his flashlight underneath Sean's car. Both Collins and I got down on hands and knees to look where he was pointing.

There was a single shoe underneath the car, just by the front wheel on the driver's side.

Collins looked across at me.

"Is that your nephew's shoe?"

In truth I had no idea and told her so. I cursed myself. How the hell did I miss that?

From its position it could not have been there before the car arrived. The front wheel would have driven over it and the shoe was undamaged.

We all got to our feet.

"I'm gonna call it in," said Collins. "I best get a detective in here."

"Sure, okay," I said. "But what about cell phone triangulation? If Sean's cell was on earlier then we can get an idea of his movement."

Collins looked at me like I was teaching her to suck eggs.

"It's one of the first things we do now. Didn't give us anything other than him coming out to here, so it must be off or out of juice or he switched it off when he got here."

But I was worried. What twenty year old doesn't keep their cell on, charged and with them 24/7?

Collins went to the cruiser and radioed in her findings. Her partner came over to me.

"You okay?" he asked. I guessed my face must have been showing my concern. I glanced at him.

"Not really," I confessed. Despite the fact I'd been in the army at Sean's age, I was still as worried as hell about my nephew.

The cop patted me on the shoulder and went over to Collins. They talked for a minute or so then Collins came over to me.

"A truck's gonna come out and take the car in." She shook her head. "CSI will check it there."

I looked at her, disbelieving. "No CSI here?"

"It's a public place, apparently not worth doing." Collins sighed. "We'll get more from the car than hundreds of false positives from this place."

Hernandez had disappeared over by the riverside and now he returned.

"Nothing there," he said, shaking his head.

"We'd see more in daylight," I stated.

"Yeah, but that's ten hours away," said Collins, taking another flashlight out of the cruiser and beginning her own slow and methodical tour of the parking lot. I followed alongside her, figuring a second set of eyes on the scene was worth having.

Other than the blood on the doorframe and the shoe under the car there were no signs of any violence.

We took ten minutes to cover the parking lot then turned our attention to the grass and dirt slopes by the river.

There were plenty of footprints, too many to be of use, but no signs of anything suspicious and nothing near to the water's edge.

"From what I'm seeing I don't think he came this way," said Collins. "Not with one shoe anyway."

I agreed. There was also nothing to make me think Sean had been forcibly pitched into the river. If he'd been unconscious there would be drag marks or heavier boot prints as he was carried to the water's edge by whoever had assaulted him.

That was assuming something violent had happened.

He might have slipped getting out of the car, knocked his head, fallen to the ground and lost a shoe in the process. The occupants of the Impala I'd seen could have been taking him to E.R.

I didn't believe it.

I felt now his sounding worried on the phone wasn't girl trouble; it was about something far more serious.

Serious enough for him to be taken by whoever had been in that Chevrolet.

But I had no idea why.

FOUR

My thoughts were interrupted by the arrival of an unmarked Dodge sedan. The detectives Collins had called had arrived. Collins and I walked over to it. Two guys got out of the car. One was around my age and the other a dozen years younger. It was clear that they and Collins and Hernandez knew each other well.

She told them the findings so far and who I was.

The older detective extended his hand, and I shook it.

"Lewis," he said, introducing himself. "And this is Detective Walsh." He indicated his younger partner, who nodded a greeting before heading over to Sean's car along with Collins.

Lewis asked me to confirm my actions again, making notes as I told him everything from my being pulled over right up to the point of Collins' and Hernandez' arrival. I gave him all he needed to know within two minutes.

"Thorough," Lewis commented, referring to what I'd just told him. "You've not been retired from the force long?"

"Just over a year."

"Miss it?"

"Not at times like this."

"Yeah," said Lewis. "I know what you mean."

Detective Walsh returned with the shoe in a plastic bag. He was still wearing his protective gloves and raised the bag for me to see.

"Recognize this at all, Mr. Riley?"

I took a closer look.

It was a black leather dealer boot with contrasting pale grey stitching. A quality item and certainly something I could imagine

Sean wearing.

"What size is it?" I asked.

"Ten."

I don't know why I asked other than it being an obvious thing to do. I didn't know Sean's exact shoe size but size ten sounded about right. But it was also right for over seventy percent of adult males across America.

"It's possible it could be Sean's but it's best to ask Claire, his mother."

Walsh nodded and left me with Lewis, who glanced around as the lights from a six-wheel low loader complete with crane swept across the parking lot.

The driver of the recovery truck shunted it around before backing up and parking adjacent to the white Focus and killing the engine. A moment later he clambered down from the cab. He was a stocky guy, a good bit shorter than me, with a bald head, a massive ZZ Top beard and lurid tattoos over his beefy arms.

Lewis went over to him and I followed.

"Before you load up can you get us in without breaking much?" asked Lewis offering the driver a pair of latex gloves.

"No problem," said the driver, squeezing into the gloves. He grinned at us and took out a strange looking tool from his overalls. It was the weirdest screwdriver I'd seen.

He went over to the car and stuck the device in the driver's door lock. I heard a clicking, whirring and grating sound. The central locking popped and he opened the door for us.

The alarm went off, but the recovery driver was already strolling around to the front of the car. He fiddled with the grille, popped the bonnet and was hidden from view.

Lewis pulled on some latex gloves of his own and leant into the car.

"All neat and tidy in here," he said.

Sean kept the little Ford clean. No trash in the foot-wells and the car smelled fresh. There was nothing in the door pockets except a zip-up case containing some CDs.

The alarm stopped abruptly and the recovery driver let the bonnet slam closed.

Lewis went around to the passenger door, opened it and popped the glove box, checking inside. Just the handbook, a locking wheel nut key, some disposable gloves and a small torch. Nothing else. Just the essentials. Neat and tidy, as he'd said.

Lewis returned to the driver's side and pressed a button on the dash to open the hatchback. The lock clunked. I let him move around to the rear of the car and open the hatch. All that could be seen was a foot pump, a high visibility jacket and a warning triangle.

He checked under the boot mat, saw nothing and shut the tailgate.

No phone. No clues.

"Okay, load it up," he told the recovery driver before turning to me. "CSI will check it out. I won't lie to you; I don't think we'll get much from his car. Walsh and I will check the shoe with Sean's parents, see if we can get some confirmation there." Lewis took a breath. "You sure you can't remember a plate for that other car?"

I shook my head. "Sorry, not even a single letter. It was a dark green Impala, recent but not the latest model. That's all I have."

"Okay." Lewis watched as the recovery driver started the truck and swung the crane over Sean's car then turned back to me. "You might as well get home, Mr. Riley. Thank you for your help and patience. We'll let you know of any progress."

I thanked him and walked back to my bike.

On the way I bid Collins and Hernandez farewell, Walsh had disappeared into the Dodge and was on the radio. In the dim illumination of the interior light, I could see he looked annoyed with whoever was on the other end of the line.

I reached the big Triumph, swung a leg over it, pulled my helmet and gloves on and thumbed the starter. The ride home was slower and I remembered nothing of the journey, or putting the bike away. I did them automatically, almost through muscle memory. There was too much going through my mind.

Something didn't feel right, but I didn't know what. I also felt tired and hollow. There seemed to be nothing I could do about the situation, and it made me feel helpless.

By then it was past midnight, but I didn't feel much like sleeping.

I slumped into my favorite chair, drank a couple of the beers without tasting them and began to watch that Bruce Willis movie I'd recorded. I can't even remember which one it was.

Evidently I must have managed to drop off to sleep in the chair, because a few hours later the morning sun streaming through my front room woke me.

I checked my phone. There were no messages.

I also noted the time.

From my years as a detective sergeant I knew that the first forty-eight hours in any kidnapping or abduction were crucial.

So far ten hours had passed and there was no news.

That was not good.

FIVE

While the phone was in my hand I considered calling Claire and Richard. Maybe they'd had news about Sean, and everyone had simply forgotten to keep me informed. It was wishful thinking. I put the phone back down, got out of the chair and wandered through into my kitchen.

I ran some cold water and washed my face, one of the best ways I know to get properly awake. Then I filled the coffee machine, the second-best way to wake up. I'd have myself a shower after getting a hit of caffeine.

It would take a few minutes for the coffee to be ready so I unlocked the side door, put my boots on and stepped out onto my driveway.

I wanted to have another look at the slashed tires on my truck.

They were both on the side nearest the house, which would have meant whoever did it would have been better hidden from view. No surprise there.

Each cut was two inches wide. I guessed they were probably from a hunting knife. It would need CSI to be sure and that wasn't going to happen just for a slashed pair of tires.

If it had been high school kids doing it as a dare, then why do the two tires; wouldn't one be enough? I walked down my driveway to the roadside and looked along the street.

I could see plenty of neighbors' cars up on their own driveways, all sitting level, all looking fine. Nobody else had been targeted by the slasher. It was just me. I wondered who I'd pissed off recently and couldn't think of anyone. Not recently. There were plenty of folks in the past but they would be more likely to burn the house down or try a drive-by shooting.

Maybe I was just due a dose of bad luck.

I'd happily take that, and more, for news of Sean turning up safe and well.

I went back up the driveway and returned to the kitchen and the welcoming smell of hot coffee. I'd only just poured myself a mug when the chime for the front door sounded.

I left the mug on the table and went through into the lounge.

Through the front window I saw a police cruiser parked outside on the road and an unmarked Chevy Caprice behind it.

It was bad news. Had to be. I swore softly to myself.

If Sean had been alive then a single unmarked car or even just the cruiser would have been enough. I fought down a feeling of nausea and opened the front door. A pair of uniformed cops were standing there. The older of the two spoke first.

"Mr. Riley?"

"Yeah." I nodded.

"I'm Gibbs, this is officer Harris." The older cop indicated his colleague. "May we come in please, sir?"

I nodded again and moved back. The younger guy, Harris, stepped through the doorway and went past me but Gibbs gestured for me to lead the way. I trailed Harris into my lounge and heard Gibbs close the door behind him. I was puzzled by the lack of any detective. I'd expected whoever had been in the Caprice to be the one on point, meeting and talking with me, not the uniformed cops.

"Perhaps you'd like to sit," said Gibbs.

"No. It's okay." I sighed. "Just tell me."

I felt the need for that mug of coffee in the kitchen so there was no point in sitting. Besides I knew what was coming next. The words 'I'm sorry' and 'we've found your nephew' and 'body from the river'. I'd had to say similar things myself to worried families too many times in the past.

But I was wrong.

The younger cop, Harris, spoke first.

"Sir, do you have any firearms in your possession?" That was not a question I was expecting. Harris must have been somewhere in his mid-twenties, so I guess tact wasn't a strong point yet. I looked at him for a long moment then answered the question anyway.

"No, not on me. Got a .357 upstairs. Why?"

"You know why," said a whiny southern voice from the doorway to the kitchen.

I turned. The detective was in plain clothes with his badge stuck prominently in the belt of his jeans. He'd gone up the driveway and entered silently through the side kitchen door. I hadn't even heard his footsteps crossing the hard wooden floor.

He was familiar. I frowned trying to recall his name and also work out what he was on about.

Then it came to me. The nasal southerner was Detective Peter Killick.

He nodded to Harris.

"Go get his piece. Bring it to me."

The young cop asked me where exactly I kept the revolver and I told him. I also told him it was loaded.

In my mind there's no point keeping an unloaded gun and wasting precious seconds loading it in the dark at just the point you might need it. Harris did as the detective asked and disappeared up the stairs. Gibbs rested a hand on the butt of his standard issue Glock 17 automatic. Relaxed and calm but ready to react.

I felt confused. I felt like a suspect.

Killick introduced himself, casually as if it didn't matter. I just nodded.

"Have you found Sean?" I asked Killick. I was still trying to figure out why they were behaving so oddly. I was being slow that morning. Probably because I hadn't got to that coffee yet.

"Why? Where did you leave him?" Killick sneered.

"What?" I snorted. "You seriously think I had something to do with his going missing?"

Killick shrugged. "Maybe so. We have to follow up on all leads.

You know that."

I shook my head, slow and disbelieving. The muscles in my jaw felt tight. They were wasting their time with me.

Killick cocked his head and spoke again, the sneer still on his lips like it was a permanent part of his expression etched on his face.

"Anyway, what's this in your kitchen? Come take a look and you tell me."

He turned in the doorway and disappeared into the kitchen. I followed, shadowed by Gibbs. On the table in the center of the kitchen and next to the steaming mug of coffee was a cell phone. The battery lay separate by the side of the handset.

It was not my phone. That was in the lounge and this one was way too new. Killick pointed to it.

"This yours?" he asked.

I shook my head. "No."

"You recognize it?"

"No. Why?"

There was a trap forming but I didn't know what it was or why it was there. It had to be something to do with Sean. Was this Sean's phone? I asked Killick if it was.

He didn't answer.

The young cop returned, brushed past me and handed my revolver to Killick. At that point I noticed Killick was wearing gloves. He sniffed at the gun.

"Okay Detective, what's this about?" I asked. "Have you found Sean?"

"This has been fired recently." He said looking directly at me.

He was lying; unless by 'recently' he meant last week at the firing range, but I didn't think so. I'd cleaned and oiled it since then.

Then the seriousness of the situation escalated.

"Okay Riley. Get on your knees and put your hands behind your head."

As Killick spoke I sensed both cops behind me tense, both

28

waiting for me to react. This was crazy and I told them so. But no sane unarmed man argues with three armed cops. I sank to my knees and put my hands behind my head.

"What's going on? You found a body? Is Sean dead?" I asked. I had to know.

Killick looked at me, that unpleasant half smile on his thin lips. He cocked the hammer of my gun, keeping it down by his side. The sound was loud in the quiet of the kitchen and I felt the hairs on the back of my neck rise.

Killick brought the revolver up fast. The first shot hit Gibbs between the eyes. The second shot caught Harris in the chest. He might have been wearing a ballistic vest, but it didn't really matter. The third shot hit him in the face.

SIX

At the time I took no great pleasure in disarming Killick, or in hitting him so hard. It was a necessity, a job that needed to be done, nothing more.

There were plenty of other things on my mind. Dealing with Peter Killick would have to come later. For the time being he was more useful to me alive than dead.

I checked his pockets.

There was a cell phone, two sets of keys, his wallet. Nothing much else.

I didn't want to hang around too long. The three shots from my .357 had been deafeningly loud in the confines of the kitchen and even from outside the house there could be no doubt where the gunshots had come from.

Killick's cuffs were in a pouch on his belt. I used them, securing his wrists behind his back. I also made sure I pulled off his gloves. I grabbed some duct tape from a kitchen drawer and stuck a long strip over his mouth, wrapping it around his head. He wouldn't be able to take it off easily. There was a small risk he could suffocate, but I could live with that. I tore off another length of tape and covered his eyes. No sense in allowing him the luxury of seeing what tools he could use to get free, or even where he was.

In being moved around he had started to regain consciousness, so I smacked the back of his head onto the hard wood of the kitchen floor a couple of times until he went limp.

I needed to get moving. My home was not a safe place anymore and I needed some time and space to think.

One set of Killick's keys were for the silver Chevy Caprice. I hurried outside, got into the big car and reversed it up the driveway parking in front of my tire-slashed Dodge pick-up. The rear of the car was now partially hidden by the side wall of the house. It wasn't perfectly in cover, but it would do. At least there weren't any people around.

At this time of the morning most folks were either at work or taking that time just after dropping the kids off at school to enjoy a coffee with friends. For me it was an ideal time to dump an unconscious body in the trunk of an unmarked police car.

It was easier to do than I expected; the fact he had a scrawny build and the trunk on the Caprice was big helped.

There was nothing I could do for the two uniformed cops. Gibbs and Harris were dead, poor bastards. I left their guns holstered but took their spare magazines. I'd got Killick's matching 9mm Glock automatic, which was enough for now, but more ammunition is always welcome.

I left my revolver on the table in the kitchen, along with Killick's gloves.

It may sound crazy, but if I *had* killed the cops why would I leave the murder weapon ready to find, complete with my prints on it? It would make no sense. Or at least its presence there may lend some credence to my version of events when it came out. Killick's gloves would also be a mine of forensic evidence as well with the gunshot residue on them.

I took Sean's phone from the table. There might be some clues I could get from it related to his disappearance. Then again maybe not. I was worth a try.

Then I called 9-1-1 on my landline. I said nothing and let the handset dangle. I closed the door and left. I didn't bother to lock it. No point. I'd rather the first officers attending the call had easy access rather than have to break in and bust my locks.

I figured I'd got seven minutes to make myself scarce, based on the best average response times.

On the way to the car I gathered a small plastic toolbox from inside my pick-up. I knew its contents would come in handy.

In the rear passenger foot well of the Caprice I found a multi-pack of bottled mineral water. The plastic covering had been ripped open and just three small bottles out of the original six were left. I stuck a bottle in the center console between the front seats, slid the toolbox next to the remaining two, got behind the wheel and started the car.

I'd only driven a couple of blocks when I began cursing myself. In the haste to get away I had not only forgotten my own keys but something else more important. Something that I should have remembered because it would be so useful for the situation I was in. I was an idiot.

It was too late to go back now.

*

Five minutes later I was parked in the back lot of an auto-tire emporium and was ripping down the headlining of the Caprice.

Global Positioning System locators had just begun to be installed during my last years on the force. In principle they were a good idea and I had no problem with them, except now it was a beacon that meant I could be picked up at any moment.

The tech guys in the police garage moaned about them. Not because sticking the transponder and the aerial inside the roof was a problem – it wasn't – but that refitting the headlining was such a fiddly job. As soon as I'd noticed the creased edges of the grey material inside the Caprice I knew what I needed to do.

By the time seven minutes arrived the transponder was on the tarmac of the back lot and I was heading in a different direction, feeling better for being rid of big brother's spying eyes.

All the mobile phones – mine, Sean's and Killick's – lay in the passenger foot well, their batteries removed and stacked beside them. No sense in being easy to locate when you're on the run.

Traffic cameras could be a problem, but there wasn't much I could do about that. I didn't fancy swapping the plates on the car and didn't think it was necessary. It is harder to track cars using traffic cameras than it looks in the movies. Besides, I knew a few unmonitored side roads I could use that would make it difficult for anyone trying to track my path later.

I drove steadily, intentionally laying a false trail before turning into one of the camera-free avenues I knew. From there I threaded the car through a series of smaller residential side streets and then cut back through a wide alley to rejoin the main route I really wanted.

I checked my watch. Sixteen minutes had passed since I'd left home. I was still in a stolen police car and still had a kidnapped cop in the trunk.

I'd not had anything to drink for a good few hours, and with the earlier tension and excitement was starting to get thirsty. I was grateful for that bottle beside me. I drank as I drove, keeping my eyes on the road and taking the opportunity to stay hydrated.

I was still trying to piece together the reasons behind the morning's events, and everything pointed to the fact it had something to do with Sean's disappearance. I realized my knuckles were white gripping the wheel and I had my teeth clenched. I tried to relax and think things through, but my mind was in a whirl. I promised myself that whoever had taken my nephew would be in for a bad time when I caught up with them. A very bad time.

I headed east on Route 26 towards Mount Hood. Forests of tall pines lined the sides of the highway and the air grew fresher the closer towards, and the higher up, Mount Hood I got.

I took the ramp onto Route 35 a few miles after Government Camp. It's a quieter, more scenic route and the traffic is lighter than on the 26. It's still called the Mount Hood Highway though. I'd taken some time and ridden the bike along it at the start of summer and enjoyed the trip.

Back then I was after a quiet road, some sweeping bends and great views. For what I had planned next all I needed was the quiet and seclusion.

There are plenty of quiet forestry roads off Route 35 as it

twists and turns south of the mountain. In fact, Oregon has more National Forest roads than any other state, so I was spoiled for choice. I looked for turnings showing little signs of use. I wanted to minimize the risk of meeting a logging crew or group of hikers.

Five minutes later I found a suitable exit. I turned off onto the packed gravel surface and followed it for a couple of miles before spotting a perfect location.

A curving dirt track led away into the forest. I brought the car to a halt just after it then reversed along the track and in amongst the trees, out of sight of the road. I switched off the engine, gathered a couple of things I knew I'd need, got out of the car and went around to the trunk.

Killick was awake. He didn't look too good, but I didn't care.

I had a craft knife taken from my toolbox with me. It was small but had a scalpel sharp blade. I used it to cut the tape around his mouth. He winced as it left two thin vertical bloody slices on his face. I then peeled off the tape from his eyes, leaving him blinking painfully.

"Want to talk?" I asked him.

"Fuck you," he rasped.

"Want to live?"

He was quiet. I could tell he was calculating what he could do, or what lies he could spin. I interrupted his thoughts in a way he couldn't have expected.

With one swift move I popped the buckle on his jeans and unzipped his flies before he managed to react.

"What you doing, man? Fuck off!" Killick tried shuffling his body away but lying in the trunk there was nowhere for him to go.

I showed him the craft knife again.

"You talk and you get to stay a man. You don't talk or you lie to me and I get cutting. Understand?"

"Yeah! Okay!" Killick gave a quick frightened nod of the head.

"First question," I said. "Is Sean alive?"

He shook his head.

"I don't know. Sorry." He wasn't sorry at all. Sorry was just a word without meaning to him. He caught the look in my eyes.

"Hey man – wasn't me! Different crew!"

"Working for who?"

I could tell he was frantically working out what he could tell me. Twenty seconds passed. He said nothing.

"Who do you work for? At least you know that."

His sneer was back.

"You don't know what—" He got no further.

I can move very quickly when I want to. Right then I had the scalpel point of the knife touching the lower eyelid of his left eye, pressing against the skin just at the point where the eyeball bulges.

I made it very easy for him and spoke slowly, carefully enunciating each word.

"Who do you work for?"

Killick trembled, his breathing fast and scared. He said nothing. He was more frightened of his employer than of me.

That was about to change.

I pushed the knife upwards.

SEVEN

Killick tried to move his head away but there was nowhere to go. He gave a high-pitched croak of panic. A small rivulet of blood trickled down the scalpel blade as it parted the skin of his eyelid.

I stopped, holding the knife steadily in position. I could sense the tip of the blade touching his eyeball.

Killick's eyes were wide open and fixed on me. He was breathing fast, trying hard not to move or blink or twitch his eyes.

They say that any information gained under duress is worthless, but I was sure he'd give me something useful given his current situation.

"Fisk," he whispered.

I guess I should have been more surprised than I was, but part of me felt it made a kind of twisted sense.

Larry Fisk. A man I might have even thought of as my friend at one time. Then again, maybe not.

We'd been partners in the Portland PD for six years, right up to the time he got promoted to lieutenant and I got a better partner. Another three years later I retired, at which point I was as glad to be gone as he was to see the back of me.

We knew too much about each other. It was like we both had a nuclear deterrent. Neither of us would use what we had on each other because it meant mutual destruction. Ex-cops in penitentiaries do not have a good time or a long life expectancy.

After I'd left I heard he'd risen to the rank of captain. Proof that it's not about how good you are at the job, but it's who you know

– or what you know about them.

I refocused on the prone form of Killick and asked my next question.

"Why were you sent for me?"

"Please Riley! He knew you could be a problem." His voice was hoarse. "I had to take you out, set it up to look like you'd resisted and shot the other cops before I got you."

"Go on."

"That's it, man. That's all I know!"

"Why did Fisk think I'd be a problem?"

"I don't know!"

I was sure he did know. I shifted the knife so the scalpel tip moved against the sclera of his eyeball. Killick screamed, or tried to. With his dry throat it came out as a cracked wheeze more of fear than pain. I'd not done any permanent damage to him. Not yet.

I ignored the wet stain spreading across the front of his jeans and the growing stink of his piss, and asked the question again.

"Why did Fisk think I'd be a problem?"

"Because of Sean! Because he was your nephew! Oh shit man! Fisk – he knew you cared – knew he'd crossed the line. No going back. You had to be taken out! Please Riley – that's all I know! I swear."

Lying prone and awkward in the trunk of the car with his piss-stained jeans Killick looked a pitiful sight. I could have almost felt sorry for him if he wasn't a cop-killing bastard.

"Why is Sean involved? Tell me that and I'll spare the eye."

Killick was panicking, his voice choked. "I don't know! I'm not in the loop – Christ, I just do what I'm told, that's all!"

"Then guess."

Killick swallowed, keeping his eyes fixed on me, not daring to move.

"Money. Probably the money."

"What money?"

"Rumor is that Fisk has got a load of dirty money stashed away, that he's got some accountant guy in his pocket who's meant to be dealing with it, but something's gone wrong."

"What's that to do with Sean?" Even as I asked the question I knew the answer. Killick confirmed it.

"Leverage. On the accountant."

"Name," I demanded.

"I don't know! I'm not involved in that side of it! Please! I swear!"

Whether he was telling the truth or not at that point didn't really matter. I knew the name.

Richard 'Dick' Cresswell. Sean's stepfather. My brother-in-law.

I took the knife away from Killick's face. The small puncture wound in his eyelid oozed and he blinked rapidly as his eyes watered. I stared down at him. He looked away, unable to meet my gaze.

Richard was some financial guru, an investment banker or similar. I thought of him as a glorified accountant. But there was no denying he was good at what he did, otherwise he wouldn't have been so successful or be co-founder of the company he worked at.

I also knew that Sean had been working part-time for him within the company's small IT department. It was some in between college arrangement. Work experience, that sort of thing.

"Who took him?" Killick knew I was talking about Sean.

"Perez and Marshall."

"Dan Perez?" I asked.

Killick gave a twitch of a nod.

I knew Dan Perez. I'd liked the guy and thought he was one of the better cops around. He was a conscientious and hard-working family man with an easygoing manner. He also had three kids if I remembered correctly.

It was hard to think he could be involved. Sad too.

Maybe the pressure of finding college funds for three kids did strange things to a guy.

"Who's Marshall?" The name was new to me.

"Linda Marshall. Transferred up from L.A. Tough bitch. Fisk

likes her. They might have a thing together. I don't know."

Killick had given me all the information I wanted for the time being.

"Stay," I told him. It was unnecessary. He wasn't going anywhere.

I opened another bottle of water took it back to the trunk and let him have a drink. See, I can be nice when I want to be.

Killick nodded his thanks.

"So what you going to do with me?" His voice was subdued.

"That depends on you." I stared down at him. "You're with me a while longer. Don't give me a reason to make it any more unpleasant."

He looked away, unable to meet my eyes. He knew I wouldn't hesitate to hurt him if it came to it, and he was right.

I gave him another drink of water then re-taped his mouth and eyes. This time I gave him one small concession to comfort and found a soft cloth to place over his eyes before sticking it down with the tape. What other kidnapper would be so considerate?

I shut the trunk on Killick, went and sat back inside the car alone with my thoughts.

Killick had been more useful than I'd hoped. I guess I should also have been grateful that he had been relatively incompetent back in my kitchen – and that he'd been by himself. If that hadn't been the case then my body would have been on its way to the morgue with Gibbs and Harris by now.

I was angry, but it was a controlled rage. It was an anger that had purpose and reason.

I was proud of my nephew. He was a great kid and I loved him. At times I reckoned I might be closer to being more a dad to him than his actual stepfather.

According to Killick, Sean had been taken by Dan Perez, which I still found hard to believe, and this Linda Marshall. The other fact, again according to Killick, was that Larry Fisk was behind Sean's abduction and my attempted murder and framing.

That was something I could believe.

From what Killick had told me, I had more of an idea of what was going on. Not a complete picture, but it was better than nothing.

Sean had been taken to apply pressure to Richard; something to do with Fisk and his shady financial dealings. I had some hope that Sean was still alive. It is difficult to use a dead hostage for leverage.

Fisk was right that I'd get involved when hearing of Sean's disappearance. He knew firsthand how tenacious I was. I understood how much of a problem that could end up being for Fisk.

Was Sean's call to me yesterday part of the setup?

If Fisk and his team had wanted me to go to Barton Bridge, why delay me by slashing the tires on my truck? Or was that the point – simply to delay me?

Which is exactly what the cops that pulled me over had done. Delay me even more. And I'd been easier to identify because I'd been on a big loud motorbike rather than driving an anonymous old pick-up truck. The tire slashing made more sense now.

I wondered if Killick had more 'evidence' other than Sean's phone that he'd planned to plant after killing me. I'd ask him next time I opened the trunk.

The cell phone. Maybe there was something on it that could be useful, even if it was staged to incriminate me.

I looked at the array of cell phones in the passenger footwell, reached down, picked up Sean's and clicked the battery back into place.

It was a fancy looking device, complete with a camera lens and a light on the back. It felt very smooth and had a glossy black screen, which now bore signs of scuffing and scratches marking the surface.

I pressed the power button and held it for a couple of seconds. The phone buzzed softly in my hand and made a chiming sound as the screen came to life. It displayed the date and time and below that a prompt to enter a PIN code.

This was a problem. I would have to guess a four-digit PIN code with its ten thousand possibilities. Another problem was battery life. It looked very low and I didn't have any compatible lead or charger.

I tried Sean's birthday. Day and month. It was the wrong code. Next the month and year. No good either. I think I'd have been disappointed with Sean if it *had* worked.

His mom's birthday, both formats, were no good either. I was reluctant to try any further in case I locked the phone. It was frustrating and I was sure the battery level visibly dropped in that time.

I was about to switch it off when the phone rang.

EIGHT

The warbling ringtone continued as I checked the display. It was an unknown caller.

I took a chance, swiped the screen to accept the call, and put the phone to my ear.

"Hi Riley," said Captain Larry Fisk.

I said nothing.

"Not going to say hello?" Fisk sounded pleased with himself, like he'd won a bet.

I kept quiet and carried on listening. I didn't want to give him any satisfaction of feeling he was controlling the call. I should have switched off, but I was still interested in hearing what he might say.

"I hope Detective Killick is still with you. Any chance of a word with him?" Fisk left a theatrical pause before carrying on. "No? Never mind." Another pause. "How are *you* holding up Riley? You need anything?" The fake concern oozed across the line making me grit my teeth. Still I said nothing.

"Thought you might be feeling upset. You know, the remorse for abducting your nephew starting to kick in. And what will poor Claire think of you now? Jesus, Riley, you took her only child! That's a pretty twisted thing for a man to do to his sister." The bastard had the nerve to snigger as he said it.

I almost spoke. He nearly had me. In fact I was so close to snarling a litany of threats down the phone at the smarmy prick; but I knew it would do no good, it would only show he was getting to me.

"Anyway, we've got your gun here. It's a nice piece. Ballistics are going to check it out, something about a couple of officers being shot. You know better than I do about that. But as you've got Killick's gun to replace it I guess you're already armed and dangerous enough."

I'd had enough of his voice. I ended the call part the way through his next sentence. Hopefully it sent the message that I didn't care what he had to say.

But I did take a moment to consider Fisk's words. I was pretty sure he wouldn't have said what he did with anyone else around who wasn't in his corrupted circle of trust.

His taunts about taking Sean were real enough. But he hadn't mentioned anything about him being killed with my gun – just Harris and Gibbs. In hindsight, maybe I'd been a fool leaving my own gun behind. I'd been thinking I was clever but instead Fisk would be able to bury the forensic evidence he didn't want and maybe even use my gun on Sean when the time came.

It was time to move on, and quickly.

The call hadn't been a fluke. Fisk must have had the department monitoring the signals for mine, Killick's and Sean's cell phones. I knew that when I'd been trying Sean's phone it would only be a short time before it would be tracked. I didn't think it would have been done quite that fast though. That surprised me and, grudgingly, I was impressed.

I pulled the battery out of Sean's phone and dropped it and the handset into the passenger foot well, started the car and rejoined Route 35.

I headed westwards back towards Route 26. The Mount Hood Highway was a nice road to travel but right now I would be too easy to find if I stayed eastbound on it and I could get boxed in from either end of the road. The anonymous silver Caprice would blend in way better with the traffic on the 26.

Part of me wanted to return to town and see if I could rescue Sean, all gung-ho, guns blazing, but that would be the best way to end up dead. Probably for the both of us.

I checked my watch. It was only 11:43am.

Sean had been officially missing for nearly sixteen hours. In most kidnap cases the first twenty-four hours are critical, but as I knew who was behind it and had now an idea why it had been done, this wasn't much of a factor.

Besides, it wouldn't officially be a kidnapping. If any ransom demand had been called in, or threat been declared, that would mean the FBI would have to be informed. Fisk would not want to have the Feds around that was for sure.

Right now it would be a missing persons case, and a low priority one as Sean was not a child.

I had to assume Fisk would keep Sean alive until what he had planned regarding leverage on Richard played out. How long that was I didn't know.

I needed time to think, to work out a plan of action that had a better-than-even chance of me staying breathing, rescuing my nephew, and staying out of jail.

I also figured that the longer Fisk took to find me the more nervous he'd get. Knowing I was still at large but not knowing where I was would have that effect. I wanted him very nervous. That way he might slip up and make mistakes.

The bottom line was that I needed to buy myself a good chunk of time and that was going to be increasingly difficult with Killick in the trunk.

I was sure he had more to tell, and maybe another uncomfortable hour would soften him up enough to talk some more. Even so, I needed to get rid of him soon.

Whether we parted company with him still breathing would be up to him.

NINE

I headed south-east for forty minutes, leaving the pine clad foothills behind and descending through a changing landscape into the scrubby high desert of the Warm Springs Reservation.

Traffic was light and I drove steadily, a shade over the limit. It looked more natural that way and it wasn't fast enough to warrant being pulled over, unless there was a really bored but overzealous traffic patrol around.

My biggest concern was that there might be a state-wide lookout for Killick's silver Chevy Caprice.

Would Fisk risk having any cops outside of his direct control, his corrupt circle, pull me over? I couldn't be sure, but I suspected not. But what would I do if that happened? If I got pulled over?

Hope for the best, plan for the worst.

I didn't want to harm any innocent cops that were just doing their job, but what if they were like Killick or Perez or Marshall? I could surrender quietly only to be shot 'resisting arrest'. I guessed I'd have to play it by ear if it happened.

The September sun was strong enough to have the air-con running as I drove. I guessed it would be uncomfortably warm in the trunk and wondered how much carbon monoxide Killick was getting. Just as long as he didn't die until I'd questioned him further.

I realized I was officially on the run. My subconscious already knew it, but it was now at the forefront of my mind. I knew I'd needed to get out of Portland, if only for a while, to get out of the way of Fisk and to gather my thoughts and come up with a plan of action.

In the mid distance I saw a police cruiser heading along the highway in the opposite direction, north towards me. I checked my speed: it had crept up. I eased off the gas a little and kept the car steady, feeling my tension rise as the cruiser got closer. I decided that if they slowed and turned after me I'd make like a good citizen and stop.

At least until they had come to a halt themselves and one of them had got out of their car. Then I'd be hard on the gas – backwards – smashing the rear corner of the Caprice into their radiator. I could count on a couple of seconds of surprise before they started firing at me but by then I'd be off like a bat out of hell.

Killick wouldn't have much of a fun time of it. Depending on how hard I hit the other car he'd be lucky to survive. He'd get broken bones that would be for sure.

Plan in mind, I prepared myself as the cruiser drew closer.

I was doing sixty. They were doing sixty. A combined speed of one-hundred-and-twenty miles per hour.

I could make out the two cops inside. One male, one female. The driver had a mustache and looked to be laughing at something the female cop had said. Her face was turned to him. I took this in within a split second. An image snapshot.

Our cars shot past each other. My eyes went to the mirror. No brake lights, no tire smoke, no sirens. Five seconds passed. Still nothing. The police cruiser carried on into the distance.

I rolled my shoulders, eased a little of the tension, drank some more water and thought about what I needed to do.

The first thing was to wring whatever I could from Killick. Then I'd decide what to do with him. I already had an idea about that.

If Dan Perez was involved, he'd tell me more. I remembered where he lived and, assuming he hadn't moved, I'd be visiting him soon enough.

With the urgency of getting out of my house there had been no time for me to think of grabbing my emergency stash. I frowned as I thought about it, annoyed with myself. It was exactly this sort of situation it was there for. So much for my training. Retirement had made me slow and sloppy. Then again, I never thought I'd need to be on the run.

Right now the CSI technicians would be all over my home so there was no point going back there yet. It was well hidden and I was fairly confident they wouldn't find it, so retrieving it later could be an option.

To do that I'd need transport to get back to Portland.

The Chevrolet was down to a quarter tank of gas, so I'd need to fuel up before going back. With license plate recognition on most gas stations nowadays that was a big risk. Swapping the plates on it might work. I'd just have to make sure I wasn't caught.

If I was caught with the car there would be plenty of fibers and prints from me in it to go with Killick's piss and blood in the trunk. Hard evidence that I'd abducted a serving police officer.

No. On balance I decided I was going to have to ditch Killick's Caprice.

I'd work out another way of getting back to Portland.

Route 26 passes through the Warm Springs Reservation on its way to the town of Madras, which was where I was headed. If ever there was a town crying out for an Indian curry restaurant, that's got to be the place.

About two-thirds the way through the Reservation I slowed and turned off the main highway and onto a narrow side road. The tires rattled over a cattle grid and crunched onto the uneven asphalt surface. Dirt and small stones clattered and rattled against the car's undercarriage.

There were no recent signs of habitation around here. A distant shack that was old when JFK was shot. A couple of ancient hoardings faded pale by the sun. The scavenged remains of a rusted Ford pick-up. It was quiet. Desolate. I doubted there was anyone around for miles.

Ten minutes later I found a dirt track spurring away from the broken asphalt. The dusty trail ran alongside a dry creek and past thicker patches of sagebrush. I drove for another five minutes, the soft suspension bouncing and wallowing over the ruts. I doubted Killick was enjoying the experience much from inside the trunk.

With the heat and fumes and movement I wouldn't have been surprised if he'd puked. The duct tape gag would make it likely he'd suffocate on his own vomit.

That would be a shame. I hadn't finished questioning him yet and I didn't fancy hauling his dead body out of the car.

I stopped by a group of stunted juniper trees and switched off the engine. Everything fell silent. All I could hear was the ticking of the car as it cooled and a couple of muffled thumps from the trunk as Killick shifted position.

Good. He was still alive. For now.

I looked around. Nothing but dry scrubland and the occasional tortured tree shimmering in the haze. As close to a desert as I could get at short notice.

This would do.

What happened next was up to Killick.

TEN

As well as mulling over my own plans I'd also been thinking about Peter Killick's future. He was a cold-blooded murderer; I'd seen that firsthand. He was also party to the kidnap of my nephew. There had to be a reckoning. There had to be some form of justice.

I unlatched the glove compartment and took out Killick's Glock. I ejected the clip and checked it. It was full. Seventeen 9mm Parabellum rounds. I reloaded the gun and racked the slide. As I got out of the car, I stuck it in the back of my jeans.

The air felt warm and dry. It wasn't perfectly still; the occasional light breeze stirred the dust, but it barely had the power to move the leaves on the surrounding trees or the sagebrush that dotted the area.

I opened the trunk and let the smell of stale piss and nervous sweat dissipate for a couple of seconds. Killick had moved around and was lying on his side in a semi-fetal position. He looked worse than when I'd last seen him. His skin was sickly pale and his hands had a tinge of blue. I guess an hour of being handcuffed in a hot trunk and being driven over bouncing roads will do that to a man. But he was still alive and that was something he needed to be grateful for.

I peeled off the tape around his eyes and chucked the rag to one side of the trunk. Killick blinked his eyes. They were red and watering. He squinted against the sun and tried to focus on me as I grabbed his shoulder, roughly turned him onto his front and unlocked the cuffs, removing them.

He rolled slowly onto his back, cradling his arms in front of him, trying to work some sensation back into them and slowly flexing his hands. It looked painful but I didn't care.

He looked up at me. I could see he was worried. No, it was more than that – he was terrified. I was glad I still had that effect.

"I bet you're thinking about what's going to happen next." I said.

He gave a small nod, realized his hands were free and tentatively raised them to the tape around his mouth, keeping his eyes on me all the time. I did nothing and let him do it. He peeled off enough of the tape to speak. I heard a tremor of fear in his whining voice.

"Look man, I can tell you more. You don't need to do this! You'd be killing a cop!"

"What's that like?" I asked him quietly. "You've already killed two that I know of."

"Shit man! He told me to! You don't argue—"

I cut him off mid-flow. "Hands out front." I held up the cuffs.

"Oh fuck, no! Please no!"

"I can beat you senseless first if you want."

Killick shook his head. He was close to sobbing but still kept his hands close to his chest.

I kept my voice level and emotionless, though I really liked the idea of giving him a beating.

"Hands."

He looked up at me and took a shuddering breath. Reluctantly, he held out his arms. His hands were shaking but at least they weren't so blue anymore. I snapped the cuffs around his wrists, showed him the key then turned and threw it away. I threw it hard and far and it landed somewhere beyond a group of prickly-looking bushes.

Killick swore long and hard under his breath. It wasn't directed at me; it was more of a reaction to his situation.

"Get out," I ordered.

It was a clumsy process but he eventually managed to haul himself out of the trunk. He slumped ass-down in the dirt, legs splayed and back leant against the rear bumper. A small bit of tape still clung to his face. He reached up with his cuffed hands and peeled it off, letting the strip flutter to the ground.

"Take off your boots."

Killick cocked his head at me like he didn't understand.

I repeated myself.

He looked puzzled but I guessed he might be feeling a glimmer of hope. After all, why would I be getting him to take his boots off if I was going to shoot him?

It took him longer than I expected but he did it.

"Socks too," I told him.

He huffed out a sigh and peeled off his socks, stuffing them into his boots. He looked back at me, nervous but curious at what I was planning for him.

"Get up."

He used the edge of the trunk to haul himself upright. His movements were still stiff.

"You see that tree to your right?"

Killick nodded.

"Walk over to it." He bent to pick up his boots. "Leave them," I growled.

His eyes met mine. Some of his cocky defiance started to return.

"Why?"

"It's how you get to stay alive."

He shrugged and walked slowly towards the tree, choosing his steps carefully across the packed earth. Partway there he let out a hiss of pain as the bare soles of his feet found a sharp stone his eyes had missed.

I dumped his boots in the trunk of the Caprice and slammed it shut.

Killick turned before reaching the tree.

"What now?" he yelled.

I ignored him and opened the rear passenger door.

I took out the remaining half bottle of water along with an unopened one, standing them both on the roof of the car. I saw

Killick lick his lips. He was thirsty now and he'd be a lot thirstier before the day was out. It wasn't baking hot but the dry air would suck the moisture from him soon enough.

I picked up the half bottle and looked over at him.

"You need to tell me more. Now's the time."

"Okay, but give me a water first. Come on Riley, please."

I lobbed the half bottle to him. He fumbled the catch and it dropped to the dirt. He fell to his knees, scrabbling for it as it rolled and managed to grasp hold of it. He knelt there for a moment and drank a couple of mouthfuls.

"So talk," I told him. "It's your chance to earn this other bottle."

"Shit. You're going to leave me here, aren't you?"

"I figure it'll take you a few hours to get to the main road. You might get lucky and someone will pick you up sooner but don't bet on it. Unless you're real stupid you'll probably live." I picked up the full bottle from the roof of the car and stared at him. "This will make it easier for you, but you need to earn it."

Killick grimaced. There were an uncomfortable few hours ahead of him, but it was better than being dead.

"Were you going to plant evidence in my house after dealing with me?" I asked.

Killick nodded.

"Yeah, but not me, I just had the phone. I was told one of the techs would sort it out. Make it believable."

I took out Killick's pistol and rested myself against the car, holding the gun easy and relaxed.

"What else do you know?"

Killick got the message. He needed to talk or there would be no extra bottle, just some pain and violence from me.

"Okay, okay. I think Fisk is planning to get out, retire, and soon." Killick held up a finger so I wouldn't interrupt his flow. "Over the last months our payoffs have been getting bigger because the risks have been getting bigger, and I know he wouldn't be doing that if he was still playing the long game."

Killick paused and took another mouthful of water.

"What sort of risks?" I prompted him.

"We've had tip-offs that have led to us putting away or eliminating lots of start-up groups in the area. There were Mexicans with a serious meth lab, a Russian arms cartel, an organization calling themselves the Black Tigers – basically a black power group moving in on the crack trade – all dealt with at exactly the right time and place."

Killick met my eyes. I could see he took some pride in what he was retelling. "We were doing a good job, y'know. Taking out the bad guys. It's what we're supposed to do, right? Making a bit of extra danger money for dealing with those motherfuckers only seemed fair. They're well-armed and fight back!"

I interrupted him.

"Where are you going with this?"

Killick spoke slowly now.

"The only group we never hit were the Armenians, and we sure saw a lot more of them showing up in town as time passed. According to Fisk there's never been enough evidence to be worth pursuing them and we always had bigger jobs to concentrate on." Killick snorted. "Couple of their respectable 'business leaders' even sponsored a charity dinner. Come on, you do the math."

"So you think Fisk is helping the Armenians become the only game in town?"

"Having the captain of a precinct in your pocket would be one hell of an edge and I guess they'd pay real well for that. What I've taken is nothing compared to that."

"Still enough to make you shoot a fellow cop," I reminded him.

"That ain't the money and you know it!" he protested. I got the idea. If he didn't do the job it could be him in the firing line next.

"So why would Fisk leave if he's in such a sweet position? Sounds like he'd milk it for all he could."

"You might think so, but we've heard that Internal Affairs have been showing some interest in the department, and if I've heard you can bet that Fisk has heard more. It's only a matter of time before those tight pricks come sniffing around with serious intent

– and I bet they're going to find something. I just know it."

I knew well enough about Internal Affairs investigations. Fisk and I had been subject to a couple during our time together in the department. To be fair their investigations were not unfounded, but they never found enough evidence to back up any suspicions. We were always very careful about that.

"So what's he going to do?" I asked.

"Hell, I don't know. Probably not come in one day and never be seen again. It's not like he's got much in the way of ties to the place. He could just up and go."

"How do you mean?"

"No family, rented apartment, no social life. Marshall's the closest he's got to a friend."

I knew Larry Fisk had never married, but at one point he'd had a good sized house with a view across the Willamette River. I even remembered having a few beers with him there on more than one occasion. Apparently he'd downsized since then.

I wondered how much Fisk had managed to stash away over the years.

I became a cop because I liked the idea of making a difference. Sure, the investigation side of the job had its appeal, but it was the times of action that suited me best. Boil it down and for me it was all about taking down the bad guys. It was only later that sidelining a few dollars here and there got to be something that you did when the opportunity arose. I suppose I could blame Fisk for influencing me on that score but know the fault lies with me. Besides, any amounts that found their way into my pocket were nothing much. I thought of the kit in my wood shop and the sting of guilt wasn't that bad.

But Fisk always had more ambition. It wasn't a stretch to imagine him with a hundred grand, but I quickly dismissed that idea. That would be chicken feed to a guy like him. Half a million?

Of course, since Fisk had become captain he would have had a lot more opportunities open to him and, backed up by what Killick was saying, it could be that he was sitting on a nest egg of over a million bucks, possibly more. Thinking about it I couldn't imagine Fisk disappearing for less than that.

"Okay," I said, returning to Killick. "Tell me who's in his pocket other than you, Perez and Marshall."

"Sorry man, I don't know. Fisk's a paranoid bastard. He uses a cell structure. No more than four in a group, so we don't get to know who else is involved."

That figured. It was just like him to do something like that.

I chucked the full water bottle to Killick. This time he caught it.

"You still shot two brother officers," I reminded him as I walked alongside the car. "There's going to be a reckoning for that, somehow, somewhere. Your choice how that goes down, but I'd suggest you might not want to meet me again."

I opened the driver's door.

"Is it true?" Killick shouted. "What he said about you."

I turned, curious about what he might say next. "What do you mean?"

"That guy that went missing. The suspected child rapist. When you were working together, Fisk said you got rid of him. Is that true? Did you really do that?"

I met Killick's eyes with a level stare. I remembered only too well.

Killick had said 'suspected' and for a start that wasn't right. I knew damn well what Luis Krato had done. It had given me nightmares. Secondly, although it was true he had been a rapist he was also a killer. None of his victims had been left alive.

He was highly intelligent and had been very careful. There was nothing concrete that could tie him to any of the six children he had abused, mutilated and killed. It was all circumstantial. It was one of those cases where it was so damn obvious he had done it, he was almost gloating about it, yet there seemed to be nothing we could do except wait for another victim to appear in the morgue.

I couldn't have that.

"Was his body found?" I asked him.

After a couple of seconds he slowly shook his head. "No, never heard that it was."

"Then I guess he must have disappeared somewhere. It's a big country." I gave him a cold smile. "Enjoy your walk. Watch out for rattlers."

I left him with that thought as I got into the car and returned the gun to the glove compartment. I turned the Caprice around and drove off, leaving Killick barefoot in the dust staring after me.

ELEVEN

As I drove I thought about what Killick had told me and sifted various options and plans through my mind.

It was very tempting to give a couple of my old Ranger buddies a call. We'd kept in touch reasonably well, at least as far as guys tend to, although the nearest of them lived up near Seattle. Even so I knew they'd help me out if asked, especially as the situation involved Sean, the son of a fellow Ranger.

But they had lives of their own, families and responsibilities, and it would be unfair to drag them into what was my fight. No, I had to do this by myself.

After deciding that, the next few steps I'd take were easy enough to work out.

Thinking of steps made me find the brake and the car skidded to a halt on the dirt track. I got out, popped the trunk and threw Killick's boots under a nearby bush. Maybe they'd become a home for a scorpion or a rattler. No great change of owner. I slammed the trunk, dropped into the driver's seat and hit the gas.

It took me less time to get back to the main highway than on my way into the scrubland, but the fuel gauge had now dropped below a quarter tank. Still enough to get me where I was going.

I reached Madras, found a Sears store on 5th Street and parked up. I checked Killick's wallet and found seventy-two dollars. That was good. I'd got more in my own wallet if needed but he could pay the way for now. I figured he owed me for letting him live.

Inside the store I bought a big sports bag in blue, a Seattle Seahawks baseball cap and a pair of tan leather gloves. I would have preferred the gloves to be black, but as the tan ones were on offer and I wasn't making a fashion statement it didn't matter. Getting those items only left me a twenty-and-change out of Killick's money.

I returned to the Caprice and put my plastic toolbox into the new sports bag, then put the Glock and the two spare magazines in there as well, hidden nicely out of sight. I left the bag on the front passenger seat, retrieved the bit of rag from the trunk, and drove off towards my next destination.

I had forty dollars in my own wallet and even adding the remaining twenty of Killick's it wasn't nearly enough for what I needed. I had to risk visiting an ATM.

I parked a good distance away on the far side of the street and walked over to a machine I'd spotted. There weren't many cameras around that area, but I knew the ATM itself would have a camera. I had my new Seahawks cap pulled low and kept my head down to shield my face from the lens as best I could. I also knew that if I used one of my regular bank cards it would send a big red 'here I am' flag to Fisk, presuming he'd set a watch on my cards.

But there was one card he wouldn't know about, one linked to an account held under the name Bruce MacLaine.

Towards the end of my time in the Rangers a small squad of us had been called upon for various missions overseas. Mainly just support roles and because Delta weren't available, I guess. A guy called Archie Howell was the lead on these. The whole team was set up with false identities for the job, including bank accounts.

I came to like Archie, if that was his real name, and a number of us kept in touch afterwards. It was Archie's advice and influence that convinced me to keep the Bruce MacLaine account up and running, even though I only kept a few hundred bucks of my own money in it.

"You never know when something like that might come in useful," Archie had said.

It may have taken over a decade to be true but there was no denying I was glad of it now.

I withdrew two-hundred-and-eighty dollars. The maximum I could have taken was four hundred so this was well below the point where the transaction would get flagged up as being of interest. On top of what I already had I reckoned over three hundred dollars would be enough for now.

I returned to the car and headed south through Madras. The Caprice was getting even lower on fuel, but it didn't matter. I wouldn't need it much longer. Even so, I pulled into a gas station on the way out of town. What I wanted was the car wash.

I avoided the pumps with their number plate recognition cameras and stuck the big Chevrolet through the wash. I bought the full treatment. I sat inside the car while the brushes whirled, put the tan gloves on and got busy with the rag wiping down any surface I'd touched. The wash program took ten minutes and left the silver paintwork looking pretty good.

I left the car wash and drove south to another place I'd noticed, amongst a series of industrial units. It was an auto detailing center. The young Asian guy on reception had a metal name badge on his work shirt. Unless he'd borrowed it from someone else his name was Ken.

He was keen and polite, even though I didn't look like I'd be much of a big spender there.

I told him that I only wanted a basic hand wash for the paintwork, but to give the interior and the trunk a thorough clean and a shampoo if needed. Ken checked his price chart and came up with a figure of a hundred-and-twenty-five bucks. To a guy like me who cleans his own vehicles it seemed expensive. I told him I'd be paying cash if that made any difference, but it didn't. In fairness to him he remained friendly and professional and told me I could pay when I collected the car and cash or credit card were fine, whatever I preferred. He also said they would need the car for around two hours to get the job done properly and give the upholstery time to dry off enough.

That was fine with me. I'd already got my sports bag with me containing the toolbox and the gun, so I handed him the keys there and then, checked my watch and told Ken I'd return at 5pm. That gave them plenty of time.

After the treatment the Caprice was getting the Forensics department would have their work cut out getting any worthwhile evidence from it. No fingerprints. Little chance of any hairs or fibers. Certainly not enough to stand up in any court.

Around the corner from the auto-detailing shop I'd noticed a diner across the street that looked decent enough. I needed a meal and some coffee and that was as good a place as any to rest a while. I walked the couple of hundred yards to it and went inside.

The smell of good cooking hit me as I entered making me realize how hungry I actually was.

I found a booth and slid into it, dumping the bag beside me. The lunchtime rush had passed but the place still had enough customers to make it feel like a popular choice. The waitress that came over had a ready smile, an easy manner and I took a liking to her. Her name tag said Annabelle and I reckoned she was around forty or a hard worked thirty-five.

"Can I get you a coffee or a beer while you look?" she asked. From her accent Annabelle was local, Oregon or Washington State. She already had the jug of coffee in her hand, so I went for the coffee.

I asked what she recommended from the menu. I was expecting her to say the steak sandwich or the burger stack, but she paused and gave me a sideways look.

"I think you'd probably like our barbecue chicken and bacon. Wholemeal bun, small fries. But it's your call – cook does a lot of great stuff."

I smiled at her. "Sounds good but hold the fries. I might check out the dessert."

"You got it." Annabelle smiled, scribbled on her pad and disappeared towards the kitchen. I sipped some of the coffee. It was hot and fresh. Not superb, and not as refined as the blend I make at home, but better than you'd find in most diners.

When the food came it was as good as she had said. I took my time and enjoyed it. When Annabelle next came and topped up my coffee, I asked her where I could catch the bus to Portland.

"Going to be tomorrow morning now," she said. "You catch it at the Circle K. It comes through early from Bend, so you need to be on your toes."

I thanked her. I didn't go for a dessert in the end. The protein and carbs from the main meal would be enough for now. I paid the check and left a twenty percent tip for Annabelle.

I wasn't worried about being recognized or remembered. Fisk and his cronies would have to be doing a lot of hard legwork to trace all my movements and I doubted he had enough resources to spare, especially this far out of his jurisdiction.

However, if I was getting the bus tomorrow morning that meant I had to stop the night in Madras. Sleeping in the car overnight wasn't much of an option after what I was getting done to it. I needed to find a motel that could hire me a room without seeing any ID.

No sense in having my name logged if it needn't be. A tall order post-9/11, and rightly so, but I felt I should be able to swing it even if I had to try a number of places before eventually finding somewhere I could stay.

I left the diner and got walking.

The first motel I tried couldn't do anything for me. The girl on reception didn't really care for the story that I'd had my bag stolen and was just looking for somewhere to stay. She was following company rules and that was that. I moved on.

Motel number two was way better. Even though the guy behind the counter couldn't do anything for me there – the same story: rules are rules and all that – but he did suggest I try the trailer park off Southwest Bard Lane and was good enough to give me directions and a crudely printed map of Madras.

The park was on the south edge of the town and it took me close on twenty minutes to get there.

The guy at motel two was on the ball. There were worse trailer parks but not many. If I couldn't get a cheap place without any ID there then I would be sleeping in the car or changing my plans entirely.

Thirty yards inside the entrance a group of white trash youths sat smoking on faded plastic chairs in front of a pale green trailer. I ignored their stares and the stink of weed as I passed.

I walked up to a prefab unit that had a 'Reception' sign screwed to it and slid open the glass door. Immediately I could smell the fat middle aged guy sat behind the counter. Stale sweat and grease. He stayed sitting behind the stained countertop, his yellowed eyes spared me a brief disinterested glance before returning to the TV.

I cut to the point. "Got a room for the night?"

He sighed theatrically. "Nothing much. Depends what you got."

"Thirty," I told him.

He snorted and said nothing. His attitude was making my fists itch.

"Your turn," I said.

"Fifty." His eyes never left the TV screen. "Sixty for linen."

"How about forty?" I had no interest in the linen, especially if this guy had anything to do with it.

"Fifty's the rate. You want it or you don't."

"Forty-five," I countered. I'd make him work for it.

He sniffed and rubbed a dirty hand under his nose.

"Already said fifty. And that's for cash."

I sighed and placed a fifty on the counter. He looked over and reached out a pudgy hand towards it. The money disappeared and he gestured to the dog-eared book on the raised counter. "Sign in, will ya."

I signed in giving a false name and the fat guy slid a set of keys to me. The number 12 was on the fob. I took them and left, glad to be back out in the fresh air.

The weed-smoking youths watched me as I walked away along the rows of trailers. One of them muttered something and the group laughed.

I found trailer unit 12 and unlocked the door. It smelt stale but nowhere near as bad as the guy on reception.

It would do for one night. I'd stayed in worse places and had no problem sleeping rough if it came to it, even though it had been a while.

I opened the windows to air the place then left. I'd got a walk ahead of me and needed to get going.

Leaving the trailer park, I noticed that half the youths had disappeared and those that were left were staring at their phones, expressions blank.

Invasion of the brain snatchers had already happened and no one had noticed. The thought made me smile.

*

The silver Chevrolet Caprice looked showroom clean. I went into the reception and saw Ken behind the counter. He was just finishing with another customer, so I sat in one of the cheap fabric seats and waited.

I didn't have to wait long. Ken came over to me with the keys to the Chevy.

"Want to have a look?" he asked as I got to my feet.

I shook my head and smiled. "No, I'm sure you've done it just fine."

"There's a plastic cover on the driver's seat, it might still be a bit damp so thought it best to leave it on."

He made no mention of the condition of the trunk carpet.

The plastic cover was a bonus. I paid, thanked him, took the keys and left. I made sure I put the tan leather gloves on before I got into the car. It smelled clean and fresh. Way more so than the trailer where I was due to spend the night. It was tempting to sleep in the car but that wasn't part of the plan. It was too risky. There was an air freshener in the shape of the logo of the auto detailing center hanging from the rear-view mirror. I unhooked it. It would be more use in the trailer unit.

On my travels around Madras I'd noticed a number of closed

stores. Some boarded, some with smeared windows awaiting new owners. I parked the Caprice around in the back lot of one of them, locked it and walked off with my bag. I dropped the keys down a nearby drain.

I wouldn't be needing that car ever again.

I went into a couple of stores on my walk back to the trailer park and bought some essentials. Or at least some items I considered to be well worth having – shower gel, towel, toothbrush, toothpaste, cereal bars and a newspaper.

By the time I returned to the trailer park and unlocked unit 12 the sun was getting low in the sky and the youths were nowhere to be seen, despite the lingering stink of marijuana in the air. There was the distant thump of the kind of modern music I don't understand or care for, but it didn't bother me. It was the sort of place where you had to expect it.

I took a welcome shower, the water warm rather than hot, and immediately felt better. I had what I was doing next already planned out in my head and there was nothing I could do until tomorrow morning. So I sat and read the newspaper until it got too dark. I had to be up early tomorrow so placed Killick's gun on the floor just under the bed, lay down and tried to get some sleep.

It was difficult because there was so much still running through my mind, but eventually I managed to settle off into disturbed and angry dreams.

TWELVE

I woke in the darkness. Something had disturbed me, not that it was a great sleep in any case. A noise from outside. Quiet and subtle, but enough to tap into that part of the brain that had been honed by millennia of evolution to sense danger. No doubt the years serving in the Rangers helped too, but mostly I credit animal instinct.

Leaving the trailer windows open enough to ventilate the stale air helped as well. I heard the sound again. Movement. Maybe the sound of sneakers on the concrete flags that bordered the trailer. Somebody was trying to move quietly and not doing a good job of it. I checked my G-Shock watch. It was a few minutes after 3:20am.

I slid off the bed silently and retrieved the gun from under it. It was then I caught a whiff of marijuana. It may have been only slight, but the pungent smell was unmistakable. Whoever it was outside didn't need to be smoking it there and then, the stink clings to clothes, especially if there's a group of you all taking a hit in an enclosed space – like an afternoon spent in another trailer.

I reckoned it was the youths I'd seen earlier. But what they were doing creeping around outside my trailer? My guess was they were out to prank me. Maybe not knock and run, because they weren't eight years old anymore, so perhaps sudden banging and shaking of the trailer intended to freak me out. With some kids it's difficult to know what goes through their heads, especially when they've been toking at the weed. I thought back to when I'd noticed them near to the reception area. I'd got the impression they were beyond high school age, at least the guys were, and could even be early twenties at a push.

Now I was fully awake my senses were alert and I focused on listening. Sure enough there were people outside. At least two, more likely three, moving around to the side of the trailer with the door. I moved as well, heading out of the bedroom and along the short corridor to the kitchenette and main living space. The difference was that I knew how to move quietly, and unit 12 may have been an old trailer but it had settled over the years and was still solid enough not to shift or creak under my weight.

It wasn't pitch black. Enough ambient light from the dim lamps scattered around the park filtered through the filthy nets that clung to the grimy windows for me to see my way through the room and make out vague shadows outside. I'd not bothered to draw the drapes. For one thing I didn't fancy touching them and another was that there seemed to be nobody else around. At least until now.

I stuck the Glock into the back of my jeans and remained crouched in the small kitchen area, waiting for the youths to do whatever it was they were going to do. I didn't have to wait long.

What I heard next changed the game.

The sound of a revolver's hammer being cocked, then the gentle rasp of a key being inserted into the door lock.

Whoever was coming in was still trying to be quiet. Trying but failing. And they had no idea I was right there, no more than four feet away from the door. I could shoot them there and then before they even opened the door. End whatever they were intending to do before it started. It would be self-defense and technically I would be within my rights to do that. But if I did shoot it would mean getting the local cops involved, and right now that was something I needed to avoid.

If you have the luxury of time to think about what to do you can end up over-thinking the situation and second-guessing yourself. I didn't have time. But I did have experience and training and I'd already decided what I was going to do.

I heard the key rotating and the latch clicking free. The handle turned and the door slowly opened, hinging outwards. Whoever was coming in led with the gun, a snub-nosed revolver, the steel glinting in the faint light from outside. They stepped inside, treading softly and totally unaware of me crouched motionless in the darkness. I was close enough to smell him. Stale grease and nervous sweat challenged the weed for dominance.

I launched hard, slamming in from the side, my right hand closing around the gunman's hand, pushing the revolver away as my left drove their head into and through the partition wall. The gunman's knees buckled but I still had his hand and the gun locked in my grip. His finger jerked, the gun fired, a flat sharp crack as the bullet harmlessly punched a hole in the wall. I gave the revolver a vicious twist and felt his fingers pop as they were forced in directions they weren't meant to go. The joints dislocated with a wet crack and he screamed, a thin high keening, as I dragged the revolver out of his ruined grasp and smashed the butt onto the crown of his head before turning it towards the open doorway and pointing it at his two slack-jawed friends standing there.

It had taken three seconds start to finish. I guess his buddies could have rushed me if they had been sharper on the uptake or less stoned, but I wouldn't have bet much on them. Besides I had surprise on my side.

"Get in here now," I snarled at them, stepping back and gesturing with the revolver. The guy I'd hit had slid to the floor moaning. Drywall dust covered half his face, turning into a gory mask as blood dribbled down from his scalp.

They had a moment of indecision, like they were trying to work out whether to do as I said or run for it. Their eyes flicked to their gunman pal huddled on the floor and then back to me and the gun. I made it easier for them.

"You turn and run, I shoot both of you." I gave them a second for it to sink in. "Now get in here."

The taller of the two came in first. He was a little taller than me but with the thin frame of a long-distance runner and an acne-scarred face that he'd failed to improve with a wispy blonde beard.

His mate was broader and was going for the shaven-headed Vin Diesel look but had spoiled it by developing a soft beer gut and a chubby face. I reckoned both of them had to be below twenty, so officially still teenagers if only just.

"Take him over there." I stepped back, keeping the gun on them, and pointed at the couch with my other hand.

They stumbled in, Acne Scars bending to help his broken handed pal, and shuffled into the living area with Chubby Diesel bringing up the rear.

"Sit."

They sat.

I went and closed the door, removing the key from the lock, still keeping my eyes on them. None of them said anything. It was like they were in shock or things were happening too quickly for them to be able to process. I flicked the light switch. I wanted to get a better look at who I was dealing with as well as see where their hands were. I didn't want to have one of them pull out another gun I hadn't seen. They all blinked as the harsh yellow light flooded the area.

"Any more guns?" I asked.

There was a mumbled "no" and head shakes from the teenagers. Broken Hand had his eyes closed. I assumed he'd passed out. He looked older than the other two, maybe early twenties. He had longer fair hair and bore a resemblance to Acne Scars but had been blessed with better skin. Probably a cousin. All of them were typical white trailer trash and in a way I felt a little sorry for them.

"Knives?"

The teenagers looked at each other. Chubby Diesel shrugged and reached inside his jacket as Acne Scars began to stand up.

"Easy now," I cautioned. "One at a time and slowly."

A minute later there were two flick knives lying on the sticky carpet out of their reach and the teenagers were sat back down and looking sullen. I collected the knives. I didn't need to ask them what they had intended to do. That was easy. They were going to steal whatever I had, which wasn't a lot but they didn't know that, and in theory it should have been easy money. Three against one, plus they had a gun and those knives if needed. I wondered how many times they had done something like this and stopped feeling so sorry for them.

The key part of their plan was just that: a key.

"First to answer gets to leave." I kept my voice calm and reasonable, making sure they understood. I placed the gun on the counter next to me and opened one of the knives. It looked sharp enough. "Wrong answers cost fingers." All eyes met mine, even Broken Hand who had come around but still looked groggy.

I took the key they had used out of my pocket and held it up. There was an orange tag on it, but whatever had been written on it had long since faded to nothing. I had my suspicions but needed them to confirm it.

"Where did you get this?"

Chubby Diesel swallowed, his eyes leaving mine and darting nervously to Broken Hand. Nobody said anything.

"No answers cost fingers too. I'll start with you," I said, pointing the tip of the knife at Chubby and taking a step forward.

Chubby Diesel shrank back in the seat, eyes going wide. "Stole it!" he blurted.

"From where?"

I could tell he was trying to think of something to say. It would be lies. I lunged forward, closing the distance in a heartbeat and stabbed the knife into his leg. He shrieked as a rosette of blood blossomed through his faded denims and the other two guys winced. I heard Acne Scars sucking in a breath through clenched teeth. I'd stuck the tip of the blade into the top of Chubby's thigh barely half an inch. Enough to be painful and get his fear going, but not that deep he was in any real danger.

"Randall!" Chubby clutched at his leg, his voice a squeak, the macho Vin Diesel image thoroughly shattered. "It's his key! I get it when we do a job."

"Go on." I stepped back, giving him room and letting him see I still had the knife with its blood-stained tip.

"Fuck!" Chubby looked at his pals, realization dawning he was on his own and it was up to him to save himself from the crazy guy with the knife. "He passes me the key when there's someone worth rolling."

"Tell me about Randall."

"Sort of like my uncle but not really. He runs the place." I pictured the unhelpful fat greasy slob I dealt with earlier.

"He gives you the key but what's in it for him?"

"We take whatever we get to him and he deals with it. Gives us a cut and we get free rent. No hassles."

I thought it might be the case. I was going to have a word with Randall, and I could be sure he would not enjoy the experience. But first I had the small problem of what do with the three guys in front of me.

*

Duct tape is a wonderful thing. I really should have bought shares in it.

I had left each of the guys in different rooms, all well secured, legs taped, hands behind backs and gagged. The two of them may have been only nineteen but by that age I was in the army and perfectly capable of being a threat, so I was cautious and took the time to do it properly.

I'd also gotten some more details about 'uncle' Randall from Chubby Diesel, so I'd left him in the main living area with the TV to watch. It was the least I could do.

I kept the revolver, a .38 with a two-inch barrel, black grips and the serial number filed off. It was in reasonable condition and perfectly serviceable but also very illegal. Right then I didn't care about that. Its size made it a useful tool.

I walked through the trailer park towards the reception area, bag in hand and all I needed with me. Feeble light from the few working lamps around the place punctuated the darkness, making it easy to find my way. I had hoped to get more sleep but the visit from Randall's boys had screwed that. Another entry in the growing list of things that pissed me off.

Randall's was the biggest trailer in the park. No surprise there. If you ran the place, you made sure you got the biggest and best you could, especially if you had to make some room for a reception area. From the info I got from Chubby Diesel, I was best going around the back, so that's exactly what I did.

A couple of old cars were parked on the patchy earth at the rear of the place, and broad wooden steps led up to a decked area with a sagging swing seat and some dead twigs stuck in pots of soil. Welcome to the Garden of Eden. I left my bag half hidden under the side of the deck. The Glock was in the back of my jeans, the small revolver in my pocket and I was wearing the leather gloves I'd bought the previous afternoon.

I knew that getting in to have a chat with Randall wouldn't be easy, at least not if I wanted to do it quietly and without attracting much attention. I'd kicked in doors on trailers before and it wasn't hard if you knew what you were doing. But it was noisy. It also helped to have body armor and backup.

I scanned along the rear of the trailer and found what I needed. A window towards the one end slightly ajar. Not an open invitation but it was enough; I could reach it and the gap was wide enough for my fingers. A little pressure and the window stay popped off the peg, allowing me to open it further. I just had to pull myself up and clamber inside whilst keeping the window open. I'm no gymnast but I managed it, and thirty seconds later I was in a small dark corridor.

When you do something like that it is difficult to gauge how much noise you've made. It wasn't a stealthy entry that was for certain and I'm sure I must have grunted while I hauled myself up and over the sill. I paused and listened for any sound of movement.

Rasping snores were coming from further along the corridor. I moved silently along the carpet to the door where the snorting wheezes were loudest.

Randall having sweet dreams.

It was time for them to become a nightmare.
I opened the door.

THIRTEEN

At 6:15am I was on the road and heading north back to Portland. As the dawn brightened so did my mood. It was a fresh day and I had a plan of action. I'd got rid of a lot of aggression over the last few hours and that helps clear the mind. Apparently you can get the same effect with something called a primal scream, but the recent screams weren't mine.

I was in Randall's piece of shit car and avoiding driving above sixty. Not because I didn't want to attract any attention, though that was good enough reason, but because the wheel shake when the needle passed sixty told me he cared as much about maintaining his car as he did about personal hygiene and moral standards.

It was good of him to let me have his car. I'd asked if it was okay to take it before I left, and he hadn't said no. If he had a change of heart later and reported it stolen it didn't matter. I doubted the local police would care much about an ancient Buick LeSabre that was worth more in scrap value than as an actual car. To be fair I would be glad to get where I was going and be done with it.

I had the windows cracked down for welcome ventilation and to air out the rank beefy odor of Randall's old sweat. There was nothing I could do about the perspiration stains on the brown velour seats and just had to tolerate sitting there for a couple of hours. I'd kept my gloves on, and not just to avoid getting any prints on the controls.

Even this piece of shit car beat getting the bus back to Portland in a number of ways. There was no need to be seen in a public place or to mix with any other passengers. Using an unknown car would make it harder for Fisk to find me. It's one thing to check on public transport, which would be hard to do regardless, but nigh-on impossible to check every car coming into the city. Plus I was master of my own destiny and could choose my route, or as far as half a tank of gas got me. There was no way I'd be feeding the junker more fuel.

I took a different route back to Portland, up the 197 and then along the I84. It may have been a longer journey but there was more traffic – easier to blend in – and it meant I'd be returning to the city from a new and unexpected direction.

*

Three hours later and the Buick was sucking fumes, the fuel light on the dash glowing, but I was back in Portland and close to home.

I ditched the car in the far side of a parking lot belonging to a pizza house four blocks away from where I lived. I left the keys in the ignition. As far as I was concerned the LeSabre had done its last journey with me. Someone else could have it now.

From there I walked up one block and across one block before turning east along the road with houses that backed on to those in my own street, and in particular my own home.

Will and Freda Reardon are a pleasant couple, late thirties with no kids. Both have some sort of professional office job so are usually at work during the day. I felt safe that there would be no one home and sure enough there were no cars on the frontage.

I walked along the side entry of the house and tried their gate. It was a tall, solid-looking, wooden affair that was securely bolted from the inside. I looked at the 'Beware of the Dog' sign and smiled. The image on the sign depicted a slavering beast that looked like the bastard offspring of a crazed rottweiler and Cerberus, obviously designed to scare any potential intruders or at least make them think twice before attempting any forced entry.

I knew better.

Millie was a springer spaniel who was more likely to lick

someone to death than bite them. She'd escaped into my yard a number of times before but to be honest I didn't mind. I'd always manage to find her a treat or other small morsel before taking her back to Will and Freda. That happy little spaniel often made me think about a having dog myself someday.

I carefully passed my bag over the gate, letting it drop as gently as I could to the ground. Then, bracing against the brickwork of the house, hauled myself up and over into the yard beyond. It was hard work, but I managed it. I was grateful for the leather gloves, though they were now getting well scuffed.

Sure enough I heard a muffled woof and the pattering of paws on concrete slabs. Millie appeared, ears flying and tongue lolling as she ran. I knelt down and beckoned her towards me. Her tail wagged madly as she bounded towards me.

Sadly, I had no treats for her, but I did give her a lot of fuss and attention before moving down to the bottom of their garden to where it butted up against mine. The little spaniel followed me, probably curious as to what I was doing and probably hoping I'd play with her. I was glad she wasn't the sort of noisy dog that does a lot of barking.

I found a small crack in the woodwork, knelt down and squinted through. There was no one around that I could see. I remained still and quiet and looking for a good two minutes. During that time Millie lost interest in me, gave a soft huff of disappointment and wandered back up towards the patio.

I saw no movement or signs of anyone at the rear of my house. The place looked pretty much as I'd left it. I don't know if I really expected there to be a police cordon or even one of Fisk's lackeys waiting for me to show up, but a little caution seemed wise.

I gave it another thirty seconds, stood up, and pulled myself over into my own yard, dropping low as I landed.

A few seconds later I was at the back wall and crouching down on the wooden decking underneath the kitchen window. I listened hard. I heard nothing.

At the edge of the decking, and well away from the seating

area, there are a series of terracotta pots of differing sizes, each containing a cactus or some other hardy succulent. In one of them is an ugly looking brute of a plant with big spines on it – a gift from the other NCOs when I left the army. It was smaller back then. Much smaller. They said it reminded them of me: ugly and hard to kill. It was an old line and over-used, but I still smiled briefly at the memory.

I went over to the pot, tilted it and felt underneath. Stuck to the base was some modeling clay containing a key. The only problem was that it was for my front door, and I'd have laid good money that if any part of the house was being watched it would be the front.

I pocketed the key and cautiously made my way back along the wall to the corner of the house. I peered around it looking down the driveway.

My pick-up was still there, canted over on its flat tires. I felt a flash of anger. I was even more sure that had been done to delay me meeting Sean, as was the pointless roadside check when I'd been on the bike.

From my current position I could see nothing else. Maybe I could have just strolled up to my front door, bold as you like, and nothing would have happened, but somehow I doubted it.

I crept down the driveway along the side of the house towards the front. The kitchen door had crime scene tape across it. I tried it as I passed. As expected, it was now locked.

As I got closer to the end of the drive, I could make out the front of a car parked on the road. A police cruiser, two figures inside, parked in easy sight of my front porch.

I reckoned it was there as a deterrent, nothing more. If Fisk had really thought I'd be coming back, and wanted to catch me, then there would have been an unmarked car positioned further away but still with a view of the place.

Unless the cruiser being there was a bluff, meant to make me think that way. Maybe there was someone waiting in the house just in case I did return.

I shook my head, annoyed. I was getting too paranoid, second-guessing myself and seeing suspicious shadows everywhere. However, a little voice inside my head reminded me that it's not paranoia when they really are out to get you and at the moment that was certainly true.

I had two aims in coming home.

One – retrieve my emergency funds. There was no doubt I'd be needing those before long.

Two – get my bike if I could. I needed quick and independent transport I could rely on.

The first problem was to get rid of the uniformed cops in the cruiser, and that meant getting them to move out of position somehow. For all I knew they were just a couple of regular guys on their shift that had nothing to do with Fisk and his crooked circle, in which case I wanted to keep them well out of harm's way. Hurting or killing decent cops was something I had no desire to do.

I retraced my steps to the rear of the house, across the yard and clambered back over into Will and Freda's garden, sending silent thanks to Will for installing such a robust fence. Millie the spaniel greeted me again and followed me up the garden wagging all the way. I made a mental note to treat her to a juicy steak sometime.

It was far easier getting out through the gate from the inside. I undid the bolts and left it on the latch, making sure the little dog was left safe inside.

From there I walked up to the next street and along past the top of my own road. I glanced down and saw the cruiser sat there facing downhill. Even from this distance and with the reflections on the rear screen I could see that the two cops were still sat in there. I carried on walking.

The houses on the opposite side of the street were single story, wooden clad, with a wide sheltered porch and a small front yard mostly laid to a variety of gardening tastes. All were set back on the rise of the hill bringing the rooflines almost level with the larger two-story homes opposite. They weren't anything fancy or big but were all in good repair and sat comfortably within the neighborhood.

The fourth house along had lathe-turned balusters below the porch railing, all recently painted white. I knew this because I'd been the one to turn, fit and paint them.

I went down the tidy shrub-edged pathway, up the steps to the porch, and rang the bell.

It took a minute, but Dolores answered.

"Hey Dean, how are you? Come on in," she warbled, a bright grin appearing on her lined brown face.

Dolores was somewhere in her late eighties or early nineties. I'd known her since I'd first visited in my role as a beat cop after she'd been burglarized. That was close on twenty years ago now and I'd kept a neighborly eye on her ever since.

Her joints may have been on the way out and she relied on a walking frame more and more, but she was still playing with a full deck as far as her mind was concerned. I helped her out from time to time with those odd jobs a practical son or nephew might do, if you had any that were willing.

"I'm not too bad thanks," I said, accepting her invitation and going in. "But I've got a problem I'm hoping you can help me with."

She grinned at me.

"Me help you for once – that's a change!"

She ushered me through and we sat down in her front room.

"Really Dol'," she liked to be called 'Dol', she said it made her feel like a chick from the fifties, "it could mean you getting in some trouble with the law."

"Balls to that! It's been years since I've got into trouble," she said, a cheeky look in her eyes. "Besides, what are they going to do to an old lady?"

She had a point.

"If you're sure."

"Of course I am," she chided. "Now what do you need me to do."

I told her.

I also told her what had been going on. Not everything, and not enough to alarm her, but the main events and enough background for her to get a picture of what had happened since Sean's disappearance.

Maybe I shouldn't have said anything, but she was that sort of a lady. I knew I could trust her and knew she'd not say anything to anyone else. Sometimes it's good to have someone older and wiser to talk and offload your troubles to.

And I'm supposed to be a tough guy?

*

I checked my watch as I made my way back to Will and Freda's side gate. The countdown on the G-Shock told me I had ten minutes to get into position.

Not a problem.

On my way through their garden I even managed to find time to give Millie some fuss, before climbing over the fence into my own yard again and along to a suitable vantage point.

Dolores was true to her word and did what we'd planned, and the gamble paid off.

I saw the police cruiser start up, perform a rapid U-turn in the road and accelerate away.

If it had been a report of a gangbanger with a shotgun, they probably would have let another unit take the call so they could stay in position, but a naked young pretty female with a kitchen knife and hiding in an old lady's garden? That was another matter.

I went along the driveway quickly enough to see the car disappear around the corner. I stepped onto the tiny front porch and swiftly let myself in through the door, threading my way through more crime scene tape and leaving it unbroken.

I closed the door gently behind me, keeping my hand on the latch and not allowing it to click. I remained standing still and silent in the hallway. The first impression was that the house was quiet.

I listened carefully then stepped into the lounge, my boots making no sound on the carpet.

I'd lived there on and off since I'd been a boy, although then it had been my parents' place. It was somewhere I always thought of as home, even during all those years in the army and then in the Rangers.

Now it was my house. Refitted and redecorated by my own hands. I knew its sounds, its smells and how it should feel.

And it felt wrong.

Perhaps it was the subconscious effect of knowing the two cops, Gibbs and Harris, had been shot down only yards from where I was standing. But it wasn't just that.

There was a soft creak from upstairs.

Someone was up there.

FOURTEEN

I knew that I didn't have a lot of time.

Dolores' call would get dismissed quickly enough once the two cops had looked around and, despite the offer of coffee and cake, the guys in the cruiser would be back soon enough. I had to move fast.

But there was need for silence too.

I gently placed the blue sports bag on the carpet and took out Killick's automatic. I had left it cocked but it was safe. The Glock won't accidentally fire; the trigger itself contains a safety. But if I did shoot it would be loud and it could attract plenty of attention.

The first thing I needed from the house was in my bedroom, so I had no choice. I had to climb those wooden treads.

I looked down at my boots. Not the quietest of footwear, though there was more a risk of the soft rubber soles squeaking on the wood than any harder clonk as I trod on each step.

I went up the stairs with the pistol ready. I went slowly, trod carefully, and took my time.

I would usually have been up the stairs in less than ten seconds. But that was under normal circumstances, and these weren't normal circumstances, so it took five times longer.

Before reaching the top of the stairs I stopped. From where I was standing, I could peer around the corner of the stair wall and into the upper hallway, the top of my chest roughly level with the hallway floor.

All the doors in the hallway were ajar. Only slightly, only maybe by a couple of inches, but enough to know there had been someone up here. That was no surprise. CSI and a couple of detectives would have made a search of the place since Gibbs and Harris had been killed yesterday. Hopefully it had been a regular check-over rather than an in-depth investigation. If they'd gone to the lengths of shifting furniture and lifting floorboards, then I was screwed.

But from what I'd seen downstairs, I doubted it.

I knew my home well. I'd refurbished most of it and was used to its atmosphere. The subtle smell of the waxed oak floors was still there but there was something else. Weak but still detectable. It wasn't strong enough to be a cologne, but I definitely caught the scent of body spray or aftershave failing to mask the odor of stale sweat.

I heard the creak again. It was barely audible, but it was there and I recognized it. It came from the leather chair I used in my small office, a room at the far end of the upstairs hallway. Like all the other doors up there it was only open a couple of inches.

I stayed where I was, close to the top of the stairs, and used my free hand to dig out a quarter from my pocket. I gave it a gentle roll along the wooden hallway. It trundled across the floor making a sound like water dribbling from a height. The noise was louder than I expected, probably exaggerated by the silence. As the coin rolled, I heard a louder creak of the office chair moving as someone shifted their weight.

I stayed shielded behind the stairway wall, eyes fixed on my office door, gun held aimed and steady.

A shadow fell across the gap in the doorway, and a split second later I realized I'd been out of the game for too long and was way slower than I used to be.

The first bullet hit the wall just above my head. The sound of the shot was like a muffled truck air brake, and even though the gun had a silencer it was still loud.

By comparison the sound of Killick's Glock 17 was immense.

I fired three times, not at the gap but spacing my shots across the door. Thin wood has little effect on 9mm rounds and they punched through as if it wasn't there. I heard a grunt of pain as at least one of them found the hidden shooter.

I thundered up the last few stairs onto the upper hallway and ran forward, firing another three spaced shots, all need for stealth gone. I kicked the office door and heard a grunt of pain as it banged half open, jamming against a body on the floor. I saw a pistol rising towards me and I fired another three deafening shots at the gunman's center mass.

The hand and gun fell, dropping hard on the wooden floor.

I shoved the door open, took the gun off him, and quickly returned to the hallway, rapidly opening doors to each of the remaining rooms.

I didn't think I would find anyone else, but it was better to check now than be sorry later. Having said that, I think if there had been anyone else waiting in one of the rooms, I would have known about it by now.

I frowned as I realized they could have shot me as I ran past. I was way out of practice, but what else could I have done?

I went back into the office and looked down at the shooter.

He was a stocky guy with a shaved head, probably somewhere in his late thirties. Patches of blood bloomed on his light grey track jacket like abstract poppies. I'd hit him a total of five times. Only slightly more than a fifty percent success rate but it was enough. His open unseeing eyes told me he was dead.

I did a quick check of his jacket pockets and his jeans, putting everything up on the desk.

If he was a cop, there was no way he was legitimate. Lack of any badge or ID was a start, but waiting in my house ready to assassinate me was the clincher. Besides he didn't *look* like a cop. More like a mid-level thug.

There was something on the stocky guy's arm, a tattoo, only just noticeable at the edge of his sleeve. I knelt down and pushed the jacket back to take a closer look.

The tattoo was a word of some kind, though I couldn't read it. It wasn't English, that was a fact; nor did it look like Russian or Arabic. To my eyes it almost looked like some kind of satanic script, but from the stylized cross behind it I guessed otherwise.

I checked the other arm and found more tattoos. A series of bladed stars and a two-headed eagle against a shield. It told me nothing other than hinting that the guy might be foreign and possibly eastern European.

I thought back to what Killick had told me. I reckoned the shooter was part of the Armenian gang.

The gun he'd used was a 9mm Glock 17 like the one I had, but his had the added bonus of a silencer. I was pretty sure it would come in useful, so I put that on the desk and quickly looked through what I'd found.

There was a cheap cell phone, the screen cracked and now as dead as its owner. Useless.

No wallet, credit cards or anything with a name on it. Just a wad of twenty-dollar bills and some change, in total a little over two hundred bucks. I left the change and pocketed the notes. They'd be more use to me than to the guy on the floor.

There was a spare full clip for the silenced Glock. I took that too.

I now had three guns and a fair amount of ammo, but I wasn't finished yet.

There was little time to waste. Those cops distracted by Dolores would be back soon enough, especially if they heard any gunshots.

Then again, although the gunfire was loud from where I was inside the middle of the house, the thick double glazing and simple fact of location would significantly muffle the sound of the shots.

I went into my bedroom and over to the built-in wardrobes, opening the leftmost door. My clothes were still there but they had been moved around like someone had been checking through them. It was the same with what I kept on the floor. The few boxes of photos were out of order and assorted magazines had spilled out from where I kept them in a neat stack.

I had a moment of worry as I shifted everything aside, but it looked like the wooden floor underneath was untouched.

A section of the woodwork could be slid open if you knew

how to do it. I'd designed and installed it myself after years of hobby carpentry. When you have enough time to develop the skill, anything is possible, and it was cheaper and less obvious than a safe.

In the gap beneath the floor, I took out two zip-loc plastic bags. There was around two thousand dollars in the one; I remember feeling paranoid each time I'd opened it and put a little more money away, but I guess it was safer than leaving it under the mattress. I have proper savings accounts at the bank too, but knowing you have some proper cash nearby is reassuring.

To be fair, when I'd stored it, I thought I might end up spending it on something like a holiday, not as funds for being on the run or rescuing a nephew. I was glad I had it regardless.

The other bag contained two passports and associated documentation. One passport was in my name and the other was a fake Canadian one in the name Bruce MacLaine, just like the account I'd used at the Madras ATM. There was also a driving license for me as Bruce MacLaine, all courtesy of my CIA pal Archie Howell.

For a spook he was all right and I hoped he was okay, though it had been a few years since I'd last seen him. Who knows, maybe he'd retired.

I put the passports back. I wasn't going to need them. The money was what I'd come upstairs for.

I reset the floor, carefully arranged the boxes and put the magazines back into place.

I was cautious going downstairs, but didn't think that anyone else would be lying in wait, not after all the commotion on the first floor.

I deposited the guns in the bag and took it through to the kitchen.

Harris' and Gibbs' bodies had been removed but their bloodstains remained. My revolver and Killick's gloves had gone as well. No surprises there. I went over to one of the kitchen units and opened the drawer. Various sets of keys were inside. I selected the ones I wanted and pocketed them. There was no sign of my spare set of house keys. I suspected that Fisk or one of his lackeys probably had taken them, unless the dead guy upstairs had used them and they were sitting on my desk in plain sight and I hadn't noticed them. It was too late to go back and check now and I didn't need them anyway.

I heard the noise of a car pulling up at the front of the house. I guessed it was the cops returning. A glance back through the kitchen door and out the lounge window confirmed it. The police cruiser had returned.

Both cops got out of the car, stared at the house and said something to each other before hitching up their belts and walking up the driveway. I saw one guy take up position looking down the side of the house past my Dodge pick-up towards the kitchen door while the other peered in through the front window.

I got myself out of sight and sat on the floor in the far corner of the kitchen. In that position I couldn't be seen from any of the kitchen windows let alone from the front of the house. I sat still and quiet and waited.

I heard footsteps coming along the side of the house. At that point a thought occurred, and it gave me a cold stab of worry.

What if these cops had my spare keys?

The steps were getting closer. I scooted on my belly across the smooth wooden floor to the bottom of the half-glazed kitchen door, gently slid the lower door bolt closed, then shuffled back out of sight.

The handle clacked as the cop tried it. He tried again and the door creaked as he put a bit of weight behind it, perhaps thinking it was stiff in the frame. It wasn't. The door was locked, I knew that from earlier.

Now came the moment of truth. I'd find out if they had my spare keys.

"Locked," the cop by the kitchen door said to his partner.

There was the sound of the front door being tried, but I heard no jangle of keys or rasp of key in the lock.

More footsteps. The cop who'd been at the side kitchen door was moving around to the rear of the house and my back yard. There was a faint squeak from the window, and I imagined him resting the edges of his hands on the glass as he shielded his eyes to peer in.

I stayed still. Out of sight. Quiet and immobile. I waited and listened.

Another small sound, then more footsteps as he walked back up the driveway. I heard both cops' voices but couldn't make out anything. Moments later there was the muffled thump of car doors closing.

I breathed a little easier, moving my head to relieve some of the tension that had built in my neck. I gave the cops another couple of minutes to settle back in the warmth of the cruiser, letting them relax and any small amount of adrenaline from their search to fade.

Slowly and cautiously I checked around me, making sure no one was still looking in. I moved, keeping low, to the kitchen door adjoining the lounge. Through the front window I could see both cops in the car. They looked like they were talking, just chewing the fat. Probably talking about mad old ladies and phantom naked chicks.

There was another bit of luck in my favor. When they had returned from Dolores' false alarm, whoever had been driving had not parked the car as far forward as before.

From where they were now sitting, they couldn't see all the way down my drive.

And that meant they couldn't see the kitchen door as I opened it, slipped under the tape and made my way towards the garage.

FIFTEEN

My garage is a solid wooden structure that I'd extended over the years, building a modest workshop on the back of it. That's where all my woodworking machinery lives. The table saw I'd bought new, the lathe was second hand but a real good one. It was one way I'd spent any spare dollars I'd picked up.

The original main part of the garage is big enough for me to fit the pick-up, have the roller door closed and still be able to work on it. Not massive, but plenty big enough.

My truck stays on the drive pretty much all the time, as the space inside the garage is usually taken up with stacks of wood I'm drying and any furniture or other woodworking projects I'm in the middle of making.

But the main reason it stays outside is my bike: a slice of British beef called a Triumph Thunderbird Storm. Harleys are nice but a bit too commonplace; I was drawn to a Victory – another British muscle bike – but the Triumph did it for me. It's a guy thing.

I used the keys I'd taken from the kitchen, unlocked the workshop side door and slipped inside, closing the door softly behind me.

The early afternoon light streamed through the clear polycarbonate roof and the small upper windows at the rear of the workshop. My tools were all still in place on the wall opposite the door and nothing looked like it had been touched.

To my right a clear double-glazed door leads into the garage and lets through a bit of light. Even so, the garage remains pretty dark unless the roller shutter door is open, and most of the time I rely on a series of fluorescent strip lights strung across the ceiling.

There was just enough natural illumination to make out the big Triumph amongst the darkness.

I went through to the garage, turning on one set of the fluorescents. The lights blinked, flickered on and most of the darkness vanished. The construction of the main door and lack of any windows meant I wasn't worried about the cops suddenly seeing light spilling out and coming to investigate.

I'd not cleaned the bike since getting back from Barton Bridge the other night. It had been late, and I'd been tired, so its normal gloss black paintwork and shining chrome pipes looked dusty and muted under the strip lights. It didn't matter. Right then I needed it for transport, not for show.

I sorted out the sports bag, making sure I had all I was likely to need and leaving behind anything unnecessary. I grabbed a couple of old towels from a side cabinet, shook them out, and used them to wrap the guns and spare clips. I was gathering quite an arsenal.

There's a locker by the entrance to my workshop where I keep my riding gear. I changed into some Kevlar-lined jeans and shrugged on my old brown leather biker's jacket. I kept my footwear as it was. Definitely not as safe as wearing proper motorcycle boots but probably more useful to me later. The new tan gloves I'd bought remained in the sports bag. They'd be no use at all if I fell off. I took out a pair of proper padded riding gloves instead and placed these on the top of the bike's fuel tank.

I slung the bag over my back and tightened the straps so it sat there snugly and wouldn't move around. I picked up my open face helmet and goggles. I was nearly ready.

The Triumph looks like a big mean bike. It is powerful and no lightweight, but it is very comfortable and easy to ride. The saddle height is low enough so you don't need to stretch your legs when maneuvering the machine, and that is a good thing as it weighs around seven hundred pounds. Not something you want to overbalance on.

I swung my leg over the bike, settled onto the black leather saddle and slid the key into the ignition barrel down low next to my right thigh.

The next minute would be some challenge. I hoped I was up to it.

I took a breath and put on my silver helmet, pulled on the riding gloves and lowered my goggles.

I rocked the Triumph off its stand, thumbed the starter and the big bike erupted into life. The bass engine note reverberated deeply in the confines of the garage. It was still running the standard exhaust and I was glad of that now. I doubted that the cops sat out in the cruiser would have been aware of the bike starting, something that would have been much different had I been running a set of loud custom pipes on it.

As soon as the Triumph fired up, I pressed the remote for the garage door opener. The roller shutter clacked and rattled as it gradually raised revealing daylight and the driveway beyond. This was the part that would get the cops' attention. I didn't know how much of the garage they could see from where they were, but I guessed it was enough.

I already had the bike in gear and eased it forward on the clutch. There was no need for any throttle, its 1700cc parallel twin engine had more than enough torque to allow me to trickle it forward onto the driveway as I positioned to pass through the narrow gap between the side of the house and my Dodge pick-up.

With the helmet on and the rumbling of the big engine there was no way I could hear if the cops were getting out of the car. I reckoned I'd know soon enough.

What I didn't want to see was them with their guns drawn, pointed at me from the end of the driveway. That would put an end to my planned escape real quickly. Anything I did with them in that position would be suicide.

So far I was okay, but it had to be only a matter of seconds before they appeared, and I was only just starting to squeeze past the big Dodge.

I decided to go for it.

I gave the Triumph a little more throttle, feathered the clutch and got my feet onto the foot pegs as it picked up speed.

They say if you can get through a gap at six, you can get through it at sixty, it's just a matter of confidence.

Now I could see them. Both men were out of the car and on the driveway. Both had their weapons drawn but not yet raised.

I changed up a gear and got serious with the throttle. The big bike roared forwards towards the advancing cops. They barely had a second to react and I was counting on self-preservation taking over rather than them taking any pot shots at me.

Luckily I counted right. They ran aside as I blasted past, both of them unsure how else to react and reluctant to shoot. There have been too many lawsuits from innocent folks being hit by stray bullets in recent years that blasting away like Dirty Harry at someone on a motorbike made them think twice.

But I wasn't looking at them.

I was concentrating ahead. I saw a compact hatchback coming down the street. It would be close, but at least there was nothing in the other lane. More luck on my side.

The Triumph shot across the sidewalk and I hauled it over, leaning hard into as tight a turn as I could and fighting to keep it balanced. I felt the fat rear tire wiggle as the speed and weight of the bike threatened to break traction and slide away from me.

I heard the blare of the car's horn. I hung on. The bike didn't let me down. It made the turn and we were through, rising upright along the straight and powering away from the two cops.

I rode hard, making a couple of tight turns on the way. I heard a siren from somewhere behind, but the police cruiser was too far back to have any realistic hope of catching up. I guessed that they might have been able to catch glimpses of me, so I went through a series of narrow alleyways they had little chance of taking, finally stopping in the empty back lot of a Chinese restaurant.

I rested the bike on its side stand, shut it off and removed my helmet.

I could still hear sirens but there didn't seem to be any heading in my direction. Just the usual background city noise.

My nerves felt stretched as taught as a garroting wire. A gunfight and riding like you're Steve McQueen on a mission will do that. I swung my leg off the bike and stood, stretching out the kinks in my back and letting my pulse rate calm down.

I awkwardly shrugged the sports bag off and rested it on the saddle. It wasn't the most comfortable thing to use when riding, but it was serving a purpose. Besides it was good and strong and could hold all I needed it to. I checked around before opening it. There was no one around nor were there any security cameras. It was as safe as I could hope for, but even so I kept my hands in the bag and the guns hidden as I reloaded.

It helps giving your hands something familiar to do as you collect your thoughts.

I'd fired nine shots from Killick's Glock, so I stuck a fresh clip into it, one that I'd taken from either Gibbs or Harris only yesterday morning. The would-be assassin had only managed to fire one shot, but I checked the silenced gun anyway. Sure enough, there were sixteen rounds remaining, but I decided to stick a full one in regardless. You never know when that extra bullet will make all the difference.

I was feeling calmer now.

But that was because I had no idea of the amount of violence that lay ahead.

SIXTEEN

I swung my leg over the big Triumph, hit the starter and set off towards my next destination.

Killick had given me useful information. Richard, Sean's stepfather, was involved and being manipulated by Fisk and the Armenians. I could confront Richard, maybe get him to work with me in getting Sean back or help stall for time. I could also find out exactly what it was all about.

It was a long shot and not a good option.

Richard and I did not get on and I didn't fully trust him. Ultimately he would put himself and his needs before Sean's, I was sure of it.

Approaching Richard was a last resort.

Another option was tracking down Dan Perez.

If he was in Fisk's circle – and, as Killick had said, been part of Sean's abduction – then there would be some talking he'd be doing for me. He might be reluctant at first, but after I got creative with Chubby Diesel's knife, he'd soon be telling me all I wanted to know.

Perez lived out the other side of Wood Village, to the east of the city. At least he did when I last knew him. It wasn't a big house, but it had enough room for him, his wife, and a couple of kids. The neighborhood was good, and it meant the children had access to some decent schools. Perez had been pleased about that. The proud father thinking of his kids' futures.

I'd been there a few times, just for occasional poker nights and a couple of summer barbeques and could easily remember how to get there.

As I rode, I wondered what had happened.

Dan Perez did not seem the kind of guy who would end up crooked. Okay, he was tough enough to do the job, but he was easy going and likeable with it. He was the sort of detective that was best suited to play 'good cop' because that came most naturally to him. He was a likeable family man and appeared to be totally contented with his lot. I really couldn't work it out.

I parked the big bike a block away, locked my helmet to it and set the alarm. It wouldn't stop a group of determined scumbags heaving it into a van, but it was a deterrent to the casual thief. It wasn't the sort of area I thought that sort of thing happened on a regular basis, but the way my luck had been running I didn't want to take the chance.

I took the unsilenced Glock out of the bag and slid it into my jacket pocket, making sure nobody was taking an interest in me and what I was doing.

The sidewalk around there was level and I made good time despite strolling at a relaxed pace. A man moving quickly and with purpose always attracts more attention, so I took my time.

It was only early afternoon and the sun still had some heat in it so I unzipped the jacket and stuck my right hand in the pocket with the gun holding it so the profile wouldn't show, keeping the bag in my left hand.

I reached Perez's house. It was pretty much as I'd remembered it.

The palings on the front porch had been painted in alternating colors of blue and yellow to match the twin swing seat standing on the front lawn. The whole place appeared to be in good repair, though as I looked closer I could see that some of the paintwork was tired and the lawn was getting patchy around the edges and underneath the swings. It was like the owners had cared about the place but now simply didn't have the time or money to keep it looking as good as it could be.

I casually checked around. I could see nothing suspicious – no anonymous cars cruising past, no unmarked vans parked at the curb – so walked up to the front porch.

I noted there was no car on the driveway and could see a couple of months of weeds poking up through the paving. This wasn't the Perez family I remembered, but people change, I guess.

I wondered if anyone would be at home.

I had to check there first. There was no way I'd be heading to the precinct station to find Perez unless I decided to give up, so there I was.

I went up the porch steps and over to the front door, rang the bell and waited.

Twenty seconds passed.

I rang the bell again. I could hear the muted chimes from where I was standing.

Another ten seconds.

Then I heard footsteps. Someone coming down the staircase inside the house.

A shadowy figure appeared at the doorway. Not a large person, so not Perez, but not small, so not a child.

The latch clicked and the door opened a crack stopping against the security chain. I saw a sliver of a teenage girl's face peering at me. `

"Yes?" her voice was reserved, cautious.

I racked my brain. When I last knew him, Dan Perez had a daughter who was twelve. She was a willowy girl, taking after her mother with her slight build. What was her name?

"Elena?" I asked.

She looked at me, surprised and cautious.

"Sorry, it's been a while," I continued. "I used to work with your father, Dan. I guess he's down at the precinct."

"Mr. Riley?" she asked, "Is that you?"

Now it was my turn to be surprised.

"You remember me?"

Elena laughed and nodded. "Yeah, I remember you. You scared me – and my little brother. No one messes with old Dean Riley, my dad used to say."

"Such a reputation," I laughed, ignoring the 'old' part. She seemed a nice kid. "I'll have to have words with your dad."

Her demeanor changed in a moment, like a fast cloud crossing her face.

"He's out. With mom. At the hospital."

"The hospital?"

Elena nodded briefly and then began to shake her head. She had trouble speaking. "I'm sorry. Did you want to come in and wait? Dad should be back soon."

I spoke softly. "No. I'm sorry. I was only passing by."

She nodded again.

I had to ask another question. "Which hospital?"

Elena told me that her mother, Maria Perez, was in the Legacy Emmanuel Center Hospital in the center of Portland. She was under the Oncology department and had a separate room all to herself.

That did not sound good.

I also got Dan Perez's cell phone number from her. I thought it might come in useful.

Then I thanked her and walked back to the Triumph.

This time I was moving quickly.

*

The Legacy Emmanuel Center Hospital was where my sister Claire worked. To be more accurate, she was a nurse in the Randall Children's Hospital that lay across from the main unit, but it was close enough.

She was always good with kids, taking after our mother on that score; certainly not like me.

Before reaching the hospital, I pulled in at a cell phone store. The ones I already had in the bag were no use to me; I needed one that Fisk wasn't easily going to trace.

I spoke with a bored-looking girl who couldn't have been much older than school-leaving age. I span her some yarn about being on holiday, losing my phone and now after something that would work pretty much straight away, so the battery needed to have some power in it already.

I honestly don't think she cared what I told her. I could have said I wanted it to trigger a bomb in a school and she'd still have had the same uninterested expression on her face. I doubted working in retail was set to be her future for long.

However, she did find me a new phone with a part charged battery, even though it was a lot more than I wanted to pay. Maybe she did have a future there after all.

My leather jacket had an inside pocket that was perfect for the small phone. The charger went into the sports bag. Then I was back on the bike and off into the traffic.

Ten minutes later I was circling the roads around The Legacy Emmanuel Center, working out where to leave the bike. I eventually found a space for the Triumph in one of the multi-story parking lots near the hospital, locked the helmet to the bike again and walked over to the main entrance. I was about to go in to the reception area when I noticed a couple of uniformed cops checking out any folks walking into the area. They were being subtle and I only just saw them in time. I couldn't go in that way.

I walked around the other side of the building towards the entrance by the atrium.

Again, there were a couple of uniforms paying too much attention to people passing through for my liking.

This was becoming more of a challenge than I thought it would be. I guessed that Fisk was anticipating I'd try to contact Claire and had assigned extra officers accordingly.

It didn't change the fact that I still needed to have words with Perez. He was the next link and he'd tell me something, whether he liked it or not.

I looked around the area and noticed the enclosed footbridge leading from the Medical Office Plaza on the far side of North Graham Street over the road and into the Medical Center itself.

Five minutes later I had managed to slip through a side door into the Plaza building and make my way up to the bridge. My hopes that there would be no other cops on duty there were rewarded. Even post 9/11 it can be surprisingly easy to get into most public facilities if you are white, Caucasian, and act like you should be there.

I found a reception desk on the third floor. It was busy but not crowded. I waited my turn to speak with the nurse behind the counter. She was around my age, and the dark bags under her eyes told me it had been a long shift. I had enough charm and gave sufficient information for her to direct me to Maria Perez's room. I found it easily.

I took the main safety off the gun and kept my hand deep in my jacket pocket and ready on it. With my free hand I softly opened the door to the room and slipped inside.

Dan Perez was sat on an upright hospital chair next to the bed, where a thin woman was lying immobile. Her eyes were closed and she was breathing shallowly. Tubes from her arms, nose and other extremities led up to bags of fluid and numerous monitors that displayed information that I could only guess at. I noticed Perez clasping her thin pale hand in his own as he glanced to look at who had just entered.

"Hello Dan," I said quietly. There was no need to draw the gun yet.

My appearance was unexpected; it showed clearly on his face. Surprise quickly gave way to a resigned anger.

"Fuck, Riley. What the hell you doing here? Is nothing sacred to you?" he growled. His hand had left his wife's but was still on the bed.

I shrugged. My mother had died in a similar way and I'd gotten over it. But that was a long time ago and I knew how time dulled the pain of loss.

Dan Perez was smaller than I remembered. Back in the day he had been a broad man, powerfully built and close to my height, full of vibrancy, life and easy laughter. Now he appeared to be a shrunken shadow of his former self.

"What is it?" I asked looking down at the frail woman in the bed.

"Liver. Lymph glands. Lungs," he said. The words were bitter. It was a merciless death sentence.

"How long?"

He looked at his watch then looked up at me, curling his lip.

"Wait and see."

I let go of the gun and took my hand out of the pocket.

"I'm sorry Dan, but you know why I'm here."

He gave a soft mirthless laugh and returned his gaze to Maria, to his dying wife.

"Sean," he said.

I nodded but he wasn't looking at me.

"Where is he?"

"I don't know."

"You were there. At Barton Bridge." It was a statement not a question. Perez looked at me.

"Yeah," he said. "Me and Marshall. Pick him up and deliver him on, just like UPS."

"You passed him on?" I asked. "Who to?"

"Not sure. I stayed in the car while she handed him over to three guys in a blue van."

"So you don't know where he was taken?" I guess I had started to sound angry and aggressive because Perez held up his hands trying to placate me.

"Sorry Riley, I'm low level, just a messenger boy. Even Killick gets to do more than me, but that's just because he's happy to get as dirty as they need."

"So why did you do it?"

Perez took a breath and shook his head, eyes drawn back to Maria's pallid face. "Fucking..." He couldn't finish his sentence.

I said nothing and let the silence hang until Perez found his voice.

"I guess you've been told about Marshall?" he asked.

I made an affirmative noise.

"She's a psycho. Clever, but still a psycho. No wonder she got transferred. And you already know Fisk well enough. Then there's others." He trailed off again.

"I need locations. I need names."

Dan Perez sat there and said nothing. He carried on holding his wife's hand and looking at her. I'd made the connections about why he'd gone on the take and felt a twinge of shame. All I'd ever done was spend the small amount I took on myself.

"Come on Dan." I spoke softly. "Names and places. All you know. I'll keep you out of it."

His eyes returned to mine for a second then went back to his wife. The only thing more important to Dan Perez than the job was his family, and rightly so. He would do whatever it took to look after them. Looking down at him I understood that now.

"Promise me that Elena and Lucas will be okay."

"What do you mean?" I said, my brow furrowing.

"Promise me," he insisted, "My kids. I want Elena and Lucas to be fine. To be cared for. Properly."

"Why wouldn't they be?" I stared at him.

He didn't answer.

I strode around the bed and hauled him up by his shirt front. I heard buttons pop. What he was insinuating made me angry.

"Listen to me and listen good," I snarled. "You're their father. You have a duty to do the best for them – so you best make sure you damn well do that." I looked down at the sedated woman and thought I saw her eyes flicker. "You owe it to her."

I let him go and he remained standing there facing me. "Unless you don't care anymore and want to let her down," I added as a verbal knife twist. The words cut him, and Perez angrily shoved me away. I didn't resist and stepped back.

He glared at me, some internal conflict flickering behind his dark eyes. I didn't know whether he was going to hit me or cry. In the end he did neither.

"Come on. Names and places," I repeated.

"Revenge?" he asked.

"Rescue – and justice. It's different."

He carried on looking at me, his eyes locked on mine. Five seconds passed then he looked away.

"Get some paper," he mumbled.

*

We used the back of an old medical chart, one that wouldn't matter anymore. As Dan wrote I went and collected a couple of coffees. He wasn't about to drop me in it, I knew that. By the time I got back, he was done.

I sat in one of the guest chairs and read through what he'd written. It was less than I'd expected. Way less. I looked up at him questioningly.

"That's all I have. We're not talking happy families here, Riley. No one at the precinct is trusted – and no one trusts each other. There's a kind of cell structure," that tallied with what Killick had said, "and I only know this from being there so long and keeping my eyes open. Only Fisk knows for sure who's involved because he controls it all and you remember how paranoid that bastard is."

I nodded, looking back at what he'd written.

There was Peter Killick: I already knew about him. I wondered if he'd got himself some new boots yet. I hadn't known his address, but Perez had.

There was a name I didn't know: Richards, a patrolman. No address.

The next name surprised me: Harris. Also a patrolman. I asked Perez to describe him, and he did. He was one of the guys Killick had shot. I guess he hadn't known they were on the same team when he pulled the trigger. This was a prime example of where Fisk's paranoia worked against him and those in his pocket.

At the top of the list was Fisk himself, though his address was still the old one that I knew. The riverside house that Killick had said Fisk had sold before getting the rented apartment. I quizzed

Perez on this, but it was news to him. He knew nothing about any apartment, but then he and Fisk didn't talk much outside work.

Underneath Perez was Linda Marshall. Perez had put a question mark next to her address, and it wasn't a complete one in any case. Just a street name. I asked him about it.

"Marshall's almost as paranoid as Fisk. Honestly I want nothing more to do with her."

"She's a sergeant, right?" I asked.

Perez nodded.

"But so are you."

He nodded again. "Yeah, but her background made her senior and Fisk told me to follow her lead. I may have been getting paid as a sergeant, but I might just as well still been a detective."

Looking at the list I knew there were more involved. Killick had mentioned a CSI technician, someone who was going to add to the evidence I'd been involved with Sean's abduction and the killing of Gibbs and Harris. The whole department could be shot through with corruption but there was only one man who knew for sure.

"Fisk," hissed Dan Perez.

I nodded.

"No, he's here!"

I looked up at Perez, disbelieving. "What?"

From where he was standing Perez could see out of the room and down part of the hospital hallway.

"He's with Marshall! They're outside, in the corridor!" Dan's voice held an edge of panic. "Go! Get in the bathroom. Now!"

SEVENTEEN

I scrambled out of the chair and ducked into the small en-suite bathroom off Maria's room, taking my sports bag and the sheet of paper with me. I left the door ajar by an inch, so I had a chance of hearing what went on.

I was fortunate in that the door to the main room was a solid one with no glass panel, so I was hidden from Fisk and Marshall's view. I was also lucky that, from where Perez had been standing, he had noticed them through the main window that looked onto the corridor.

He could have easily said nothing, let Fisk and Marshall suddenly walk in and me be cornered, but maybe the possible risk to his wife swayed his decision. I couldn't be totally sure but gave him the benefit of the doubt.

I heard the door to Maria's room open and then Fisk's voice.

"Can we come in?"

I didn't hear Perez say anything but assumed he'd nodded, because a moment later I heard the sound of a door closing and Fisk speaking again.

"Riley's here."

I felt cold. The gun was out of my pocket and aimed at the gap. There was silence for a moment and I imagined Perez pointing towards the en-suite door.

Then I heard Dan Perez's voice.

"You sure?" he said.

A female voice answered.

"One of the boys downstairs thought he saw him, and we've

found his bike in the parking lot. He's here all right." She had an East Coast city accent, possibly New York or New Jersey. I guessed this was Linda Marshall. "Reckon he's here to see his sister, like we thought he might. We've got someone on her. He ain't getting anywhere near." Her voice grated on me.

It came as a surprise that Claire was in and at work. With Sean 'missing' I thought she would be waiting at home, but I guess in today's world of cell phones she could be wherever she wanted, and being in work would help keep her occupied.

It was also a stroke of luck for me. I hadn't originally intended to see Claire; I'd gone to see Perez. But if my bike was being staked out, I now needed some alternative transport, and that's where I could use my sister's help. And besides that, I wanted to let her know I was going to get Sean back.

I stayed quiet and still and listened.

"Thought you ought to know," added Fisk. "Just in case he comes looking for you."

"Why would he?" asked Perez. "I haven't seen him in years."

"Killick might have talked. Riley was good at that, getting folks to talk."

In the bathroom I smiled without humor. If I had my way, Fisk would find out firsthand just how good I was at interrogation before I was through with him.

It could be over in seconds. They wouldn't expect it. I could pull open the door, shoot Marshall, take Fisk and make him tell me where Sean was.

But I had no escape plan. Nothing beyond immediate action. Getting out of the hospital with an unwilling hostage that was also a police captain would be bordering on the impossible.

"What do you want me to do if I see him?" said Perez.

Right or wrong, I decided to wait.

There was a half second pause before Linda Marshall spoke.

"Put him down. You need to make the shot count, but it'll be self-defense. We'll make sure it comes out that way."

"We don't need him running around causing trouble," said Fisk.

There was the tread of feet and the sound of a door handle. Fisk and Marshall were leaving.

"Hope your wife gets better soon." Marshall spoke the words but there was no sentiment or emotion behind them.

Perez's voice was flat. Matter of fact. "She's dying."

"Then I hope it's quick," snapped Fisk. "We've got work to do."

Fisk had never had a kind or considerate personality but that was cold, even for him. It sounded like the stress was getting to him.

I heard the door bang shut. I waited, still keeping the gun ready.

The door to the en-suite opened slowly. Perez was standing there, his hand on the door.

"Are you going to kill them?" he asked.

I lowered the gun. "Maybe. Part of me wants to, but it's best for them to face trial and the truth be heard." I didn't add that I wanted to clear my own name too, but that was secondary to getting Sean back.

"You going to turn me in too?"

"Should I? How deep are you in?"

He shrugged. "Deep enough to be guilty. Deep enough to go down. But as I said, not deep enough to be inner circle."

My hand tightened around the gun.

"So why do it? Why get involved?" It was a stupid question.

Perez barked a short mirthless laugh. "Because of her. Why else?" He met my eyes. "We don't have enough insurance and I need the money. Good enough?"

"Jesus! You're a fool Dan. You know getting into Fisk's pocket is a bad move. There had to have been other ways."

"What, like secretly making crystal meth?"

That made me smile. I shook my head at him and sighed. "I don't know. I'm not blaming you. But you're still a damn fool."

Dan Perez looked back at me, at first annoyed, but then a smile of his own appeared briefly and reluctantly on his face. For a moment I remembered him how he used to be. It soon vanished and I felt sorry for the guy.

"Come on," I said and ushered him out of the small en-suite and back into Maria's room. "You stay here with her."

"What are you going to do?" he asked.

"Get Sean back. Try to sort out the whole damn mess. Try not to get killed in the process."

Perez nodded. "Good enough. If you can do it."

He sat down and took his wife's limp hand again. Even with my limited knowledge I could tell from the monitors that things weren't good. We had to be talking about days at the most, if not hours.

There was something I had to ask before I left.

"I saw your girl Elena earlier. Are they going to be okay? The kids?"

Dan nodded. "My sister will be with them by now. It's best they don't see her like this. She wouldn't want it."

I looked back at him. I wanted to say something but really couldn't find the words.

In the end I gave him a brief nod and a thin smile that felt too tight on my face. I was about to leave the room when a thought occurred to me. I turned and asked Dan a question.

"Would you do something for me?"

*

I knew from what I had heard during the exchange between Fisk, Marshall and Perez that Claire, my sister and Sean's mother, was being watched. I would be seen as soon as I approached her, and Fisk and Marshall would know and within moments it would all be over. There would be too many innocent bystanders around to risk making a stand and I didn't want that.

After leaving Maria Perez's room I made my way along the corridor towards the far end of the hallway. I went through the far door into the empty stairwell and sped down four levels to the basement before heading across towards the other side of the building.

If Perez had done as I asked, and made his call letting them know he'd seen me nearby, then Fisk and Marshall would now be concentrating on the wrong area of the hospital. It didn't matter that it was solid confirmation I was there, since they had already told Perez they knew I was around somewhere in any case. I had lost nothing and gained the advantage of misdirection.

Another opportunity presented itself as I noticed a porter exiting from a door marked 'Laundry'. I caught the door before it closed and snuck into the corridor beyond.

A few seconds later I was in the roar of the steamy laundry room, surrounded by various white coats and pale blue smocks and pants. A couple of Asian guys spotted me, but I smiled and waved at them and made sign language that I was looking for a lost pen. It was what sprung to mind at the time, and it seemed to work as they shrugged and carried on with their work ignoring me.

I quickly searched through a sheaf of white coats hanging on a rail, found one that looked the right size and took it. Hospital camouflage. The only downside was ditching my expensive biker's jacket. Maybe I'd be able to get it back when this was all over. I transferred the phone into the sports bag and, as the pockets in the white coat weren't nearly big enough to accommodate the pistol without it showing, I had to stash it in there as well, carry it with me and hope I didn't need to get to it in a hurry any time soon.

I also found a clipboard and took that. It didn't matter that it had a cleaning rota on it. A middle-aged white guy in a white coat carrying a clipboard in a hospital just had to be a doctor. It was a better disguise than looking like a lost motorcycle courier.

I left the laundry room and returned up a level via the nearest stairwell, exiting into the main hallway before heading out and across the wide tree-lined courtyard that separated the large main medical center, and the Randall Children's Hospital where my sister worked.

The area had a few benches placed between the trees and half a dozen folks were sat in them enjoying the autumn afternoon sunshine. It wasn't a busy thoroughfare but there were enough people passing through, so I didn't stand out.

I was halfway across the area when the twin doors to the Randall Children's Hospital thirty yards ahead slid open. A broad, bearded uniformed cop stepped through them, striding with purpose towards me.

EIGHTEEN

I kept my eyes on the way ahead and avoided looking directly at the big cop. I was just a doctor on his way to the next building and his duties there. Just part of the hospital scenery, that's all I needed him to think.

The cop kept moving towards me along the wide tree-lined pathway. His hand was not near his sidearm, nor did he give any indication he was preparing for a confrontation.

I kept walking. Calm and steady.

The cop kept walking. Still swiftly, still with a purpose. If he had identified me then maybe he'd wait until he was past me before turning, drawing his gun and issuing his challenge.

I got ready. The environment would play to my advantage. The amount of space in the area, the proximity of the trees, and with the bystanders around: these would give me time, room to move, and enough cover. I would be evading, not shooting back if I could help it.

He passed by on my right, a couple of yards separating us.

The moments after we passed each other felt like an eternity. I was now two thirds of the way across the courtyard. I resisted the temptation to look behind me and continued walking towards the Children's Hospital, towards the relative safety of those automatic double doors.

Another five long seconds, another five yards closer, and still no challenge.

Moments later the doors parted. A patient on a gurney was wheeled through accompanied by an orderly and a nurse, all three in quiet conversation. I paused briefly to let them pass and this time could not resist looking back.

The cop was disappearing through the far doors of the main medical center. A little of the immediate tension eased, but I knew I was taking a big risk trying to see Claire and could not afford to be complacent.

There was even a chance she might turn me in. I hoped she still had enough trust in her big brother not to do that straight away.

One reason for seeing her was that she deserved to know the truth about what was going on, or at least as much as I knew, and to know that I was going to get Sean back. The other reason was that, with my bike being watched, I needed her help. More to the point: I needed her car.

I chose the first of the three elevators just by the main entrance and pressed the call button. A few seconds later the doors opened. Right then I knew lady luck was not on my side.

Two uniformed cops were standing there: a short tubby guy with thumbs tucked into his belt and his younger, taller, thinner colleague. Tubby was the cop that had delayed me the other night.

Both were looking straight at me.

Of course, the other night I had been wearing a helmet and wasn't dressed as a doctor.

I smiled, stepped in and they moved back. I pressed the floor I wanted. My sister worked on the sixth floor, but I pressed the button for the eighth. The cops carried on watching me. The brushed stainless-steel doors slid closed. We were the only ones in the elevator, so perhaps lady luck wasn't being too unkind. In the dull reflection I saw Tubby's brows furrow. His hand moved away from his belt and towards his gun.

I stabbed the elevator stop button before driving my elbow back hard into his face.

His nose broke and he staggered back, blood streaming down mouth and chin. He was still fumbling for his gun as I slammed him into his taller partner and they both crashed into the rear doors.

Jim Freeman was the first sergeant I'd had after joining the US Rangers back in '88. He kept on at us all about how finesse didn't matter – it was all about results. Fight hard, fight dirty: it didn't matter as long as your opponents went down.

Tubby was staggering, off balance and still between me and the taller cop. A hammer blow to his ear with my left fist dropped him to the floor, down but not out.

The other cop pulled his gun free. It was a bad move in such close quarters. I went in hard, shoving his gun hand aside and smashing my forehead into his face, feeling his nose give.

Breaking the nose is always a good opener in a fight. It dazes your opponent and gives you a bit more time to act, even if it's not as good as a kick to the head or a boot in the balls.

Tubby grabbed my left leg, intent on pulling me down. I twisted, kicking out with my right. The toe of my boot connected with his bloodied face. Dealing with the other cop at the same time meant it wasn't as hard a kick as I wanted. Tubby grunted but held on.

The tall cop flailed his left arm, trying to hit me in the head. I blocked with my right, then pistoned my fist into his face. Three hard fast blows. Each one smacking the back of his head against the elevator doors. I felt his gun hand lose strength and savagely twisted the automatic out of his grip, a couple of finger joints popping as I wrenched the gun away.

Tubby's fingers dug into my thigh as he fought to clamber up or drag me down. Either way, it didn't matter. I smashed the butt of his buddy's gun on his forehead. He moaned and let go of my leg. I hit him again like I was driving a six-inch nail into oak, and he slumped to the floor without a sound.

A fist hit my cheek. A lucky blow from the tall cop that caught me by surprise, and I almost dropped to my knees. There was enough power behind it to let me know he was still in the fight. That had to change.

I used the gun, scything around fast and connecting with the side of his head with enough force to knock him sideways. He fell, sprawling to the elevator floor. I followed up with a brutal kick to the stomach that drove a retching gasp from him.

A low groan from behind me let me know that Tubby was more resilient than I'd expected. I turned to see him on the floor, pulling out his gun. He was hurting and slow. I snapped out a kick to his hand, breaking fingers and sending the gun clattering against the metal wall.

He rolled onto his side, wailing and clutching his hand as the agony hit.

I went in hard. A kick to his groin like I was punting a football from the hundred-yard line. He doubled up, vomited and lay still.

In the few seconds it took to get my breath back I wondered how far deep in Fisk's network of corruption these guys were. Sure, they'd deliberately delayed my meeting with Sean, but that was a world away from kidnap and murder.

I did the right thing and put them both in the recovery position. Both cops would live but they wouldn't be waking up for a while yet.

I took their guns, popped open the roof of the elevator, and chucked their weapons out before hauling myself up into the area beyond, taking the sports bag with me. I left what remained of the clipboard behind. It had got trampled in the fight and wasn't much use for anything anymore.

It wasn't totally dark in the shaft; dim emergency lights lifted the gloom just enough to see my surroundings. The shaft housed all three passenger elevators, each solidly supported within their own metal guide rails. Steel cables hummed as they moved swiftly between floors. All except the one I was now standing on top of. I knew it wouldn't be staying that way for long.

I reckoned the cops would be out for a good long time. The problem would be someone from the hospital's janitorial staff investigating the stopped elevator. I figured I'd got no more than a couple of minutes before that happened and by then I needed to be well out of the way.

Fortunately I did not have to clamber up steel cables. A metal ladder was set into the side of the shaft, and it was an easy task to climb upwards.

I was halfway towards the top of the building when the cops' elevator started moving again, descending towards the ground floor. I picked up the pace of my climb, concentrating on the steel mesh walkway at the top of the shaft.

The elevator stopped. I couldn't hear anything over the background noise of the rest of the machinery and the other two elevators in the shaft.

I kept climbing. The unconscious cops would have been discovered by now. I wondered if anyone would open the top of the elevator to see where I had gone. It would be a very brave or foolish person to do that, given I'd taken both cops' guns. They wouldn't know I'd left them on the roof of the elevator; I could be standing right on the top of it ready to shoot whoever poked their head through first.

However, I knew the hospital would now be put on alert for a violent intruder. The increase in security over what Fisk had already put in place would make my life even more difficult but that had been unavoidable.

The way I saw it, Fisk had only a few options.

The most extreme measure was to evacuate the hospital and bring in a load more officers and SWAT team to find me and bring me down.

It might even work, but I doubted he had enough resources to cover the evacuation of the hospital and there was a good chance I could still get away in the confusion. That would turn into a very high profile and public humiliation for the whole department, let alone Fisk. Even if they did manage to catch me, I doubted he wanted the chance of me talking to anyone outside of his control.

He already had a strong police presence across the whole hospital, so he might pull them all to cover just the Randall Children's building. That would make sense.

I reckoned he'd want those cops loyal to him to be the ones taking me down. Like he'd said to Perez, he wanted me to be shot resisting arrest.

But how many bent coppers did he have at his disposal? A dozen? Twenty? I'd only taken three out of the game so far, with Killick and the two cops in the elevator, and that could still leave plenty ready, willing and able to bring me down, no questions asked.

I reached the metal walkway and hauled myself up onto it, seconds before all three elevators came to a halt. The rumbling of the machinery didn't totally die away but there was a noticeable drop in the sound level.

I stopped and knelt down, my hand going into the bag and finding the assassin's Glock with the silencer. From somewhere below there was a clang followed by a sliding rumble. I couldn't see from where I was, but I guessed a set of doors into the shaft had just been opened.

A torch beam found the metal ladder and followed it upwards. I heard voices that were too muffled to make out any distinct words. Then the torch moved down and out of my sight. I remained still.

More voices, then the sliding rumble again. The doors closing. I risked a look over the edge of the walkway. I saw nothing: no open doors.

I took out the gun, re-zipped the bag and ran for the door at the end of the metal walkway. The door had a lock, but it was on my side. I placed the bag to one side and yanked the door open, covering the opening with the gun.

It opened onto a stairwell landing. There was no one there. I stepped through the door, taking the bag with me. This part of the stairway was simple painted concrete. To my right the stairs led down to a solid white door. Ahead, across the landing was a door with the sign 'Roof Access Only'. Even with a quick glance I could see it had wiring leading to it, which meant someone could tell remotely if it was opened.

I grimaced and turned to check the door I'd just come through. No wires. That was a relief, but I couldn't rest easy yet.

I went down the stairs to the white door. Again, no wires. I tried the handle. The door was locked, and not just from the inside. It was a mortise that would need a key regardless of what side of the door you were on. However, as the frame was wooden and the door opened away from me, I used my size eleven boots.

The frame around the tongue of the lock broke and the door burst open, shaking on its hinges. The stairway there was far less utilitarian, there was even thin carpet on landing, though on this top floor the walls were plain. The lighting was still bright, but it was softer and on the next level down I could see artwork and framed posters on the walls.

There was no-one on the upper landing. I peered over the handrail checking for any rapidly approaching figures bearing guns and a will to use them.

It was quiet. At least for now.

I put the gun away again, closed the door as best I could with its busted lock, and made my way down to the next level. On the way, I took off the white coat.

Not only had it got seriously blood spattered during the fight in the elevator, the climb up the shaft had added a patina of dirt and grease to it. As a doctor's disguise it was useless now.

The metal ladder had been filthy and my hands were almost black with grime. I kept the white coat loosely bunched over my hand carrying the bag, hiding the dirt as best I could. I could do nothing about my other hand, as I needed it free for opening doors.

There was a small family lounge down on level eight that had so few people there it was as good as empty. I found the nearest washroom, locked the door and began scrubbing my hands. I'd ended up having to hit the shorter cop way harder than I first thought to put him down and now my knuckles throbbed. Grime mixed with spots of blood in the basin as I cleaned away the filth as best I could.

It wasn't perfect, there was still grease and dirt ingrained in the various cracks and lines of my hands, and they are a pair of rough and knocked about paws in any case. I could pass for an engineer, but it would be hard to fake being part of the medical staff.

I splashed some cold water over my face and neck, drying off with a couple of paper towels. The cool water was refreshing and welcome. I took a moment to collect my thoughts, looking at the hard lines of my face and cold eyes reflected in the mirror.

"What have you got into?" I whispered to myself.

At least that was something I had some idea about.

"More to the point, what are you going to do about it?"

At that moment I had no answer.

NINETEEN

I left the washroom and the family lounge, taking the stairs down a couple of levels. I kept my eyes open for any police presence as I went but saw none.

It had now been twenty minutes since I'd encountered the cops in the elevator. Probably a couple of minutes less since they had been found. Fisk would have got to know at least fifteen minutes ago. That was plenty of time to get his troops organized and in place.

So where were they? What was he planning?

It occurred to me that he was probably wondering the same thing about what I was going to do.

The sensible thing would be for me to get the hell out of the hospital, get away, live to fight another day.

But that wouldn't get me nearer to finding Sean, which is why I'd come back to Portland and why I was taking these crazy risks.

Besides, I'd had enough of being pushed around as part of this game. It was time I started pushing back.

It stood to reason that Fisk would have stationed cops on all the choke points I'd have to pass through when leaving the hospital. That would mean they would be close by each exit. If I remembered the plan of the building correctly, that meant covering five busy doorways.

He'd also make sure there were two cops at each point; he knew I'd deal with one easy enough and there was the added advantage of two pairs of eyes being better than one. That was a commitment of ten from the total of those officers he had available.

I wondered how many could be left to patrol the building. Maybe another ten? Maybe just him and Marshall?

Ultimately I was just guessing at Fisk's tactics and had no true idea of the numbers of cops involved. I had to focus on my own plans.

I paused on the landing between levels seven and eight, extracted the phone I'd bought earlier from the bag, and powered it on. It was a basic model and seemed to take an age to come to life. I checked the display. The battery was one bar over half power, but the signal was non-existent.

I made my way back up to the family lounge on the eighth floor.

There were still a few people around, but no cops, and no one paid me any attention. I checked the phone again. It had a signal.

I called the hospital reception. I told them it was Mr. Dean and was looking to speak with Nurse Claire Cresswell about an urgent matter regarding Patrick. I hoped the use of Sean's middle name as well as my own would get her attention.

The receptionist asked me to hold. I held, listening to the tinny melody playing as I waited and keeping my eyes on my surroundings and the entrance to the lounge. A minute passed and they came back on the line advising me they were trying to locate her, and would I like to leave my phone number so she could call me back.

I told them I'd hold as it was important that I speak to her. The receptionist went away and I was treated to a couple more minutes of the music again. It did not calm my nerves.

"Hello?" It was Claire. "Mr. Dean?" Her voice sounded unsure.

"Hi Claire, it's me." It was good to hear my sister's voice. "Can we—"

"Where are you?" she said, cutting me off. "What's going on?"

"I need your help," I said, ignoring the question. "But first I need you to listen."

I heard her take a steadying breath.

"Okay."

I kept it brief. I needed to speak to her face to face and without any police shadow.

There was a pause before she spoke.

"Tricky." I could tell she was thinking, considering options. I didn't know what anyone had told her and hoped she wasn't planning on setting me up. I frowned. Not Claire though, she wouldn't do that.

"Is there a cop there with you now?" I asked.

"Nearby," she confirmed. "But I can do it. Where are you?"

I told her I was in the hospital but not exactly where.

"Meet me by the main stairs, level five. It'll take a few minutes."

"Got it," I said, and she ended the call. I powered the phone off, preserving the battery.

My mouth felt dry at the thought of wondering what I was going to say to Claire and how she might react. I took a minute to get myself a drink from the water cooler and decided it had to be done regardless.

I strolled down the stairs to level five, taking my time and glancing through the glass in the stairway door on each level as I went. I saw no cops.

Claire was as good as her word. She was standing opposite the level five door dressed in her nurse's uniform, looking both worried and harassed. Stray blond hairs escaped from her headband and trailed over her face. It reminded me of our mother, but the determined set of her jaw was father's legacy for sure. I couldn't see any cops nearby so took a chance, went through the door and walked over to her.

She stared at me as I approached, the expression hardening into a glare. I met her gaze and saw her anger fade slightly. There were dark circles under her red-rimmed eyes that told me she had been crying more than she'd been sleeping.

"Walk with me," I told her, nodding along the corridor. She didn't move and I paused. "Please Claire."

She moved to stand in front of me and looked me direct in the eyes. "What's going on with Sean?" she demanded quietly.

I met her stare and kept my voice low enough so that any passers-by wouldn't hear. "I don't know yet. It's what I'm trying to find out."

Claire's mouth tightened.

"I'll tell you what I know, but not out here," I added.

"Okay," she sighed. "Follow me."

The fifth floor of the Randall Children's Hospital had two long main corridors that ran parallel to each other, joined along their length by five short linking corridors.

Claire led the way along and then into one of the adjoining corridors. As we turned the corner, I glanced back in time to see a uniformed female cop appear from the area by the elevators, looking around as if searching for someone.

We were around the corner and out of view before she could catch sight of us.

"I think I just saw your personal police escort," I said.

Claire turned her head as she spoke. "Which one? The big guy or the girl?"

"The girl."

Claire said nothing for a moment, she was checking through a small bundle of keys.

"They've both been taking it in turns hanging around 'for my protection'. Probably from you I guess." She smiled without much humor. "At least they haven't been getting in the way, just one or the other always there, nearby."

We'd stopped by a nondescript solid white door. Claire slid a key into the lock. I heard a faint rattle. Nothing happened.

"Damn," she muttered, trying another of her keys.

I had my back to the wall, not leaning on it but standing so that I could check out the length of the short corridor in both directions. The few room windows and glass panes in some of the doors gave a limited reflection into a small section of each of the adjacent long corridors.

It was enough for me to notice the dark police uniform of the female cop. From what little I could see, she looked to have stopped and was talking to a nurse.

"We need to go," I told Claire, making the urgency clear in my voice. I saw the nurse gesture in the direction of the corridor we were in, and the cop began to move.

"Got it!" Claire swung the door open and I followed quickly inside. She immediately shut it and locked it behind us on the turn latch.

The small room had a sharp astringent smell that was a mix of plastics and cleaning chemicals. It was also very dark, with just the faint glow of the door exit lamp and a slit of light underneath the door from the corridor outside for illumination.

Even in such dim light, I could see Claire reaching for a light switch. I grabbed her wrist to stop her and with my other hand placed a finger on her lips.

She stopped, holding still. I took my finger away and let her hand go.

Whether a light from this room could be seen under the door in the brightness of the corridor beyond was doubtful, but it wasn't worth taking the risk.

It was the same with speaking. Anyone passing by in the corridor wouldn't hear quiet voices from the room, but a determined listener with an ear held against the door was a different matter.

A dark shadow fell across the slit of light under the door. The handle was tried a couple of times and the door bumped softly in its frame. Claire froze and stared at it. I considered the silenced gun still in the sports bag beside me and how quickly I could get to it.

The shadow moved away.

I heard voices outside, a confident female voice asking a question, a man's muffled reply. The cop and a passing orderly I guessed.

The shadow returned and the handle rattled again. I decided to leave the gun where it was in the bag. I didn't want its presence to frighten Claire, and if the cop did come in I was pretty sure I wouldn't need it in such close quarters.

I left Claire and went to the door, grasping the locking turn latch between my thumb and forefinger as solidly as I could. There was the unmistakable sound of a key sliding into the lock, and I felt pressure on the latch as whoever was outside tried to turn the key.

I had more leverage and strength than whoever was outside and held it firm. The pressure stopped. I heard the man say something about a different key and the cop saying not to bother.

We waited. Ten seconds passed and there was no more noise from the door. We waited another twenty before turning on the light.

It was another ten before Claire spoke.

TWENTY

"They said you took him." Claire's bright blue eyes bored into mine, like she was trying to see the truth in there without me even having to speak.

I gently placed my hands on her shoulders. "You know I didn't." I wanted to say more but she looked away and I felt her start to shake.

"Richard's spending all his time at the office. Says it's unavoidable. He keeps saying Sean will be fine and not to worry." Claire shook her head. "I was so angry with what you said about him not caring about Sean, but you were right."

"No. I spoke out of turn." I gave her shoulders a gentle squeeze. Her big brother was there for her.

We remained standing there quietly for a couple of seconds, then Claire shook her head.

"Oh God, what's happening?" she said, the tremor in her voice threatening to break into sobs.

"I'll tell you what I know, but can't take long," I said, keeping my voice low. "And I'm going to get Sean back."

Even though I said the words, right then I didn't know exactly how I was going to do that.

Claire looked back at me. "You know who's got him?"

I nodded, letting my hands drop from her shoulders. "I've got a pretty good idea."

Claire's eyes shone, becoming glossy with tears. "Is it something to do with Richard?" Anger now mixed with her grief giving a harder edge to her voice.

I frowned, unable to hide my reaction. "Probably."

I glanced at the door, collecting my thoughts about what to tell my sister. She didn't need to know everything, but she deserved enough to put her in the picture.

"Richard is being used by Larry Fisk." I saw she recognized the name, a slight grimace crossing her face. "Working on some kind of financial arrangement probably linked to an organized crime group. Sean was taken as leverage over Richard to make sure he does what they want."

There was a look of frightened desperation on Claire's face. "So Sean is being held by the mafia? What are they going to do to him?"

I could have told her that, once Richard did what they asked they would let Sean go, but I knew that wasn't going to happen and Claire would be able to tell I was lying. I had to say more, but how much? I needed her to trust me.

"From what I've found out, Fisk is involved with some Armenian syndicate. Like Russians but not. And not the mafia as you would think it."

"Worse?" she asked.

I shrugged. "It doesn't matter. Less organized. Less powerful. Still a problem."

"And Sean?"

"I'll find him. I'll get him back." I promised her.

"How?" she demanded.

"Best you don't know. Let me handle it."

At least now I had the outline of a plan of action forming in my mind. It wasn't a great plan, in fact it was a fairly desperate course of action, but it was all I had right then.

She shook her head. "Oh no you don't." That determined set to her jaw was back again. "He's my boy, I'm going with you!"

I motioned for her to keep her voice down. For now, it was useless to argue. She was stressed and wound up. I knew she would do whatever it took to get Sean back. Even breaking the law, perhaps even killing, and I couldn't have that. It was one thing for me to have to make those decisions, but she was a nurse, a healer, a mother. She needed to stay out of harm's way, to stay clean.

However, for what I had in mind, having her help would make things far easier. Besides, I trusted her. She was my closest family, and ties of blood are always the strongest.

Claire looked at me, head cocked expectantly and arms folded ready to hear what I had to say.

"Okay," I conceded reluctantly. "I could use your help."

"So what do we do?" she asked.

I'd gone to the hospital to find Perez, the aim being to get more information, which I'd done.

What I hadn't expected was to find Fisk and Marshall there in the hospital too, or the extra cops around the place. I knew that Fisk and Marshall were behind it all and, in my eyes, fair game, but I didn't know which of the other cops around the place were in Fisk's pocket and which were straight and just doing their job.

I was pretty sure the cops in the elevator were bent, as they'd been the ones stopping me the other night, delaying my arrival at Barton Bridge. They had to be under Fisk's or Marshall's orders. I felt very little guilt having hurt them.

I needed more information, I needed to find out where Sean was, and Fisk would know this. I therefore needed the opportunity of some uninterrupted quality time with my old buddy.

But I knew the chances of me getting caught were now way higher than any odds I had of taking Fisk.

Claire remained looking at me, trying to guess what was going on in my head.

"So what are we going to do?" she asked.

I met her gaze, noting her use of 'we'.

"You sure you want to get involved? It's one thing for me to—"

"I'm already involved!" She cut in angrily, then lowered her voice again. "When I got the call that Doctor Riley wanted to see me it wasn't too hard to figure out, so I gave Cagney the slip before turning up."

"Cagney? The female cop." I gave a brief smile.

She nodded. I could tell she'd made her mind up. She was too much like me. There was no use arguing about it. Anyway, if she was willing, her help meant that the chances of turning the situation to our favor were better. They still wouldn't be great odds, but it was an improvement.

"Okay," I said. "Do you have your car, the minivan, with you today?" I asked.

"Yes. The keys are in my locker."

I nodded. Not so good but not unexpected either.

"Can you get hold of some kind of sedative or tranquilizer? Something that works quickly?"

"Why? I ought to know?"

"For Fisk," I told her.

Claire thought for a second before replying.

"I'm no anesthetist, but I reckon a dose of Ketalar would work well enough. I don't have access to it, but I know where it's kept. I can get it and some syringes."

She didn't need to add that her actions would probably cost her job. If it meant getting Sean back safe and well, I knew she'd pay that price willingly.

"Good." I smiled at her. "I bet Cagney is getting frantic by now, and I'll bet she's also put a call in to Fisk or Marshall – not that she'd want to admit losing you – so they'll be edgy too. They'll all be on the lookout for you."

Claire carried on looking at me as I continued thinking aloud.

"We need to get you back to your cop, have her believe that there's no problem, that you just needed some time alone. Go and have a quiet coffee and a chat together – in an empty room, just the two of you. She'll report back to Fisk and Marshall and that should calm things down."

"What then? I can't get the Ketalar with her there with me all the time."

"I'll turn up and deal with her."

I saw the look of concern on Claire's face as she imagined what I meant.

I shook my head. Even if she was part of Fisk's corrupt little club, I guessed she would only be a minor player. I had no intention of killing her.

"Tied, gagged and out of the way is what I have in mind," I said. I didn't mention that I'd be pointing a gun to help make that happen. Claire didn't need to know that.

"I'll need to know where you are," I added.

"Call me on my cell."

"Didn't think they were allowed in here?"

She shook her head.

"It's okay in most places, just not next to sensitive equipment. Here—" Claire took out a ballpoint pen from a pocket, grabbed my hand and jotted down a number, "—call me on this and I'll let you know where we are."

I gave her an approving smile. My sister was resourceful and quick thinking.

"We can do this," I told her. "We'll get him back."

"Or die trying," Claire murmured, looking at my battered knuckles.

"Let's avoid that if we can." I'd do my damnedest to make sure that she'd be okay even if I wasn't. She was my little sister and I'd look out for her. I gave Claire's arm a brotherly squeeze and she looked up at me again.

"Ready?" I asked.

She nodded. "Call me in fifteen minutes."

I checked my watch. "Fifteen minutes," I confirmed, setting the countdown on the Casio G-Shock.

She went to the door, turned back to look at me for a long moment. Then she switched off the lights, opened the door and walked into the bright corridor beyond.

The door closed and I was left in the dark.

TWENTY-ONE

I relocked the door and waited.

Two minutes passed as I thought about what needed to be done and tried to account for all possibilities.

I'd got the bare bones of a plan – or at least a good idea of what I was going to do – as I was talking with Claire, but she'd only got to hear the first part of it. It didn't matter. She'd get to know the rest if the first steps succeeded.

Even in the darkness of the large storeroom I was able to unzip the sports bag and recheck what I had in there. I had plenty of firepower for what was needed without resorting to the excesses of a machine gun or assault rifle. Overkill in all senses of the word.

I zipped up the bag and slung it over my shoulder before moving to the door. I checked my watch. Six minutes gone. I opened the door and slipped out into the corridor.

A couple of nurses and an orderly glanced at me as I emerged from the storeroom. With the bag on my back, they probably thought I was pilfering supplies. It didn't really matter, and no one challenged me.

I walked to the north corridor turning left towards the stairwell on the west side of the building. As I turned the corner, I caught a glimpse of a dark uniform further back up the main corridor.

There was a set of automatic double doors ahead of me and I tried to see who it was from the reflection in the glass. It was one thing when looking at an oblique angle from the side corridor, but from straight on it was impossible. What I could see was a child of eight or nine in a stretcher being wheeled towards the doors by an orderly. There was a nurse alongside and all three were talking. The child was smiling, which I took to be a good sign.

I waited for the doors to open and stepped to the side as they came through, giving them a smile myself. I also took the opportunity to check back towards where I thought the uniformed cop was approaching from.

A brief glance was all it took. It was the broad cop with the beard I'd seen when crossing the courtyard below.

He was walking along the corridor in my direction, but not moving fast. He hadn't seen me. It looked like he was just patrolling.

I passed through the double doors and carried on towards the smaller west stairway, breathing a small sigh of relief when I turned the corner out of his sight.

I knew Claire worked on the sixth floor, so that was a good a place as any to wait. I went up the stairs one level and checked the countdown on my G-Shock.

I had another couple of minutes to wait. The stairway might not have been as big as the main one, but it did have the advantage of windows. I rested the bag on the floor and looked out of the window at the world beyond. The earlier sunshine had gone leaving the afternoon sky an overcast aluminum grey, washing out the parts of the city I could see. Even colors of passing cars seemed muted.

There was the familiar feeling of tension I'd experienced each time I'd gone into action in the Rangers, and later as part of Portland PD whenever making an arrest, especially if it might be a challenging one.

It wasn't fear. There was an apprehension, a knowledge that I was about to face danger, but it was overwhelmed by the feeling of being ready for action. Of excitement.

I checked my watch again then switched my phone on.

I read the number Claire had scrawled on my palm and keyed it in.

The ring tone sounded for a few seconds then Claire answered. She sounded exasperated.

"Sorry Julie," I assumed Julie was a friend. "It's a bad time. There's a lot going on here."

"Tell me about it," I replied, smiling.

"There's something about my crazy brother going on, and–" she paused and I heard a muffled "okay" before she continued, "–I can't tell you right now, but let's meet up soon." I guessed her police shadow was right close by.

I needed to know where she was.

"Where are you? Which room?"

"Right, we'll put a date in the diary," she said, "How about at six on the twenty-fourth?"

Six. Twenty-four. Excellent. I smiled.

"Floor six, room twenty-four. Be there in three minutes." I told her.

"That's great, see you – bye," she finished hurriedly and ended the call.

I picked up the bag and casually walked out onto the sixth floor, scanning the room numbers as I went.

It took two and a half minutes to find the short corridor that led to room twenty-four. Even though it was a staff-only part of the building, the door to the corridor was unlocked and I was able to walk straight in.

I locked the door behind me on the latch.

On the right, a door opened into a compact kitchen area. I glanced through the vertical glass panel set into the door. At the far end of the room were some cupboards, a sink, kettle and coffee machine. A vending machine was tucked along the far wall selling snacks that were too sugary or too salty to rightfully be sold in a hospital.

The door to room six-twenty-four was right next to the kitchen. A small staff lounge. I heard Claire's voice from inside. I took out the silenced Glock from the bag and opened the door.

Claire was across the room, back against the window and with a mug of coffee in her hand. Opposite her was the female cop, also with a coffee in her hand. She started turning towards the door.

"Don't," I said, pointing my gun directly at the cop's face. I didn't want her to try anything heroic or stupid, and I definitely didn't fancy having hot coffee thrown at me.

The cop kept still, eyes flicking between me and the gun.

I saw that she was quite young: mid-twenties perhaps, and probably not long out of the academy.

I moved into the room and closed the door with my heel, all the time keeping the gun steady on her.

"What's your name?" I asked.

"Hayes," she replied. "Barbara Hayes."

"Okay Officer Hayes, using your free hand take out your gun and toss it here," I told her. "Slow and easy."

She was sensible; she did as she was told. Her automatic dropped to the thin carpeted floor in front of me, a Glock model 19, smaller than the 17 and more suited to her grip. She kept her free hand raised palm out at waist height, coffee still held steady in her other hand.

"Easy Mr. Riley," she said. "This can't end well. I heard you were a good cop once. Think of Claire here."

My smile held no humor. "Who fed you that line? Fisk?"

She looked confused for a moment.

I shook my head, the smile gone. "Never mind." I continued looking at the cop as I spoke. "Claire, take Officer Hayes' drink off her."

Claire put her own mug down on a low table before stepping towards the young officer. Hayes handed her the cup and it joined Claire's mug on the table.

"Now your cuffs," I told Hayes.

She moved her hand to the back of her belt, still keeping calm and her movements slow, plucked the cuffs out and threw them onto the floor in front of me. I crouched and picked them up keeping my eyes on her face and the gun rock steady.

I nodded. "Okay, Officer Hayes, you're going to walk to that pipe then turn and face me."

I indicated a two inch painted pipe in the corner of the room that probably was something to do with the heating system. It looked tough and sturdy and impossible to move.

Hayes shrugged and did as she was told. I followed and snapped one cuff around her wrist, all the time keeping the gun pointed at her head.

"Don't get any ideas. It's not worth it," I told her.

I got Claire to feed the cuffs around the pipe and snap them over Hayes' other wrist so her hands were secured behind her back and she couldn't move far from that big pipe. I took her radio, put it in a pocket and stepped back.

"Sit down," I ordered.

She slid to the floor, back against the pipe and knees raised but eyes still defiant.

"Are you in Fisk's pocket?" I asked her.

She frowned, glaring at me. "What are you saying?"

"That you earn a little extra for helping the Captain with special duties, or to look the other way when told to?"

"Fuck you! The only bent cop in this room is the one I'm looking at."

Her response had been so immediate and natural I was inclined to believe her. If she was that convincing an actress she wouldn't still be a uniform cop, even a fresh-faced youngster like her. I lowered the gun and spoke quietly to Claire who had moved to stand at my side.

"What are the chances of someone walking in here?"

"High," she replied. "We need to lock the door."

"Done that, but we need to stop anyone trying to get in and calling the janitor."

"Okay – hang on." Claire left the room and I heard her opening doors. I divided my attention between Hayes and the door to the lounge.

A minute later, Claire was back.

"Out of order sign," she explained. "The sink backs up so often we've had one laminated. I've also switched the lights off out there."

"Good work," I told her, taking the opportunity to bring in

the bag from outside the room. There were items in there I'd be needing soon.

"So are you working together now?" asked Hayes. The question was directed at Claire.

"If it gets my son back," Claire retorted.

Hayes looked up at her saying nothing, then lowered her eyes.

I took Claire to one side. "How quickly can you get that anesthetic?" I asked quietly. "And we need a wheelchair and a blanket too."

"Want me to fix you a sandwich while I'm at it?"

"Chicken salad would be nice." I grinned at her.

A small smile crossed her face. "Fuck you Dean Riley," she said softly and opened the lounge door. "Give me fifteen minutes. I'll knock."

I looked over at Hayes. She sat quietly, her eyes on Claire and me. I used the weighty bag to prop the door open and followed my little sister to the door at the end of the stub corridor. The smile had disappeared, instead she just looked worried.

"You gonna be okay?" I checked with her.

Claire nodded and unlocked the door. "Fifteen minutes," she said, then she was gone.

I locked the door behind her and returned back to the small lounge and the captive Hayes. I closed the leftmost set of blinds so anyone looking in through the door glass at the end of the corridor would have a hard time seeing much beyond, but I'd be able to see them.

"What now?" Hayes asked.

"We wait."

She remained silent for a whole minute before speaking again. "You gonna kill me?"

I looked at her, meeting her eyes. "That's not my plan." The gun was down at my side. There was no need to keep it pointed at her.

Hayes managed to hold my gaze for a couple of seconds before looking away. "Was shooting Gibbs and Harris part of the plan?"

She was plucky, I gave her that. Trying to keep me engaged

and distracted from the door, even though she may be treading dangerously and putting herself at risk was brave. I was tempted to tell her the whole story, but now wasn't the time. I needed to stay focused.

"I didn't shoot them. Killick did," I said, reaching into the sports bag and locating the roll of duct tape. "Under Fisk's orders," I added.

"Bullshit!" whispered Hayes, her eyes back on me again.

I shrugged and went over to her. "Officer Hayes, I think you're okay. If I had more time I'd tell you more, but right now I'm going to need you to be quiet for a while."

Hayes looked at the roll of tape and then at me. "I can be quiet," she said.

"No." I shook my head. "You know what I have to do. Let's make this easy and it'll be over sooner."

She inclined her head, eyes revealing an undercurrent of fear. I wrapped a double loop of tape around her head just covering her mouth.

"Still breathe?" I asked.

Hayes nodded.

"Going to behave?"

She tilted her head and raised an eyebrow. Whether it was a 'yes' or 'go to hell' was hard to tell.

"Don't give me a reason to tape your eyes," I told her.

A shake of the head and she lowered her eyes to the floor.

I left her and went to stand by the open lounge door, dividing my attention between Hayes and the door at the end of the corridor.

I waited. There was nothing else I could do.

I was very much dependent upon my sister now.

TWENTY-TWO

Everyone knows that time drags when you're waiting. And if you're on alert or in a tense situation with your mind keyed up and running fast, it *really* drags.

After half an hour I checked my watch to find that only nine minutes had passed since Claire had left.

Hayes continued to sit quietly. A couple of times I caught her looking at me, like she was trying to work me out or make sense of what I'd said to her.

The full fifteen minutes came and went.

That was no surprise. I had doubted that Claire would be back before then. Unless you've been in the military and have the experience, everyone always underestimates how long things take, and Claire had a lot to accomplish.

It was a little over twenty minutes before I saw her peering in at the end door.

As I got to the door I could see she had managed to get hold of a wheelchair and there was a pale blue blanket folded on the seat. There were people passing by, but Claire was alone. I unlocked the door, held it open and she wheeled the chair in.

"All okay?" I asked as she passed, locking the door again.

She let out a slow breath. "Could have been easier, but yeah, okay."

We parked the chair in the small lounge. Hayes looked at it and then at Claire and me. Maybe she thought it was for her. She was wrong.

I took Claire out into the short corridor, and we spoke quietly.

"The anesthetic?" I said.

Claire carefully reached into her pocket. "Here it is," she said, showing me two small bottles of fluid and a couple of syringes. "Hopefully this should be enough. There's a limit on what I could get."

"Well done." I smiled at her.

"I checked the dosage. How much to give depends on how heavy someone is."

"That's going to be a best guess."

"Yeah, I thought it might," she frowned. "We'll stick with 1mg per guessed pound to be safe. Better to give a bit less than too much."

"I'm not sure about that. This needs to work, and quickly too."

"It will. They'll be out in thirty seconds and be under for five to ten minutes."

"Assuming they get enough," I said doubtfully.

"Listen Dean, get it wrong they're going to die." Claire held my gaze, making sure I understood. "Anyway, who's the nurse here?" she added, emphasizing the point.

"Okay, I got it," I reassured her. "1mg per pound."

"Good," she nodded. "You can administer another injection when they start to come around, but if I'm there I'll do it."

I hadn't had the time until then to bring Claire up to speed with the rest of my improvised plan. I gave her the outline of what I intended. It meant I still needed her help. It also meant her getting more deeply involved, although I had an idea that might help protect her should the worst happen.

She was shaking her head slowly in disbelief before I'd finished.

"You're serious?" she said.

I nodded.

"And you're sure about this?" she whispered. "I mean *really* sure?"

"Fisk is behind it all. He's the key. Him and Marshall."

"Not that. I believe you about Fisk. It's just your plan..."

"Got anything better?" I asked.

Claire ran a hand over her mouth, a sure sign she was having doubts. After a moment she gave a long sigh and looked up at me again.

"Okay. For Sean." Her voice caught as she said it.

"One thing," I said. "Remember you're being coerced by me and doing this under duress. I've told you I'd kill Richard if you didn't help."

She gave me a sad smile. "You've tried to think of everything haven't you? Not sure it would wash, but thank you."

We returned to the lounge and made our preparations.

*

I took Hayes' radio out from my pocket and thumbed the transmit button.

"Fisk," I snarled. "Captain Larry Fisk. This is Dean Riley. Let's talk."

I heard nothing but static. Five seconds passed. I pressed transmit again. "Fisk – if I don't hear from you in ten seconds, I'll shoot Officer Hayes in the knee. All you got to do is speak."

Another five seconds passed. I took out the silenced pistol. Then the radio cracked.

"Riley, you old, mad dog. Keeping well?" Fisk managed to keep his voice controlled, putting false humor in there to annoy me, though I could still detect an edge of tension. "Had some family troubles I hear."

"We should meet. Talk about it." I tried to avoid speaking through clenched teeth. "You up for that?"

"Well, I can't see that happening anytime soon, unless you want to turn yourself in, but I'm guessing that's not your intent. Care to tell me what you do have in mind?"

My rage and frustration boiled over.

"I'm going to find you. We ARE going to–"

The gunshot was stark and loud in the room. Claire was holding Hayes' Glock 19, a curl of smoke rising from the barrel.

I let out a cry of pain and dropped the radio.

Claire snatched the radio up from the floor and pressed the transmit button.

"I've shot him!" she cried, "He's bleeding! Oh God!"

"Where are you?" came Fisk's terse voice over the radio.

"Sixth floor, room six-twenty-four. Come quickly!"

I stared at my sister. Our eyes met. We both knew a line had been crossed and there would be no going back.

TWENTY-THREE

Claire lobbed the radio onto the padded seat of the couch then handed me the gun.

"I hate these things," she said.

"You did well." That was certainly true. The timing of the shot had caught me off guard – and I was expecting it – and her panicked words had hit just the right note. I really hoped the ruse would work.

If Fisk came with a big police entourage the plan would have to be adapted pretty damn fast. But I knew he'd never meet with me unless he had the upper hand and the opportunity to finish me. That meant coming with only those cops on his bent payroll.

Claire and I had to move fast. I unlocked the door at the end of the corridor. Hayes' gun was back in Claire's hands. They shook a little as she held it. I didn't think that there was much acting involved this time. I got in position.

Thirty seconds later I heard a door banging open outside, then moments later the door to the stub corridor and the sound of many hurrying feet.

Marshall barged into the lounge first, gun drawn, immediately pointing it at the slumped figure covered by the blanket that Claire was aiming Hayes' gun at. Fisk followed swiftly and gently took the pistol from Claire's trembling hands. A third officer in uniform remained in the doorway. It was the bearded cop I'd seen earlier.

I came out from the unlit kitchen moving swift and silent and, before the cop in the doorway could react, I had a gun at his head. The snub .38 revolver in my left hand pressed into his ear, in my right hand the trusty Glock 17 with silencer swung to cover Marshall.

"Drop it!" I said, the command applying to everyone in the room.

The cop I was effectively using as a human shield let his pistol fall to the carpet and slowly raised his hands. Marshall was crouching by the blanket-covered body, back towards me, her gun hidden from my view.

Fisk had the gun he'd taken from Claire in his hand. In one smooth move he pressed it against her temple.

"How about *you* drop it?" he sneered.

Shit. He was a swift as a snake.

Fisk used his spare hand and maneuvered Claire in front of himself, playing the human shield game himself. Claire winced as he twisted her arm.

I ignored him and shot Marshall where she crouched.

Even with the sound suppressed by the silencer the crack of the shot was still loud, and the bearded cop flinched as the bullet smacked into the meat of Marshall's left buttock. She yelped and sprawled forwards onto the carpet, pulling the blanket off the drugged form of Hayes.

Shooting people in the ass isn't something I make a habit of, but the way she was crouched it seemed the safest option. It would hurt like hell, but she wouldn't die.

I felt the tall cop tense.

"Don't," I whispered to him, applying a little more pressure with the revolver. He understood and tried to relax.

Fisk raised his voice. "Give it up Riley!"

"Toss the gun Marshall," I said. "You too, Larry."

Marshall lay semi-prone on the floor, breathing hard. She still had her gun, though it wasn't currently pointed at me. Fisk moved the Glock 19 he'd taken from Claire, digging it into her back. She let out a whimper.

"Riley, you're not listening," said Fisk. He seemed to be enjoying the situation, the sadistic bastard. Perhaps he thought he had the upper hand somehow. "Drop your weapons or little sister gets shot through the spine."

"Toss the gun Marshall," I repeated, ignoring Fisk.

Marshall did nothing.

My gun cracked again as I shot Marshall through the sole of her boot. She howled.

"Don't make me ask again," I told her.

She threw her gun. It wasn't anywhere near me, but it was out of her reach.

"Fuck you!" said Fisk, pulling the trigger of the gun digging into Claire's back.

It clicked empty.

I pointed my obviously loaded gun at him.

"Now you, Larry. Drop the gun and let Claire go."

Fisk swore under his breath and chucked the empty gun to one side. Claire stumbled away from him.

"Get the guns," I told Claire.

She started by collecting Marshall's pistol. I remained where I was, one gun aimed at Fisk, the other still against the bearded cop's head.

"Now your own piece. Finger and thumb, nice and slow."

Fisk's eyes narrowed.

"This can't end well Riley. Think about what you're doing."

I shot the carpet at his feet, making him flinch. My human shield twitched but remained as still as he could. I centered the gun back on Fisk's face. He licked his lips nervously. We stood there another three seconds until my finger began to tighten on the trigger.

"Okay! Okay!" he said, slowly pulling back his jacket to reveal his gun.

"Still using the Beretta?" I asked.

"Yeah, what of it?" he replied. He used the finger and thumb of his off hand to slowly draw out the automatic. He knew me well enough not to try anything stupid right then. The Beretta hit the floor with a bit more care than he'd shown to the gun he'd had against Claire.

"That means you probably still have the .32 at your ankle."

"Jesus, Riley!" Fisk sounded exasperated but there was a nervous edge to his voice as well.

"You know what to do," I said.

He slowly knelt down, pulled his pant leg up and carefully withdrew a hammerless .32 revolver from his ankle holster. I gestured with my gun and he tossed the small gun by the Beretta then slowly got back to his feet.

"Get those hands back up," I told him.

His eyes flicked between me and the big bearded cop acting as my shield. With my .38 pressed against him I could feel any movement he made. Sensibly the cop kept still.

Fisk raised his hands.

Claire collected all the discarded guns, finishing with the uniformed cop's in front of me. She moved steadily, making sure not to get in my line of fire.

"Marshall – arms out and lie still," I said, sensing her moving. Marshall moaned and stopped moving.

"What now?" sneered Fisk. "We reminisce about the good old days? I know if you wanted me dead it would have happened already, so what are you after?"

"We'll get to that," I told him.

There was a careful dance to perform first, and I choreographed it using the silenced Glock to control the unwilling performers. Claire played her part perfectly, taking guidance from me at each step, but acting reluctant as if she was an unwilling participant.

Marshall got handcuffed where she lay. She was incapacitated and bleeding, but not badly. She'd feel faint as the adrenaline wore off. Claire firmly taped her mouth and eyes. Hayes had recovered consciousness but was still groggy from the dose of Ketalar we'd given her. Evidently the dosage had been spot-on, thanks to Claire. She also got an improvised tape blindfold too, with a bit of toweling as a concession to comfort.

The bearded cop lay on his side on the carpet facing the side wall, wrists bound to ankles using two sets of cuffs. It did not look comfortable. He had been treated to a set of duct tape accessories around the head too.

That left Larry Fisk.

He sat in the wheelchair that Claire had brought earlier, wrists and ankles taped down.

A minute later and his head was head lolling from a strong dose of Ketalar. This time I'd added a little extra to be sure he was well under, and for a good time too. Claire draped the blanket over his body, conveniently hiding the restraining tape around his arms.

With everyone incapacitated I smashed the radios, collected Fisk and Marshall's cell phones, popped the batteries and dropped them in my ever-heavier sports bag.

I took all the magazines for the Glock automatics I had with me, weighing the bag down even further. There was enough 9mm ammunition to fight a small war, but I had no space or need for any of the other guns.

I took them apart, disabling them, before chucking each gun down the back of the vending machine in the kitchen. It wasn't perfect but it would take a few minutes to get them if the three captives figured out how to get loose, or when someone found them, and even then the guns wouldn't fire anymore.

I wheeled the comatose Fisk out of the room, Claire following, carrying the blue sports bag.

She locked the door behind us.

We were good to go.

Provided we didn't get caught on the way out.

143

TWENTY-FOUR

Claire had given Fisk another small shot of the Ketalar before we left. He was out for the count and was breathing heavily like someone in a deep dreamless sleep.

I'd thoroughly taped his wrists to the arms of the wheelchair and secured his legs to the uprights. All of this was covered by the blanket, expertly tucked around him by Claire. There was no way he'd be getting out of the chair in a hurry.

We made our way to one of the larger elevators in the middle of the building designed to be big enough to take a couple of stretchers. We let an orderly wheeling an empty stretcher get out first before I wheeled Fisk in.

Other than us the elevator was empty.

"You'll need to check the exits." I told Claire. "Find one without any cops."

I wondered how it would look, pushing a grown man in a wheelchair around a children's hospital, but kept that thought to myself. There was nothing that could be done about it.

"Don't worry," she said. "I've got an idea."

We reached level one and the doors opened.

The silenced Glock, now reloaded with a full clip, was tucked in the wide back pocket of the wheelchair along with Fisk's jacket to hide its shape.

My right hand was by the gun, ready just in case any of Fisk's officers were standing outside the elevator doors.

Our luck held; there weren't any. Just medical staff and patients. We got a few curious glances as I wheeled Fisk out but nothing more than that.

Claire led us out, turning right at a busy nurse's station and along the north corridor. She started talking to me about electrolyte levels and hydration. I nodded, not paying much attention. I understood she was talking as part of an act. My concentration was on our surroundings and looking out for any dark police uniforms that may be around.

Moments later we had reached the end of the corridor and a solid door. I looked at her expectantly.

"Fingers crossed," she said and tried the handle. The door opened.

"Lucky," I noted.

"Should be locked but it's a sneaky smoker's exit." Claire held the door open and I wheeled Fisk into the narrower corridor beyond.

Five yards away were a set of double glass doors. In the grey light of the late afternoon, I could see a pathway and grass and trees beyond them. I trundled Fisk towards them.

Claire came past and checked the doors.

"Damn," she muttered.

"Problem?" I asked.

She nodded. "So much for the sneaky smokers plan. They'll set off a security alarm when I open them."

"So we'll have to get out quickly."

"And I don't know who else is around outside," she added.

I took a breath, frowning. It was a risk we'd have to take. I didn't fancy heading back and trying any of the main exits. That felt like asking for more trouble than we'd get this way.

"Let's do it," I told her.

Claire put her hand on the release bar and looked at me. I nodded. She pushed the bar.

The door opened with a bit of effort on Claire's part. I couldn't hear any alarm but guessed a light or buzzer would be sounding on some security panel somewhere.

I bumped the wheelchair out, Fisk's head lolling as we crossed the threshold, and moved with a purpose along the pathway. I was glad to finally be out of the building but knew we were far from safe yet.

We turned right alongside a landscaped garden area, heading towards a couple of the parking lots. One of the main entrances to the hospital was coming up on our right. It was set back into the north-east corner of the building and a short distance away from the pathway. I checked it out, continuing to push the unconscious Fisk with Claire at my side, partially shielding me from view.

Outside the entrance were two cops, standing together and both alert, but with their attention on the entrance and anyone coming out of the building.

If either of them looked over their shoulder they would see me pushing Fisk. Then again there were enough people about that we might just blend into the background.

I kept moving.

We crossed North Gantenbein Avenue and went into a multi-tier parking lot.

Claire drew me to a stop. We were out of sight of any passers-by. She took a moment to check Fisk. He still appeared to be unconscious, but she pulled up an eyelid and examined his response in any case. She looked up at me and frowned.

"He's still under but probably only for another few minutes." She handed me a capped syringe already loaded with another dose of the Ketalar. "Here – if he starts murmuring or moving his head then give him half of this, wait for a minute and then inject the rest."

"Okay, but I thought we were heading to your car?"

"It's too risky. I'm parked over on the other side of the hospital. I'll go get it and pick you up in a few minutes. Stay around here and look for my van."

"Still the blue Chrysler?" I asked.

Claire nodded. "That's it. But it's best I stop over on that road over there." She indicated the one-way North Monroe Street that ran alongside the parking lot. Then she turned and walked back out of the lot, leaving me with a bag full of guns, the wheelchair and Fisk.

TWENTY-FIVE

I found a secluded spot in the corner of the parking lot structure where I could see both roads, parked the chair and waited.

I glanced at my watch. I couldn't be sure but thought Claire had been gone around four minutes. I'd been keeping aware of my surroundings, but my gaze kept returning to Fisk the way you'd keep your eye on a quiet rattlesnake.

There was movement under the blanket. He had started to move his hands but his head remained lowered and his eyes closed. I moved over to him. His head twitched as I approached. The syringe came out, I uncapped it and stuck it in his neck where Claire had shown me. Fisk twitched and let out a faint grunt of pain as I injected half the contents. He whispered something I didn't catch and within fifteen seconds he was back to sitting still and breathing steadily.

Just over a minute later I gave him the rest of the injection. This time he made no sound. I figured he'd be no problem for at least another dozen minutes now and turned my attention back to the roads outside.

A cop limped out from the garden pathway Claire and I had used. He was the taller of the two guys I had hit when in the elevator. I thought he was doing well to be back on his feet already. However, he had a bandaged nose and moved as if he was full of hurt. As he walked along he kept one hand on his holstered gun.

He paused across the road, looked around then hobbled off south along Gantenbein Avenue.

On the opposite side of the road I saw a light blue Chrysler minivan coming the other way. There was no way he could fail to see it. The cop paused, tilting his head, using the radio at his shoulder. I tensed.

The minivan drove past him and he didn't turn.

I caught a glimpse of Claire at the wheel. It was time to go.

I wheeled Fisk to a side exit, moving swiftly, and emerged into the autumn light in time to see the brake lights of the Chrysler as Claire turned the corner then pulled to a halt a few yards away.

She hadn't been able to park and the minivan was paused in the road, hazards now flashing. Fortunately the street was wide enough for most cars to pass on the far side. Claire saw me in the mirrors, got out of the van and slid open the side door.

It is not an easy task getting an unconscious body out of a wheelchair and into the back seat of a car, but we managed. It helped that I didn't care if Fisk got hurt during the process, but it was still an awkward job. I got in after him and told Claire to get going as I roughly strapped Fisk into place and re-taped his hands together with more duct tape. The roll was getting well used.

Claire drove away gently. We had already drawn attention from a couple of folks returning to their cars and there was no need to raise their suspicions further with a tire-squealing getaway.

Ultimately I wanted to get to Marine Drive that ran along the Columbia River. I knew of an empty derelict houseboat there. At least it had been empty nine months ago.

I told Claire to drive north on Vancouver Street, then cut across on Martin Luther King Boulevard. It was the quickest and most direct route. Time rather than stealth was more important right now.

"Are you sure?" she asked.

"It's the best place I can think of for now." That much was true. I wanted somewhere out of the way where Fisk and I could have a long talk without being interrupted.

"Won't they be on the lookout for this van?"

"Maybe," I said. "But right now there'll still be confusion and arguments over who's in charge. We should be okay for a while."

She gave me a quick look that told me she wasn't convinced. To be honest, neither was I. It all depended on how the department would respond without Fisk and how much Marshall would expand the hunt for us. Would she get the whole department on the case or remain with those officers she could trust not to ask awkward questions.

We also had what amounted to a high value hostage, so any first response would be cautious. Negotiate first. Shoot later. Again, I hoped I was right.

I'd taken the gun with the silencer out of the bag and rested it pointing at the meat at the back of Fisk's thigh. If I had to shoot it wouldn't hit any arteries, but it would sure hurt.

Eight minutes into the journey Fisk spoke. I hadn't been aware he'd woken up. His eyes were still closed and his speech a little slurred.

"Big mistake, Riley. You've played and lost."

"How do figure that? I have you and a gun pointing at you."

Fisk opened his eyes. He was not on top form, that was for sure, but I guess repeated shots of Ketalar would do that. I could see him trying to collect his thoughts.

Claire's eyes darted to me in the rear mirror.

"Without me around it'll go bad," murmured Fisk. "He'll die."

I guessed he was talking about Sean, but didn't want him to confirm that right there and then with Claire up front driving.

"All you have to do is tell me where he is," I told him.

"I don't know. Not my idea."

I knew he was lying. I pressed the muzzle of the silencer into his leg. I wasn't gentle.

"Where is he?"

He glanced down at the gun.

"You won't do anything. Not in here. Blood on the seats. Not clever." As his head cleared his voice became more controlled.

I snorted a derisory laugh.

"Do you really think I care about upholstery stains? I'd happily shoot you in the liver and let you bleed out slow."

Fisk met my gaze. He knew what I was capable of. He blinked and I carried on.

"You have two choices, Larry: tell me where Sean is, or I'll make your death long and slow."

Fisk sighed. "Even if you find out where he is, what are you going to do? The whole department will be looking for you. You're a wanted man."

"I'll find a way."

Fisk made a non-committal sound. It was like he knew I'd try but also knew I'd probably fail.

I saw from the surroundings passing the window we were getting close to the old houseboat now. "I'd say you've got five minutes before our talk gets serious."

"Gonna torture some lies out of me?" he sneered.

"If that's what it takes."

"That's one way of letting Sean die."

"What do you mean?"

"What time is it?" Fisk turned, craning his neck to see the digital clock on the Chrysler's dashboard. "Oh," he said, as if there was a small but disappointing problem, like getting ham in your sandwich instead of pastrami, coffee with low fat milk instead of cream.

Or someone you didn't care about getting killed.

"What do you mean?" I asked again, twisting the gun and reminding him of its presence.

"If I don't make a call…" He let the implication hang in the air.

Claire's eyes bored into me through the mirror.

"Keep your eyes on the road," I told her. "He's lying."

"No I'm not." Fisk was looking at Claire.

This was something I hadn't anticipated and now I felt stupid. Fisk knew he had us now. Even if it only bought him time, he'd managed a small victory.

"When do you need to call?" I asked.

"About," he looked at the time again, "seven minutes ago."

TWENTY-SIX

Claire made a choked gasp and pulled the van to the side of the road in a chirp of tires. She turned in her seat and glared at Fisk. "If Sean's dead I'll kill you myself."

"There is some leeway," Fisk smiled. "Ten minutes or so."

"Let him do it." Claire's voice was brittle with emotion.

I wanted to shout at her to continue driving but was torn. If Fisk was telling the truth, then I had to take the chance.

I swore under my breath, tucked the gun behind me, well out of Fisk's reach, and unzipped the sports bag. It was a dangerous situation and I had lost an element of control, but I'd have been more worried if his hands and feet weren't still taped.

"Come on! Come on!" Fisk urged.

It felt like ages before I matched the battery to his phone and powered it on. The swirling logo and welcome chime taunted me with its slowness.

"Give it here!" he insisted waggling the fingers of his taped hands.

I paused. "No."

"What?!?" he exclaimed.

I heard Claire whimper and her eyes boring into me.

"What's the unlock code?" I asked Fisk.

He sighed. "Zero-nine-one-one."

I keyed the number. It was rejected.

"Give it to me," he said. I stared at him.

"Code."

"For Christ sake!" screamed Claire.

I shook my head, refusing to look at her.

"Code," I said again.

"No," said Fisk.

"Let him have it – Dean, please!" Claire was crying now.

"It's what he does. He's clever."

"Do you want Sean to die? Is that it?" Fisk snarled the words at me. "Some uncle. Some brother! Jesus, Riley, you're playing with his life. You're fucked up inside."

"They're tracking the phone right now Claire." I kept my voice soft. "He's just buying time, trying to panic us into giving him his phone, maybe make a call to Marshall–"

"You dumb fuck!" Fisk spat, interrupting me. "You still have her phone! How–"

I punched his nose. Not a bone-breaker, but enough to shut the prick up and make his eyes water.

"Like I was saying, if not Marshall then someone else. Keep the line open long enough to make a trace. When he guessed that I would check his call log first he starts stalling."

The way Claire looked at me told me she didn't know if she believed me or not – but I'd better be damn right or I'd lose my sister as well as my nephew.

Fisk had his hands holding his nose as he slowly shook his head. "Don't do this Riley. Don't throw this away."

"Code."

Fisk sighed angrily. "Four-three-nine-five, and hurry will you!"

This time I believed him. It was the date he'd joined the force.

I keyed the number Fisk had given me. It was correct. I went into his recent numbers list and looked for a pattern. There were regular numbers but nothing that looked like it was made on any schedule.

"Number." I asked.

"Speed dial nine. Can't remember the number."

I pressed nine and held it for speed dial. As soon as the number was displayed, I hung up and pulled the battery. I still remembered the number from six years ago and didn't want a direct connection to the police department's techs.

I looked at Fisk but spoke to Claire. "Told you he was lying."

"Can't blame me for trying," said Fisk.

Claire's attention was fully on Fisk now. Her words were directed to me but the venom in them was all for Fisk.

"Don't kill him, Dean." Fisk looked over at her, puzzled. "Just cut off his hands and feet. Then blind him."

Fisk knew he'd overplayed his hand and tried to recover.

"Look, that was stupid, I know – but Sean is still alive. I swear."

Claire put the Chrysler back in drive and pulled back into the traffic. Neither of us said anything. I dropped the phone back in the bag and pressed the gun into Fisk's kidney. I said nothing. I just looked at him.

Even in the air-conditioned cool of the minivan Fisk had started to sweat. He didn't look at me. Instead he kept his eyes on Claire.

"He's safe, I promise you. He was taken as leverage, that's all."

Claire's hands gripped the wheel harder but she said nothing. If I had been driving and she'd been in the back, I wouldn't have given much for Fisk's chances of not being shot.

"What leverage?" As soon as I asked the question, I suspected the answer.

Fisk took a breath. "Look, it all comes down to the money. Where it comes from, where it goes, making figures balance and look legit. Richard's name came up as being the man to go to. A recommendation. He'd got the skills to do what was needed, and of course he'd get a small cut of the funds to make it worth his time."

The van weaved slightly but Claire corrected it. I could hear her trying to control her breathing as Fisk continued.

"But it was suggested that a little extra insurance was needed, something to make sure Richard did the right thing, which is where Sean comes in."

The way he casually explained it, like dealing with a commodity, made me want to shoot him there and then.

Fisk caught my look. "Hey, when it comes to it, I'm only a fixer.

It was someone else's idea."

"Who?" I asked.

"One of the bosses: the Armenians, I guess. It came through on the contact phone." For once I believed him, even though I would have put money on it being Fisk's idea. Combining leverage on Richard and being able to frame and get rid of me would be just his sort of plan. Maybe I was letting old animosities lead me to conclusions that I expected, rather than being able to see what was really going on. I still had a lot of pieces to put together, but it had been a long day and I was dog tired.

"Where's Sean?" I asked.

"It's not that simple—"

"Yes. It is."

Fisk sighed and said nothing. I tapped him on the knee with the tip of the silencer.

"Knee or balls?"

That got him talking again.

"Look, Marshall has the connections for that line of work. I let her deal with it."

"So what good are you then?" I said, moving the tip of the silencer up between his legs. "Never wanted kids, did you?"

Claire brought the minivan to a halt, the tires crunching on the dirt.

"Dean..." she said.

"What?" I asked keeping my eyes on Fisk. He knew his time was running out with me and he was scared.

"You said there was an old houseboat..." said Claire.

I turned around, peering out through the windshield at the view beyond.

A series of rusty pontoons lay in the water at the edge of the river but there was no sign of any houseboat.

It had gone.

TWENTY-SEVEN

I let out a frustrated breath and turned my attention back to Fisk. "Something missing?" he asked, a slight smile at the edges of his mouth.

"Like I said, if Marshall has Sean, what good are you to me?" I said, bringing him back on track. "You're running out of options, Larry."

"No, we can deal, there's more–"

I shoved the gun into his crotch.

"NO! No!" He tried to shrink away but there was nowhere to go. "Look if I give you the account numbers I have and you change the access codes she'll have to deal! You'll have full control of those accounts. You can use that. She'll want the money more than she does Sean."

"Doesn't Richard already have all the account numbers and access codes? I would have thought he needed them to do his part of the job?"

"No, no." Fisk shook his head. "It's part of a consolidation process. Money's coming in from multiple sources into a holding account. Then when all payments have been made it gets transferred out again into a whole new set of accounts. Richard's job was to set up those new offshore accounts and make sure that, when the holding account is full, the transfers to those accounts take place without attracting the interest of any federal financial investigation. He doesn't need the access codes to put money in them, just to get it out."

"Which he would know is illegal, so Sean is taken to make him co-operate," I added.

Fisk nodded.

"Is Sean going to be let go once it's all done?" said Claire.

Fisk looked at me and said nothing.

"Is he?" Claire demanded.

I moved the gun to point directly at the top of Fisk's kneecap.

"WILL THEY LET HIM GO?" screamed Claire.

Fisk hung his head. "I can't answer that."

"Loose ends," I said softly.

Fisk remained quiet. Claire was trying to control her breathing. I knew she was both scared and angry.

"So we have to convince Marshall to trade Sean for the money," I said.

"That's the best option," said Fisk.

I thought for a moment, feeling both Claire's and Fisk's eyes on me.

"Why doesn't Marshall have the codes, or at least her own account?" I asked.

"Linda has her own account. I can't tell you much about that other than it'll only be a couple of million at best."

Only a couple of million I thought. What sort of figures were we talking about here as a total? I also noted the use of her first name and wondered if Fisk had some emotional attachment to her.

Fisk continued. "She also has the codes for some of the other accounts but not the account numbers. It's the same with me. It's kind of like an insurance policy, to make sure our clients don't dispense with our services too early."

"How does that work?" I didn't understand.

"The order of the access codes is in account number sequence," explained Fisk. "Without knowing the account numbers they are useless, and vice versa. When we get our cut we send the codes and it's job done."

"But how can you set up access codes for each account if you don't know the account numbers?" asked Claire from the front seat.

"Easy," said Fisk. "I was sent a secure login and had to setup whatever access codes I wanted against a list of hidden account numbers."

"And you trusted that?" I wondered aloud.

"You should try a little trust," snapped Fisk looking sharply at me. "It might end up saving your boy's life."

I frowned. If the derelict houseboat had still been there, we could have carried on the conversation inside, away from prying eyes. As it was, we were simply parked at the side of the dirt road like lost tourists. We'd have to move soon.

As if to emphasize the point a pair of trucks rumbled by, kicking up dust as they passed the idling minivan. We couldn't stay there much longer.

"So who are your clients, the ones getting the money?" I could guess but wanted Fisk to confirm it.

"A group of highly motivated Eastern Europeans," he said.

"Armenians?"

Fisk raised his eyebrows. "Good guess."

"So what's your suggestion?" I asked Fisk.

"I give you the codes I know. You trade those however you want for Sean."

"And in return?"

"You let me go. I disappear. You never see me again."

I reckoned he probably had a fair amount stashed away already, and that was in addition to whatever would be hitting his special personal account set up by Richard. He'd said that Marshall would *only* be getting around two million, so I reckoned he must be on for around five million, maybe more.

What he offered was a good option for him. Getting away with your life and a heap of money was better than a jail term or ending up dead.

I carried on looking at him. He continued, knowing he had to add more.

"Look, I'll record a statement that you were set up, get you off the hook. Sound fair?"

"Why don't I just trade you directly to Marshall or the Armenians for Sean? You've got the codes. Why not deliver direct?"

Fisk shook his head emphatically. "No. No deal. We're too far down the line now."

"Go on," I said.

He sighed, like he was dealing with an idiot child.

"Taking me changed everything. Marshall will think I've ratted her out by now, that you've made me tell all–"

"Which you have." I interrupted.

"Okay," acknowledged Fisk. "And the Armenians will think I've been compromised. Sure, they'll take me and get the codes but then I'll just be another body in the river."

I changed tack, following up on the flaw I'd noted earlier. "Why not get the account numbers from Richard? You already have the access codes in account order sequence, you get the accounts and that's a lot of money right there for the taking." I stared at Fisk. "You've got to have thought of it."

"There are some people you don't mess with. Not unless you like looking over your shoulder for the rest of your short life."

I knew he was referring to the Armenians, not Richard.

Claire shifted in her seat. A beat-up SUV rolled past us on the track, travelling slow. I looked around, wondering where we should go but still with plenty of questions for Fisk.

"Turn us around," I told Claire. "Let's be ready to move."

She got busy maneuvering while I threw another question Fisk's way.

"Who has Sean? Marshall or the Armenians?"

"Both," he said. "From what I know the Armenians have him, but they'll still take guidance from Marshall. For now."

"You know you stay until Sean gets out."

Fisk huffed, not happy with that.

Claire finished turning the van.

"There's another option," said Fisk. "You change the access codes to what you want, then you can set me loose. You won't need me."

I looked at Fisk. "I like the sound of that," I said.

Fisk caught my meaning and paled slightly.

"Once you have access to changing the codes you let me go."

"Go on," I said.

"Okay, we'll need an internet connection to do this."

A thought crossed Claire's face. She looked at me.

"Internet cafe?" I asked her, guessing her thoughts. I was wrong.

She gave me the look that computer savvy youngsters give to an older generation, despite there being only a handful of years between us.

"No, I don't think there are many of those still around now, Dean. There's a laptop on Richard's boat. It's a good connection. It's where he works sometimes."

It sounded like it was our best option, but I was still digesting one nugget of her information.

"Richard has a *boat*?" His business had rewarded him far better than I realized.

*

Claire took us back along the track, rejoined the highway and drove steadily along Marine Drive, parking at McCuddy's Marina.

I was surprised and relieved by how close it was. The less time we spent on the road, the better. The journey had only taken five minutes start to finish.

It was still enough time for me to think about how the exchange would work. I still needed to know how to make contact with whoever was holding Sean, then arrange a way of exchanging the information – as in the account access codes – for Sean himself.

Hostage exchanges are always tense and tricky situations. There never seems to be an easy solution that all parties are happy with. Like Fisk had said, there always has to be an element of trust.

But I didn't trust the Armenians, I didn't trust Marshall and I didn't trust Fisk.

PUSH BACK

It turned out that my instincts were right.

TWENTY-EIGHT

The next immediate challenge was to get Fisk onto Richard's boat, preferably without raising too much suspicion. He'd have to walk there, and that meant freeing him from the tape. I took the switchblade out of the bag but didn't cut him loose yet. Instead, I spoke with Claire.

I needed her to open up Richard's boat, check that the laptop was still there and then come back. I also asked her about the keys for the boat, but she'd already thought of that.

There was a spare set Richard kept in a lockbox at the back of the boat. Before Claire went, she took the keys out of the minivan's ignition and passed them to me.

"Ten minutes," she said, then hesitated, remembering the hospital. "Maybe twelve."

I smiled at her. "Okay."

She got out of the Chrysler and walked across the parking lot towards the boat ramp. I turned my attention back to Fisk. He was looking at me thoughtfully.

"Here's how it's going to go," I told him.

"I know," Fisk cut in. "When Claire gets back you're going to remove the tape, I follow her to the boat staying a few yards behind. If I try anything you'll put a bullet in me. That it?"

"Pretty much."

"Even in public. In daylight?"

The downside of the early autumn weather blessing us with mild weather was that it was still perfectly light outside. It was only 6:30pm and the sun wouldn't set for another hour. For walking

Fisk to the boat, I'd have preferred it to be dusk at least.

"No hesitation," I confirmed.

Fisk looked away from me and kept quiet. That made me more uneasy than if he'd carried on talking.

The minutes passed. I kept myself aware of the surroundings, as well as Fisk's every move. I continued to sift plans and options, but I'll freely admit I'm no great plan maker. I like the simple approach. That's why I have always been happy to remain a sergeant – in both the Rangers and the police. I had also been a detective though, so that must have counted for something.

I heard police sirens approaching and pressed the muzzle of the gun into the side of Fisk's belly.

"Better hope they don't stop here," I told him.

The sirens got closer, the wail increasing in pitch. There were at least two vehicles coming, possibly more. I adjusted the angle of the gun against Fisk. He closed his eyes. Sweat beaded on his forehead.

I heard the brief roar of powerful engines as the police cruisers sped by on the road behind us, their sirens dropping to a lower pitch as they passed.

Fisk let out a slow breath. He opened his eyes and looked at me.

"You'd do it too, wouldn't you?"

I stared back at him. I said nothing. A vein pulsed on the side of his head and he looked away.

Claire was returning. I spotted her leaving the boat ramp and hurrying towards the minivan. She looked worried. I willed her to slow down. A casual stroll is far less noticeable than someone nearly about to break into a jog. There were a few other folks around; not many, but enough to make me cautious.

She reached the car and shuffled into the driving seat, turning to face me and leaving the door open.

"No laptop." She sounded breathless.

I wasn't surprised. Over the past minutes I'd come to the conclusion that Richard would be pretty foolish to leave his laptop unattended on a boat.

"You've got the keys though?"

She nodded.

"I'm going to need a computer of some sort," said Fisk. "No computer, no swapping codes."

"Don't worry about that," I told him.

He sighed. It was an exasperated sound.

I passed the minivan keys back and to Claire and told her what we were going to do regarding getting Fisk to the boat. Then I cut and removed the tape, freeing him.

"Do I need to say anything?" I asked.

"Nope," was all he said.

I got out of the van and took the sports bag with me, putting it over my left shoulder, then draped the hospital blanket over the pistol in my right hand.

Fisk watched me and the gun, then followed, shuffling across the seats and getting out of the same door next to me. I gave him enough room so he would have little chance of any misguided heroics. He shut the door behind him.

Claire locked the Chrysler, walked around the front of it and across the parking lot towards the boat ramp.

"You know what to do," I said to Fisk.

He walked after Claire, keeping a good four paces back. I followed him a little closer. Down the boat ramp, the solid wooden boards of the jetties spurred off leading to separate avenues of boats.

It took just three minutes to reach Richard's boat.

There were bigger craft around, but not many. I saw Fisk giving it an appreciative look before we got on board.

It was a modern cruiser: at least forty feet long, bow to stern. The upper hull and superstructure gleamed white and the chrome handrails shone. Below the gunwale and down to the chine, some two feet above the waterline, gloss black paintwork bordered with a red stripe gave the boat a rakish, sporty appearance. It was easy to see that Richard cared for his boat more than his cars.

I expected the interior to be all black leather, ebony and chrome, but it wasn't. The upper deck and cockpit seating areas were clad in a white faux leather, complete with a black band sweeping across the backrests. Claire led us from the back of the boat down into a kitchen and seating area. An arch in the far wall led through to a bedroom under the prow of the boat. The floor looked like cherry wood planking and the cabinetry, also cherry, had a deep gloss. I was also surprised to see a white leather wraparound sofa. It was still stylish but had a homely feel to it.

I told Fisk to sit and he did, reclining in the far corner of the sofa. I dumped the heavy sports bag near to the cabin steps, well away from him.

"What now?" he asked. He knew he'd bought himself some time and maybe even a way out. Unfortunately it meant he was starting to get cockier than I liked.

"You stay quiet and be a good boy," I told him. I reached into the bag and pulled out the roll of duct tape. There was just enough left.

"What? Again?" whined Fisk.

I ignored him and passed the gun to Claire. She was reluctant but took it anyway.

"Do you know how to use that?" said Fisk from across the cabin. The guy really liked the sound of his own voice, especially when he could use it to be patronizing.

"Squeeze, don't pull," said Claire raising the pistol so that the bore of the silencer lined up on his left eye.

Fisk kept quiet.

I went over to him. I was in the way of Claire's aim but that was okay. If he tried anything I was more than capable and ready to stop him.

"You try anything, you get hurt. Understand?"

He sighed. He understood.

"Come on. Just get on with it."

I did. I made Fisk pull up his trouser legs and cross his ankles before I taped around them, directly onto bare skin. It would be much harder for him to break free from that position. It would hurt more too.

Then I did his wrists. It wasn't the best solution. I knew if I left him alone he'd be free in thirty seconds, but it was better than having him loose to start with.

I finished and stepped back to admire my handiwork.

"You got shares in this stuff?" he sneered, raising his taped wrists.

"Want me to tape your mouth?"

He shook his head and kept quiet.

I dropped the sparse remains of the tape back in the bag and extracted my 'burner' phone and charger. I plugged it into a nearby wall socket. The phone gave a faint beep as it began charging.

I went over and spoke quietly to Claire. It didn't matter that Fisk could still hear us.

"I'm going to need you to do some shopping." I dug into the blue sports bag again, took out a wad of my emergency money and passed it to her. She handed back the gun, glad to be rid of it.

"What do you need?" she said.

"Laptop computer. Nothing fancy. Just as long as you can connect it to the internet and our friend over there can use it."

"I'd prefer a MacBook," chimed Fisk. I gave him a look that spoke of more duct tape and a side order of pain, but he carried on. "Of course I am assuming you know how to get on to Richard's Wi-Fi." I really was getting tempted to tape his mouth, if only to stop his smarmy tone, but I couldn't escape the fact he was right. "Most people tend to be quite security conscious these days," he added.

Claire gave me a worried look.

"Don't worry," I told her, moving us both out of earshot of Fisk. "We'll cross that bridge if we need to."

She didn't seem convinced. The adrenaline and anger that had helped her along earlier had faded, leaving her looking tired and apprehensive.

I put a hand on her arm.

"Look I know you've gone through a lot already, but I also know you're strong. I wouldn't ask you to do this if I didn't think you could."

It had very briefly crossed my mind to leave Claire guarding Fisk while I went out, but I'd quickly dismissed that idea. Even with wrists and ankles bound he was still dangerous. Not so much a problem for me but there was no way I wanted to leave my sister in that situation.

There was also the fact I was a wanted man and it was far more likely that it was my face being the one looked for rather than Claire's. Even so, there was still a risk she might be picked up.

I reckoned that there would also be a police BOLO, a 'Be On Look Out', for the Chrysler minivan. On the plus side it did have a bland anonymity in its favor.

I spoke quietly and outlined a plan of action for her.

Portland airport was nearby. I calculated it would take around fifteen minutes for her to drive there and park, leaving the van in long stay. Getting it away from McCuddys and Richard's boat and making it more of a needle in a haystack of needles would be a good move.

Provided she got there without being stopped.

At the airport she'd get a cab into town, to one of the bigger malls. There she could buy what we needed. Then it would be a cab ride back.

All told I reckoned she'd need a couple of hours at the outside.

Before she went I gave her the number of the burner phone, just in case. She gave me the keys to the boat, a hesitant kiss on the cheek, then she was gone.

There was no denying I was worried about Claire; I was depending on her again and hoped the pressure wasn't too much.

I didn't know it then, but the next time I'd see her would be back in hospital.

TWENTY-NINE

There was a fridge on the boat. I checked inside and took out a couple of half-liter bottles of water. I unscrewed the caps and handed one to Fisk. I took the other.

He thanked me. For once it sounded genuine, and from the way he drank I could see he was thirsty.

I hadn't done it out of any kindness. It was time for him to talk and I didn't want any excuses of a dry mouth or parched throat to stop him. I let Fisk drink. It looked awkward with his hands taped.

I sat at the other end of the curved couch, keeping my gun hand relaxed but ready. With the other hand I powered on the burner phone. Finally, the main screen appeared with a simple start menu. I found the audio recording option, selected it and placed the phone halfway between myself and Fisk.

He looked at the phone, then at me. He'd finished drinking for now and the bottle was over half empty.

"Time to talk," I told him. "First off, tell me again why Sean was taken?"

He repeated what he'd said earlier, about leverage on Richard.

"If you wanted leverage on Richard, why not take Claire? Richard cares more about her." I said.

"She'd be more readily missed. Besides, when Sean called you—" Fisk stopped.

"Go on."

Fisk sighed and looked away, weighing up what he could say.

"Sean found out something was wrong, probably when doing some computer upgrade in Richard's office, and after he called you that's when the order came through."

I must have looked puzzled because Fisk continued.

"Richard's office was bugged; that's where he called you from. I guess it made sense to get him out of the picture. Take Sean, stop him talking to you, get leverage on Richard. Neat and tidy. Setting you up was a bonus."

That made me want to go over to Fisk and kick him repeatedly in the balls until he vomited blood, but I kept myself still and remained sitting on the white couch.

I tried a different question.

"Why was Killick framing me for Sean's murder?"

"You sure you want to know?" said Fisk quietly.

I nodded, slowly, once. Fisk shrugged.

"Even taking Sean, preventing your meeting up, would mean you'd get involved. So if we had Killick take you out of the game it was problem solved and we'd have someone to pin everything on. It's no secret you were ex-Special Forces and know how to kill. Then there's all those confessions you got when on the force. You were always known for being able to 'physically motivate' suspects. Nobody wanted to get on your bad side, but nobody was sure how to get on your good side. Maybe you'd finally gone off the deep end."

"Really?" I asked, low and dangerous.

"Another option was you having an accident riding that bike of yours. Something messy. Couldn't get hold of a truck in time though.

"Thanks," I said without any trace of sincerity. "Tell me about Linda Marshall."

"What do you want to know?"

"All you've got."

Fisk told me. From the way he spoke he wasn't thinking he'd see her again. Evidently he had checked her file which was to be expected in his position as police captain.

Linda Marshall had been a lieutenant working vice down in Los Angeles. She had a good arrest record but poor administrative skills, as Fisk put it. There had been times where the amounts of money or drugs seized did not tally with records. It wasn't ever that much, a couple of thousand here or there, but it was enough to have Internal Affairs start taking an interest.

Fisk met my eyes. "Sounds familiar, doesn't it."

I didn't respond. It was only ever money I'd taken, and when there's a hundred thousand dollar pile who's going to miss a few hundred bucks here and there? Besides, that wasn't what I felt shame for from my time on the force. I'd done something far worse, and Fisk knew it. I was surprised he hadn't brought it up. Unless he thought it would be pushing my buttons too far. And he might have been right.

Her arrests and takedowns were all quick, brutal and effective. She was tipped for rapid promotion to captain herself before the Internal Affairs cloud began hanging over her head. One young I.A. investigator pointed out that she'd never managed to arrest any members of an Armenian Power group operating in L.A. and asked the question whether she was getting intel from them or the Russian mafia. Her response was understandably hostile, yet it was logged that she remained calm, denying such involvement.

Marshall's demotion to sergeant came about after someone leaked a recording of a pre-raid briefing where she made specific mention that any petty cash gathered during the bust was to be pooled and shared equally. Despite protests that it was a joke, and being supported by most of her team, getting away with a disciplinary and the demotion was lucky. She had been sloppy. It could have been a lot worse.

Suspicion about who had made the recording and passed it to Internal Affairs was short lived. It was easy to tell from the angle and location of the footage and the fact that the officer in question had since been transferred out of the team. No one likes a snitch.

Whether it was related or not, the ex-team member's son got killed by a hit and run the following week. The car was found burned out. It had been stolen from the Glendale area on the day of the hit and run.

Glendale was a known Armenian Power territory. You didn't have to be Columbo to make the connections.

After that, Marshall had been applying for jobs around the country but it was Fisk who saw her potential. He saw that she got results. I knew that he didn't care how and that a bit of corruption was acceptable.

But I got the feeling that Fisk had thought he'd netted himself a barracuda and ended up with a great white shark.

"So she's your number two," I said.

"In effect. She has the connections, and the drive. I was going to promote her back to lieutenant before I left. Let her run the show."

"Why leave?"

"I have my reasons but they're not for this tape," he said, nodding towards the phone. It was still recording as it charged.

"Who can she call on? Who will she trust?"

"That's two different questions, Riley," said Fisk. "She can call on the entire department if needed, and I'll bet she's needing. But that's only to find us, and she'll have a real hard-on to do that especially after you shot her in the ass.

"For anything more than that, there's maybe a dozen who would just do as they're told, take the money, do the job and say no more."

"Is Perez in there?"

Fisk shook his head. "He's on the sidelines. He's taken his fair share to look the other way but he's no friend of Marshall. No, your biggest problem would be four guys in the SWAT team."

"Go on," I prompted.

"Lane, Santos, Jenner and Dawson. Dependable. Work well as a team. Share the same ethics."

"Figures," I said.

"They're some mean and dangerous motherfuckers. You could say they're Marshall's go-to guys if something needs to get done. Dawson's a sniper. He's good." Fisk's words were matter-of-fact, like he'd seen Dawson in action, which he probably had.

I thought about that for a second. It was not comforting. I'd done some sniper training while in the Rangers. I was okay, nothing more. There were plenty of other guys better than me. We all knew how dangerous a good sniper was. The target would be dead without even hearing the shot.

It didn't even occur to me why he was volunteering the information.

While we had been talking, the sun had set and dusk had settled over the marina. It wasn't pitch dark outside, I could still see over to the boarding ramp, but it had that grainy indistinct monochromatic look that evening brings.

I stood up, pulled the cabin's small curtains closed, and found the switch to the lights. The boat might stand out illuminated in amongst the docking berths but there was little else I could do unless we sat in the darkness, and I wanted to make sure I could see Fisk.

I was expecting some caustic comment from him, but he kept quiet.

I sat down again, careful not to let my shadow fall across the curtains. Fisk's comment about Dawson being a sniper was still fresh in my mind.

I'd figured I'd got enough now. I took the cell phone and stopped the audio recorder.

"So how's it all going to happen?" asked Fisk. "With me, once I've given you the access codes?"

"You give me the means to make the deal," I emphasized the next part. "Once I have Sean, you get to go. As agreed."

"As simple as that," he said. I could tell he wasn't convinced. "And the exchange for Sean...?"

There was only one way I could see it working. I didn't like it, but my options were limited. I was about to tell him when the burner phone rang.

I didn't recognize the number, but I wasn't expecting to. I answered the call.

It was Claire.

"Dean, they've got me," she sobbed.

THIRTY

"Who?" I asked, fearing the worst.

"Central Precinct. I'm in the station now. Apparently I'm a person of interest to the North Precinct. It's been put city wide. You're my phone call." She was trying to remain calm but the nerves still came through across the line. "What should I do?"

"Is Marshall there?"

"No. I've not seen her. It was regular uniform that got me, just as I was going into the mall."

I thought for a moment. I expected Marshall could still be at the hospital being patched up. The bullet wounds I'd inflicted weren't life-threatening but would be enough to incapacitate her, though she'd still be able to issue orders and coordinate operations.

At least Claire was in a different precinct to the one Fisk was the captain of, so unlikely to be in any direct danger.

"Okay. Say you'll only speak with Dan Perez from North – and just him alone. Tell him everything you know except for our location."

"Everything?" Claire sounded unsure.

"Yes, everything – except for where I am," I stressed. "You dropped me off at the airport and I'm going to call you later. Got it?"

"Yes. Okay."

"Remember – only talk to Dan Perez. He's our best bet. Hang in there, Claire. I'll sort this out. I promise."

I felt a twinge of guilt getting Perez involved, especially after what I'd seen with his wife at the hospital, but I knew he would do okay by Claire.

Claire said okay again, sounded like she wanted to add something else but instead said goodbye and hung up.

Of course, no sooner she was off the phone than I thought of more things I should have told her, things to help her story, but also that I was proud of my little sister and was even more determined than ever to get Sean back for her.

As I sat there, I became aware that Fisk was staring at me, his face serious. He took another sip of water. He'd heard my side of the call and might even have caught bits of what Claire had said. He knew the situation.

"Sounds like we have a problem," he said.

I said nothing.

"We need a computer to sort out those access codes."

"I still have you," I reminded him. "With your codes. I can still trade."

"What about our deal? You hand me over and I'm a dead man."

I stared at him for a moment. I could tell he was thinking about what he could do, what his options were.

"Better hope we can find a computer soon then," I said, unplugging the phone. The power was at about two thirds. It would be enough. I put it in the bag then turned out the lights in the cabin. Even with the curtains closed there was just enough grey light filtering in to still see Fisk.

Although I'd said to Claire not to give away where I was, I had the unnerving feeling it might already be too late.

Marshall knew that Claire was with me, she would know all about Richard, and it would be easy enough to find out he owned a boat and where it was moored.

Maybe I was being too paranoid but it's what I would have done if I were in her position.

I went over to the galley units and checked the drawers. I found a couple of cooking knives and took those, dropping them into the bag. Fisk eyed me warily. They weren't for use on him, in fact quite the opposite. I was removing them so Fisk couldn't use them to get free or stab me.

Ideally I wanted to find some rope or cord to tie Fisk up more securely. A fresh roll of duct tape would also be great. I'd even have accepted some string. I found nothing and cursed my stupidity for not taking a spare set of cuffs when at the hospital.

I had to trust that I'd bound Fisk enough and he wouldn't risk trying to get away for a minute or so.

I went to the cabin door.

"Don't try anything stupid," I told him.

"Okay." He said it the same way teenagers say, 'Whatever'.

I took the gun, slowly opened the door and listened. Above the lapping of water, distant traffic was the thump of faint music from a nearby bar. If there was anyone creeping around outside, I wouldn't have been able to hear them.

I shouldered the bag and closed the cabin door behind me. If Fisk got himself free he could lock the door from the inside. That didn't bother me. I had the keys and could still get in. The downside of that setup was that, even though I could lock the cabin door, it could still be opened from the inside.

I was not happy about having to leave him unattended but felt I had little choice. I figured he'd be more of a danger and liability if I cut his feet free and had him come with me.

No, the main deterrent against him doing anything was that I had a gun and was prepared to use it. The best he might find would be a dinner fork.

Richard's boat was solidly built and the few steps to the rear deck didn't make a sound as I went up them. I trod cautiously, surveying the jetties and what I could see of the boat's surroundings. I saw nothing suspicious, but still felt like I was being watched.

I turned slowly, crept up the few steep steps to the upper deck with its white seats and fancy cockpit and crossed to the wheel station. I placed the sports bag in an open stowage bin, stuffed the silenced pistol awkwardly in the back of my jeans and took out the keys to Richard's boat. The ignition was easy to find even in the deepening dusk. Lights appeared on the dashboard and an 'engine start' button illuminated.

I pressed it. There was the distant whine of starter motors spinning then the engines caught, coughed, and settled to a soft burbling idle.

Now it was time to move fast.

I cast off the mooring lines, returned to the cockpit and eased the boat forwards out of its berth and away from the jetty. I had to keep the speed low and span the wheel, steering into the lane between the row of berths and the long wooden walkway of the next row of jetties. It was getting darker now though I could still make out enough. Against all marine and river regulations I kept the lights off.

Glass exploded around me as the side window erupted inwards, shards peppering my face. I crouched low and heard another burst of automatic gunfire. Holes shredded the fiberglass as I shoved the throttle open. The boat's engines roared, prow rising as it accelerated.

The staccato bark of the machine gun ripped the air and bullets tore through the superstructure around me, more glass shattering. A length of solid-looking walkway lay directly ahead of the speeding boat. I spun the wheel to the left and the boat responded, heeling over as it turned hard. I kept it pointed in approximately the correct direction as it continued powering forward. The right side grazed the walkway and I corrected by feel. The boat swayed, settled, then picked up speed as it entered the river proper.

The gunfire had stopped and I risked sticking my head up for a glance forwards. It was lucky I did. We were powering directly towards the side of a larger vessel. I yanked the throttle back and turned the wheel hard right. The nose dipped and the whole craft yawed drunkenly. I fed in more power and it bit into the turn with more purpose. We made it past with more room than I expected and I kept the wheel where it was, taking the boat through one-eighty degrees and pointing it upriver, where I knew there would be less traffic.

I had a couple of seconds to gather my thoughts. The first of which was that my right arm felt cold, maybe from the shattered side windows around the cockpit. Then the pain started and I looked down. My shirt sleeve was bloody. I'd been hit.

I throttled the boat back to a sensible law-abiding speed, found the switch for the forward lights and flicked them on. I knew that if I'd carried on sailing blind Marshall wouldn't need her hit squad, I'd end up killing myself by accident.

Then I checked my arm. I was bleeding from a ragged hole in the triceps area. From what I could see, I'd been fortunate. I reckoned a bullet with most of its force spent was embedded there. There was no exit wound and I wasn't in any imminent danger of bleeding out. It still hurt like hell but there was nothing I could do about it right then.

I kept the boat heading east along the river, trying to recall the geography of the area. I could see lights along the shoreline but didn't really know where I was going. I'd have been fine on dry land but my knowledge of what lay along the waterside was sketchy at best. I needed some kind of map or chart to get my bearings.

Some pain killers would also come in handy.

I slowed the boat further, thinking I might be able to stop and drop some kind of anchor or hold station somehow, when I caught the rasp of an outboard motor followed by a thump against the rear of the boat that I felt more than heard.

Immediately I shoved the throttle wide open and span the wheel to the left. It saved my life.

A three-shot burst punched neat holes in the wheelhouse roof as the gunman was thrown off balance. I was moving before he had time to recover. All I had time to take in was a black clad figure with a white face and an MP5 submachine gun. He was halfway up the steps, and it was a wonder he hadn't fallen backwards off them. The boat roared and twisted like a harpooned beast, but I managed to run across the deck and kick the gunman hard in the face.

Even through my boot I felt his teeth loosen. He fell off the steps, sprawling onto the rear platform. I also lost my footing and slammed down onto the deck. I didn't land on my wounded arm but still banged the elbow, sending a fierce jolt of pain through me.

I shifted my weight, clawing at the pistol stuck in my jeans' rear waistband with my left hand. My whole right arm felt useless. Below, I saw the gunman spitting blood and untangling his MP5.

Shooting left-handed at an odd angle while lying prone and on a bucking boat wheeling in circles, it was no wonder I missed with the first two shots. But he wasn't that far away from me, and I had plenty of bullets left. I half emptied the clip at him before the gun jammed. The gunman was wearing a ballistic vest but those don't do much to protect your legs and groin. I could hear his howls over the roar of the engines.

I crawled over the deck towards the cockpit, reached up and cut the throttle. The boat still turned but the wild ride had slowed enough for me to quickly rearm myself. After that I'd check to see if we were about to crash.

The jammed gun got chucked in the stowage bin and I yanked Killick's Glock 17 from the bag.

Before I could do anything, what felt like a sledgehammer hit the bullet wound in my right arm and I fell to the deck, damn near blacking out.

Fisk dropped the metal boat pole, drove a kick into my stomach, then pried the gun from my numb hands.

"Hello Riley!" he snarled.

THIRTY-ONE

" Over there, on the floor." Fisk gestured with his free hand, keeping the pistol steady on me, no mean feat as the boat continued swaying on the river swell. I crawled over to where he'd indicated and rested my back against the edge of the padded seat.

Where had he come from? I knew he hadn't come out of the cabin by the rear door. There had to be a forward hatch. I'd been stupid to miss it. That would be a mistake I'd probably pay for with my life.

Fisk upended the sports bag in the stowage bin, the contents clattering against the plastic, before tossing the bag away across the deck.

The first thing he picked up was my phone, the one I'd recorded his 'confession' on. He looked at me then threw it through one of the broken side windows and into the river.

The boat had settled into a lazy drift and the moans from the wounded gunman had stopped. Against the backdrop of the idling engines, I heard the sound of an approaching outboard motor again. Fisk kept an eye on me as he went over to the cockpit, turned the wheel and fed a bit of power to the engines, stabilizing the boat. I heard a muted thump as the small R.I.B. that had been following bunted against the rear platform.

Fisk went back to the stowage bin. This time he carefully took out the unregistered .38 revolver I'd taken from the kids at the trailer park.

"Yours?" he asked.

I shook my head and said nothing.

He examined it as best he could in the dim lights of the upper deck.

"Very naughty," he murmured, a half-smile on his face. He looked over at the man climbing up the steps. This guy was another dressed in black semi-combat gear with an MP5 machine gun slung across his body. He was short and wiry and moved with that catlike grace that a lot of special ops guys have. His features were Hispanic. I guessed this was Santos, one of the SWAT guys Fisk had mentioned. That would mean that I'd shot Lane or Jenner or Dawson the sniper. I hoped it was Dawson.

"Lane's dead," said Santos, speaking to Fisk. "Bled out," he added shooting a hate-filled look at me. I suspected that was what he wanted to do to me, bleed me out real slow.

"Secure the boat," ordered Fisk. "Take us upriver, nice and easy. You know where." Santos nodded and stepped over to the cockpit area. The beat of the engines rose and I could feel the boat make headway against the current.

Fisk was looking at me. He was thinking, considering what to do. Deciding how to kill me, I was sure. I stared back at him, fighting the throbbing pain in my arm and trying not to let it show.

"I guess I should kill you now," he said at last. "Dump your body overboard. That would be sensible." He came over and sat on one of the seats near to me. He still had the illegal .38 in his hand and was far enough out of my reach to dispel any thoughts of heroics. I sat there and said nothing.

Fisk sighed. "I just can't do that."

A sharp wave of pain hit me and I turned the grimace into a pained smile.

"You're thinking torture?" he asked. He was enjoying the situation now our roles were reversed.

"Get on with it then," I told him.

"Soon," he assured me. He rested the muzzle of the silver gun on my kneecap. "Knee?" he asked, smiling. "Or balls?"

"Where you like. You've got the gun." I tried to think about my options, but they were few and I was in pain. There was a strong chance I'd be in even more pain soon.

Fisk removed the gun and got to his feet. "Maybe if you misbehave. Stay there Riley. Be good." He went back over to the stowage bin and placed the gun on the side next to him before gathering the parts of his own cell phone and putting it back together. I took a moment to check my arm as best I could. It had stopped bleeding for now. I'd left a bloody trail across the deck that looked worse than it actually was. I might have lost somewhere between a quarter and a half of a pint of blood since being hit, but no more than that.

"Well, who'd have thought it!" Fisk said, addressing his comments to me. "Three bars of signal." He dialed a number and put the phone to his ear.

"Fisk here, put me through to Marshall." There was a delay, then. "Yeah, yeah, I'm fine." I could only hear his side of the conversation punctuated by pauses. There was some news I could tell he wasn't happy about.

"Perez, yes I know." I guessed they were talking about Claire. A thunderous look clouded his face. "No – I don't care if it's their precinct, get someone else there. Deal with it." Another pause, then, "I'm going there now. Get Dawson to meet us at Troutdale. One hour."

Fisk ended the call and looked at me. There was a cold anger in his eyes there that stemmed from more than just the phone call or being drugged and kidnapped. It was something that ran deeper, a buried seam of resentment built up over the years.

A vein throbbed at Fisk's temple.

"This would have been so much easier if you'd died," he sighed angrily. "Or if you'd just kept running. But you had to be the hero, didn't you? You had to return."

"I thought you'd remember what happens when someone pushes me," I reminded him. "I push back, harder."

"Really?" he said. "Well okay Rambo, want to know what happens now?"

"Not really." My voice sounded husky. I cleared my throat. I also did not appreciate the Rambo joke.

Fisk continued regardless, a sadistic smile emerging through his animosity. "You're going to see Sean." He picked up the revolver and came back to sit near to me. There was still no way I could reach him without being shot first.

"Though I should kill you right now. You're dangerous. More so being wounded. Like an old lion refusing to give up." He snorted a mirthless laugh at his own joke. "Riley the crippled old lion. I could shoot the other arm, your knees of course, maybe hurt you a bit more in other places, before letting you die. What do you think? What would *you* do?"

I said nothing.

Fisk nodded as if I'd just given him a sound piece of advice. "You're right, too easy. But what we can do – what we *will* do – is get you to murder your own nephew using this naughty unregistered gun you've brought along. Probably a gut shot. Let him suffer a bit first."

I shunted myself sitting more upright and immediately Fisk had the gun pointed center mass at me, his finger putting pressure on the trigger.

"You're a fucking twisted creep," I snarled, channeling the throbbing of my arm into anger. Fisk ignored me.

"Afterwards you won't be able to live with yourself, so you'll eat a bullet. Neat and tidy. It's a good plan. I like it."

I didn't. Not one bit. But something inside nagged at me to keep him talking. Find out what I could, even if I was taking it to my grave.

"So you do know where he is then?" I said referring to Sean.

"Christ! You're still the dumb grunt who prefers heavy lifting over brain power aren't you. Of course I know – I arranged it." Fisk's condescending sneer suited his rat-like face. "Without me those fucking Armenian retards would be lost. They may operate the 'business' side of things–" he made air quotes as he said 'business' "–but I'm the guy that enables it to run smoothly – and

183

they know it."

"A valuable member of the team I'm sure," I said laying on the sarcasm. "Shame your best work is for a crime gang rather than the force."

That needled him. His eyes narrowed, the sneer remaining.

"I run a good precinct. Those that don't like the way I work can put up or get out. At least nobody has gotten the wrong kid killed since you left."

I knew he'd bring it up at some point. My biggest regret and biggest shame. An event that made me question my abilities as a detective and the methods I used to get to the truth. After nearly three years it still haunted me and was one of the reasons I decided to retire. I just couldn't face doing the job and making the same mistakes again.

It was something I'd never made amends for, and it was looking increasingly likely I never would.

Fisk took my silence as a cue to continue.

"And yeah, I'm valuable. Seven figures valuable that'll soon be rising to eight."

I had been in the right ballpark with my recent guess of five million, probably more, and knew now he'd be at least doubling that.

"I never knew being a bent cop could pay so well," I commented.

Fisk's eyes flashed with anger, and he smacked the barrel of the silver .38 across my face with the speed a viper would be proud of. I felt the sting of blood on my cheek and was thankful he hadn't hit me in the mouth. It took me a moment to realize he was speaking again.

"Don't talk to me about being bent, you fucking hypocrite!" he mimicked a whining tone. "A little bit here, a little bit there, not too much." He was in a full-on rant now. "If you'd had the balls to go big you wouldn't still be in your shitty little house with your redneck chicken-fucker pickup truck. Fact is, despite the 'I was a US Ranger' macho bullshit you're just a pussy." Fisk emphasized his point jabbing the gun at me. "Having you around was a liability.

How can you trust a guy who's afraid to take enough to cover buying a round at the bar?"

He sat back on the seat and took a calming breath.

"You know, at the start I thought we'd be friends. But all you did was piss me off and hold me back. I'm going to enjoy seeing you die then I'm going take an expensive vacation."

"Aren't you forgetting something?" I interrupted.

"What?"

"Claire knows what's going on. She'll talk to someone at North Precinct. Do you really have the time to deal with anything other than getting out?"

Fisk snorted.

"Whatever she says can be dismissed as a result of the stress of her crazy brother filling her head with lies. She'll be transferred to Central and held in connection with the abduction of a senior police officer." He leaned forward far enough for me to smell the sourness of his breath, "Dangerous places, holding cells. Never know what might happen before an officer can intervene."

I was sorely tempted to grab for the gun and grapple him to the floor but knew there was little chance it would have ended well for me.

"What about Richard? Losing his stepson and wife gives you no leverage. If he controls what's happening with the money it might all disappear."

"No I don't think so. Because how will he get to hear anything about it until after he's done his work?"

Fisk had a point. I blamed my stupidity on shock and loss of blood.

"I reckon the shock of hearing about it afterwards could make him hang himself," said Fisk. "Nothing to live for. Another loose end tied up neatly."

"And you've got people that can arrange that?"

"People everywhere. One of them even works in Forensics."

"Lucky you," I grumbled.

He smiled.

I said nothing. I'd lost.

THIRTY-TWO

The engines slowed and I felt the boat start to turn.

"We're there," said Santos from the helm.

Fisk got to his feet, standing a safe distance from me. He spoke with Santos, confirming the actions they would take over the next few minutes. Mundane stuff. Tying up the boat against the jetty, best way to disembark, disposing of Lane's body. That sort of thing.

Fisk got me to shuffle across the deck and lie flat on my belly in the area next to the cockpit. He told me to spread my arms and legs like I was some performing starfish. I did as instructed. It was tough work moving my right arm. He nudged it with the toe of his shoe and I let out a grunt of pain.

"Hurts, does it?" he said without sympathy.

I didn't care. Something on the short cockpit bulkhead in the space under the seat had caught my attention. I groaned and used the pretense of shifting with the pain to move myself closer. It wasn't the first aid kit I was interested in. There were a couple of bright yellow and orange cylindrical tubes clipped in place. Signal flares. I could just reach the first one.

Fisk turned to Santos and told him to keep the boat steady and watch me. He'd go, tie off the boat and see if Jenner and Dawson had arrived. The rumble of the engines trembled through my body as Santos feathered the reverse throttle, taking the boat gently backwards.

Getting my fingers to work took some doing. There was a numbness creeping into them that was at odds with the pain at the top of my arm. Slowly I managed to unscrew the orange protective cap from the bottom of the one signal flare. From where Santos was standing, I guessed my arm was shielded from view by the cockpit seat, even in its folded-up position.

I heard Fisk shout "Hold!" and the big diesels dropped to an idle.

The plastic cap dropped into my hand and I placed it on the floor. A small ball on a cord dangled from the end of the flare.

"Secure!" yelled Fisk.

Santos cut the engines. The only sound was him moving. I wondered what he was doing.

Then Santos was kneeling at my side, his hand pressing hard on the middle of my back as he leant over to whisper to me.

"Lane was my friend. I'm godfather to his little boy. Can't let what you did go unpunished."

I heard the click of a knife blade locking into place. I suspected that it might not be big, but it would be very sharp, and he'd know how to use it. But, unless he was a leftie, I suspected he would switch hands as it was his right hand currently pressing on my back.

"Might just take your ear. The captain won't mind that."

"You sure?" I said, taking firm hold of the flare cord. "Hadn't you best check." As he started to answer, I tugged down. There was a faint crack and my hand smacked into the deck. A jolt of agony ran through my arm and across my shoulder.

The flare ignited with a hiss. I felt the pressure of Santos' hand on my back slacken as he looked around for the source of the noise. I tried to ignore the pain, grabbed the flare and rolled as best I could onto my left side. I half expected to feel his knife slash into me as I moved.

The flare had been enough of a distraction and I'd caught him off guard, but it was far from over yet. The knife swapped hands. It was an evil looking thing; maybe four inches, dark steel, mean and purposeful. I had no desire to see it any closer and jabbed the flaming red flare towards his face. Instinctively he fell back, slashing with the blade, only just missing my fingers.

I used the chance to rapidly shuffle away, to gain a bit of space, using my left arm to brace myself as I managed to rise onto one knee. Santos was on his feet, knife held ready, eyes squinting against the fierce brightness of the flare in my hand.

I stood up, passing the flare to my left hand. Santos echoed the move, swapping the knife to his left hand and reaching for his pistol. Tactically a good move, though for a critical second he was vulnerable. I went for him.

It wasn't a graceful move. I lunged brutally, deflecting his knife hand and thrusting the burning flare at his face. He staggered back but I still crashed into him. This was a simple matter of physics. I was bigger, weighed more and had momentum. He fell backwards, his head banging against the bulkhead of the cockpit as we both sprawled on the deck. I lost hold of the flare and it rolled away. I managed to remain on top of Santos, adrenaline fighting the screaming pain in my arm as I pinned his knife hand. Santos' right hand scrabbled for his gun, pinned between us.

I hit him in the face with my free hand, but at such close quarters it lacked force. I felt his hand close around the gun and I changed tactics, grabbing the side of his face and driving my thumb into his right eye.

Santos howled, abandoning any idea of the gun and bringing his hand up in an attempt to stop me. He wasn't quite quick enough and I felt his eyeball burst under the pressure of my thumb. The howl became scream. One that would bring Fisk and anyone else running back.

I had to end it quickly.

I let go of his face. He thrashed and moaned, trying to fight me off. I could feel his knife hand coming free under my wounded right arm.

The flare was still aflame on the deck nearby and I grabbed it. Santos gripped my throat and squeezed. I thrust the flare's flaming incandescence up below his jaw. His pain-filled moans turned into an agonized bubbling scream as I put my weight behind it and the two thousand degree heat burnt up through soft flesh and into his mouth. The flame sputtered wetly as his tongue vaporized and bloody steam rose from his open lips.

He died a few seconds before the flare did.

I was already on my feet; maybe a little unsteadily, but up none the less. I saw Santos' MP5 dangling from a hook on the far side of the cockpit. Evidently he'd taken it off before threatening to cut bits off me. I hadn't even noticed.

I took the gun and relieved Santos of his two spare magazines for the MP5 knowing I'd need them soon enough. I also retrieved the first aid kit from under the seat before heading over to the rear of the deck, sitting down out of sight behind the low rear wall at the back of the cockpit area.

I carefully peered out checking the surroundings behind the boat.

The R.I.B. had been discarded somewhere along the way, and Richard's battered cruiser was tied stern first to the side of a rusting metal barge that served as a mooring point. The barge was long and low but sturdy.

The only lighting on this temporary dock came from red marker lights spaced along its length. I guessed they were a legal requirement for marine safety. They gave just enough illumination to be able to walk along the metal-plated surface of the barge without losing your way and finding yourself treading water. At the far end of the barge a narrow metal walkway with thin handrails linked it to a wooden jetty that looked like it had been made out of railway sleepers. A long shack had been built on the left side, partway along it, its details lost in the shadowy gloom.

Closer to land the lighting was better, but not by much. A floodlight mounted at the top of a tall pole cast a sickly yellow glow on the ground around it and the broad wooden planks where the jetty joined the land. Everything beyond the reach of the light shrank into the surrounding darkness, although beyond it I could see the outline of a wide building at least two stories tall with similar yellow light spilling out from its right hand side. At the angle and distance I was viewing it from I couldn't make out any more. I reckoned it was probably an old dockside warehouse.

As I scanned the area I was also rapidly checking through the first aid kit. I found some pain killers and dry swallowed them. I wasn't expecting miracles, but it would help take the edge off the throbbing in my arm. I took one extra, figuring my body could cope with the raised dose and would benefit from the reduced pain.

It was still quiet behind the boat, so I took a moment to use Santos' knife and cut off my bodied shirt sleeve. I inspected the bullet hole as best I could.

It hurt like hell and blood trickled over my fingers as I felt the area. The bullet was in there but fortunately not too deep. There was no way I was going to try and get it out, that would have been a good way to do more damage to myself and maybe end up passing out.

I used an antiseptic wipe from the first aid kit to clean around the wound, which was bad enough, forcing me to breathe sharply through gritted teeth. The hole was still seeping as I applied a self-adhesive absorbent gauze pad from the kit. It still needed more attention, and I spied a length of bandage in the kit that would help.

The pain was getting less but my arm was stiffening. That wasn't so good. I had to keep it moving. I told myself I'd had worse, which was true. Although then I had been thirty-five years younger and attended to almost straight away by a Ranger medic: Claire's first husband and Sean's father, Mike.

That thought gave me a renewed incentive. There was no way I could let him or Sean or Claire down. Or forsake my past as a US Ranger.

I recalled the Ranger creed I had taken so many years ago. So much of it held true for what I had been and was still facing. I silently recited the acronym to myself, preparing for what lay ahead:

Recognition that I could have walked away from the situation, but I hadn't. I knew the hazards and came back to face them and do the right thing.

Acknowledgement and acceptance that I would use my skills and training to fight harder and faster than any other soldier.

Never shall I fail. My family needed me, and I would give my all.

Gallantry was something that had been instilled in me from my childhood years and it was something that came naturally. In the Rangers it applied more to showing courage and honor on the battlefield, but I also felt it applied more readily to showing the correct politeness and respect to women. I felt a pang of guilt thinking about Officer Barbara Hayes back at the hospital. If I got out of this I'd have to make some amends, a personal apology at least.

I refocused on the mantra.

Energetically I would meet my enemies and with all my might.

Readily I would display the fortitude to fight on though I be the only survivor.

Thinking through the creed did me good and I was surprised how much it energized me.

I was finishing up wrapping the bandage around my arm when I heard footsteps approaching along the metal barge.

The low wall at the rear of the cockpit would give little protection from any bullets. They would punch straight through the fiberglass, taking shards of it with them. I was better getting well away from it. I shuffled further into the cockpit itself and knelt, keeping myself still and listened hard.

I heard someone swearing softly and Fisk say something in return, but I couldn't tell what. The voices stopped. I felt the rear of the boat dip ever so slightly, then a voice.

"Santos?" It was Fisk.

I switched the MP5 to burst fire and aimed at the head of the steps. I heard Fisk mutter a curse and was sure I heard my name mentioned.

I kept quiet and remained still. They knew something was wrong because there was no response from Santos. They would be wondering where he was and where I was, and if I'd killed him why hadn't I untied the boat and made my escape. Only Fisk might think I'd be so stubborn and tenacious to stick around. I let them worry and sweat in silence.

There were stealthy footsteps on the ladder to the cockpit. The top of a head appeared above the edge, and I fired. At least two bullets out of the three-round burst found their mark. There was a brief spray of gore and the figure dropped out of sight thudding onto the deck below.

Shouts and gunfire erupted, tearing chunks out of the fiberglass wall and the back edge of the deck. I was far enough back to be protected by the narrowness of the angle they were shooting from, but it wouldn't be long before they changed their approach.

I had to get them off balance.

I reached up and turned the keys in the ignition. Keeping my eyes on the top of the steps, I found the starter. The boat's big diesel engines coughed into life, uttering their steady watery burble. I found the throttle, pushed it half open, and the boat moved forward a couple of feet before jerking to a halt, engines growling.

I went prone and was crawling away from the cockpit over to the far right side of the deck when a hand with a machine gun appeared over the top of the steps and raked the control area with sustained fire.

Instruments shattered, glass, wood and fiberglass splintered. I kept low and still until the shooter's magazine emptied. It didn't take long, barely a couple of seconds, then I scooted forwards on my belly towards the steps, using legs and left arm to propel myself as best I could.

I was halfway there when the hand with the machine gun appeared again. It was pointing directly at me. I squeezed the trigger of my MP5 as soon as it appeared, saw a spray of red as part of the hand disappeared, then both the hand and gun were gone.

A chilling thought occurred to me. I hoped they didn't have grenades. If they did, I was fucked.

I hauled myself closer to the steps, ignoring the throbbing of my arm. It was okay as long as my hand could point a gun and my fingers squeeze the trigger. Even over the snarl of the diesel engines I could hear the stifled moans from whoever's hand I'd shot.

Flicking the fire switch on the MP5 to fully automatic, I shoved the muzzle over the edge of the steps and pulled the trigger. I held the gun sideways, so the recoil forced it into a lateral arc that sprayed the lower platform. It emptied and I pulled away from the edge, fumbling to eject the magazine. One man was screaming below and there were sounds of hurried movement.

The spent magazine dropped out and a fresh one clacked into place. I risked a glance over the edge to the back of the boat.

I saw Fisk staggering across the flat of the barge. I couldn't tell if he'd been caught by a bullet or jarred his leg jumping off the boat. On the platform below, the guy with the mutilated hand was bleeding from the shoulder and the leg. He was being supported by a colleague, perhaps more of a friend as he hadn't just left him behind and run like Fisk had.

It was doubtful they could both make it across the gap to the old barge as Richard's boat continued straining against the moorings, water churning in the gap between.

I yelled at them to drop their weapons. Maybe that was my subconscious thinking of gallantry and giving them a chance to surrender. Either way it was lost on them.

The supporting guy turned, using his wounded colleague as a shield, and fired at me. I treated them to a burst from the MP5. The guy with the wounded hand took the brunt and fell to the deck, all strength gone from his legs. His uncaring friend stumbled back and toppled into the water.

I got to my feet, ran to the smashed cockpit and shoved the boat into reverse. I didn't fancy trying to jump the gap any more than the other two guys had. As the boat went backwards, I heard a terrified scream. The note of the engines dipped for a fraction of a second, the scream stopped and the beat of the engines recovered. The boat thumped hard against the side of the barge, and I cut the ignition.

I set the MP5 back to three-shot-burst. I still had at least half the magazine left as well as the full one. I also took Santos' Glock. He had a spare clip for it, so I took that too.

I wasn't wearing a tactical harness like Santos, and didn't have the time or inclination to take it off him, so I had to stash the guns and ammo where I could on my regular clothing.

I did have room for that evil little knife of Santos's. I collected it from the decking, pressed the release, folded it smoothly closed, and slipped it into my left sock. Then I used a strip of sticking plaster from the first aid kit to tape it to my leg. It might take a few hairs with it as I drew it, but I didn't want it falling out at an inopportune moment.

I knew Fisk had taken the .38 revolver; however he had left Marshall's cell phone.

Without knowing the pin number or the passkey shape or whatever security was used to lock her phone there was no way I could make a call.

Except to emergency services. That is always available.

It was time to get some official help.

I placed the call.

THIRTY-THREE

In my mind the call took way too long but I had to be clear and make sure all the details were understood. Once done I left Marshall's phone, still powered on, in the shattered cabin and went down the steps to the back of the boat.

The rear platform was bloodstained, littered with shell casings and had two bodies sprawled on it. One didn't have much of a face and the other one was the guy with the wounded hand, though that was the least of his worries. The way his eyes were open and unfocused he had no more worries at all.

Both men were dressed similarly in black canvas cargo pants and dark sweaters. I also noticed the guns they had been using. They looked like Russian AKS-74U carbines, or decent copies of them. Brutal, reliable and effective, if a bit crude. And very illegal.

I stuck with the Heckler and Koch MP5. In my opinion a more accurate weapon and far more compact and fit for my purpose. It was also a gun I was very familiar with.

Down in the water at the back of the boat I saw the residue of bloody froth and caught a glimpse of what could have been part of a leg. I didn't stop to investigate. The gap to the barge was no more than a stride away and I was soon jogging across its rusty metal surface the way Fisk had gone. I couldn't see any blood on the way so he couldn't have been hit. A twisted ankle at the worst. Shame.

I was almost at the metal walkway when I remembered that it wasn't just Fisk on the loose. He'd turned back up at the boat with three guys who were definitely not cops.

That meant Jenner, one of the other SWAT guys, and Dawson,

the sniper, was around somewhere and I was heading for an area with no cover that was a direct route to the buildings beyond.

Now I was closer to it I could make out more of the long wooden shack that clung to the left of the jetty. The sides had been painted black at some point – possibly with creosote to preserve it – most of the glass in the sparse windows had been smashed, and the tin roof sagged alarmingly. It looked like a death trap, but it was a better option than running up the jetty into a hail of bullets.

Or a single high velocity headshot from a sniper rifle.

I checked the shack's door and almost laughed. It had a padlock on it that was pointless, as the wood around the latch was rotten. I kicked it and went inside, into the dark, and nearly fell through the floor into the water below.

It wasn't totally pitch black in there, but it was close. Faint light from outside filtered through the stained and aged windows, but there weren't many of them. It took a few seconds for my eyes to adjust to the gloom. I could see that I was in what amounted to an elongated shack, possibly once a fish sorting warehouse back in the day. Someone had decided to remove a lot of the floorboards and those that were left I had little trust in. The joists were still in place, spanning the building like exposed black bones, and some dozen or so feet beneath the gaps I could make out the water at the edge of the inlet glinting in the meager light.

I gently closed the broken door and took stock of the situation.

The choice between approaching along such an obvious path with a sniper on the loose and making my way through a dark and unstable building was no choice at all. I had to go through the building. I'd have some control over my destiny, even if I did end up bruised and in the water. It was better than a head shot from somewhere unseen.

The MP5 had a small tactical light, a torch, clipped to the picatinny rail underneath the barrel. I used that to sweep the area, careful not to let the beam shine through any windows and give away my position.

I turned my attention to the floor. I was best to stick to the edges of the building where the wood was likely to be stronger. I switched off the tactical light and let my eyes readjust before moving. I trod carefully, testing each step as I went, and reached the opposite side of the room from the door. Now it was a case of repeating the step lightly and process all along the far wall until I got all the way to the end of the shack. I'd figure out what to do next after I got there.

It got easier as I went along. My eyes became more accustomed to the darkness and the solidity of the floor improved. I reached the end wall, found a gap between the boards and peered through.

About twenty yards away, ahead and to the right, a block-built structure jutted out from the larger ones behind it.

It was only twenty yards from the end of the shack to where the wooden jetty met the land. Right by the pole with the light. If I went for it, I might make a dozen yards before taking a bullet. If I was very quick and very lucky, I might even make the full twenty.

It was a killing zone.

If I had been seen entering the shack it wouldn't be long before somebody decided to start shooting. Against a couple of Armenian thugs with AKSUs the wooden walls would quickly get shredded, and me with them. And even if I hadn't been seen, I was sure it wouldn't be long before Fisk sent someone to investigate.

Then again, maybe Fisk was content to wait it out. Let me come to him. Through that killing zone.

I was stuck with nowhere to go and the clock still ticking.

THIRTY-FOUR

There was another way.

I had to think outside the box, or in this case outside the shack.

Through the windows on the far side of the shack, looking away from the jetty, I could see that the shoreline had been carved out to make a square inlet, like a crude harbor. A brick wall had been built where the inlet met the land, rising some ten feet from the surface of the dark water. The area beyond that was flat and without any nearby cover. Assuming I could climb up the slimy bricks like some semi-aquatic spiderman, it would be too easy to be noticed. I wouldn't be going that way.

The muddy riverbank some thirty yards away from the shack glistened in the faint light that managed to reach it. It would be awkward to climb but its shallow angle would help. The upper reaches of the bank were covered in bushes and once behind those I'd be out of sight.

But first I had to get over there.

I lowered myself through one of the gaps in the floor, my booted feet finding a diagonal cross beam. My right arm wasn't that much help, but I was still able to use it if I swore quietly through gritted teeth. The underside of the shack was a web of support beams. It looked like whoever had built it had never wanted to risk it collapsing into the water, then over the years other folks had added their own reinforcement. Right then they had my gratitude. It was like a climbing frame down there.

It was slow going, the wood becoming far more slimy and algae-covered as I got closer to the water. I had to pause at one point as I felt the Glock riding out of the back of my jeans. I decided to put the main safety on, just in case. I knew it should have been fine with just the trigger safety, but the way my luck was going something would happen and I'd shoot myself in the ass. At least the MP5 was safe, adjusted and slung close around my shoulders.

The river wasn't as cold as I expected, though it was cold enough. I didn't want to spend any longer in there than I needed. I lowered myself in and pushed away from under the long shack into the opaque water, heading across the short distance of the small inlet in the opposite direction to the buildings. I swam as quietly as I could, but it was awkward and painful.

It took me just two minutes to cover the thirty yards to the other side of the little inlet, and then clamber up the dark muddy shore and get behind the scrubby overgrown bushes. I took another couple of minutes to recover afterwards. I was wet and filthy, and my wounded arm was stinging like crazy.

I checked through my weapons making sure they were free of any water and silt. On the way I'd lost the spare clip for the Glock. I hadn't even noticed it fall out. At least everything else was fine, and a little water wouldn't do much harm in the short term.

Ahead of me was a tall power pylon, its cables disappearing into the darkness across the river. I waited and took time to listen.

Above the faint hum of the power cables I was sure I could hear the distant sound of an engine. From the pitch and speed, I guessed it was a generator. I turned my head, trying to get a bearing on it. From what I could make out the sound was coming from the rear of the warehouse, now behind me.

It would be as good a place as any to start, but I had to get there first.

I pushed through the bushes heading east towards the pylon and away from the warehouse, MP5 held ready, and came out onto the edge of a patch of crumbling asphalt that ended at a non-descript packed dirt area.

The idea was to circle around. Come in from the least expected direction.

I skirted the line of bushes to where a packed dirt track led back towards the warehouse and the cluster of buildings adjacent to the jetty. The main drag of the road continued onwards but I took the route towards the warehouse, moving slow and cautious.

I felt reasonably sure I wouldn't be spotted, unless there was a sniper with a night scope looking in my direction right at that exact moment. At least if that was the case I wouldn't know about it until too late. And then I wouldn't be worrying about anything ever again.

I put the thought out of my mind and carried on towards the group of buildings near my side of the warehouse. There was more shrubbery to the south, on my left, in front of another low building that had a collapsed roof and smashed windows. Parked in front of it were the decayed remains of an old pick-up truck sat on its axles, wheels long since gone. I reckoned it hadn't moved since Reagan was in office.

The building was quiet and looked long abandoned and a danger to anyone entering. Couple that with its location and it made a poor tactical choice for anyone to be in. I ignored it and carried on.

I went past the low building, got closer to the big warehouse, and my field of view opened up. I couldn't see the barge, jetty or the floorless shack but I did have a full view of the side of the warehouse.

From this closer vantage point and even on this unlit side of the building it was possible to see that it was taller than I'd first thought, probably three stories high and without any windows.

A single-story wooden structure had been built against the side of the warehouse, the gable end in line with the rear wall. It was only about a third the length of the warehouse and had been painted blue at one point in its life. The paint had faded and was peeling but all the windows looked intact, and I could see a door part-way along its length.

Beyond that, and closer to the river, was a battered forty-foot metal container and a couple of old metal dumpsters, all against the block walls of the warehouse.

Unless you have had the training it is difficult to remain still for very long. Even though my training had been back when I'd been in the army, I could still do it. I expected that Dawson the sniper, if he was out there, would also be able to do it.

Within sixty seconds I spotted the first guy who couldn't do it. Thirty seconds later I saw his mate adjust position.

The first was standing restlessly in the shadows behind the furthest rusty dumpster. I couldn't see what gun he had, but if you have bright blond hair, you really should be wearing a woolen hat at night.

The other was lying prone on top of the container and partly shielded by some pallets that had been discarded on the top there. I could only see his legs, and it was when he moved them, stretching out the kinks, that I'd noticed him. I guessed he had his gun lined up on the walkway.

They must have seen me go into the long wooden shack but that had been well over ten minutes ago and I expected they were getting restless. From their positions there might have been a small chance they could have seen me climb up the shore across the thirty yards of inlet but with what I could tell from their body language they thought I was still hiding in the shack.

Now I'd seen them I wasn't worried about them. Dawson was my biggest concern. I imagined he was positioned somewhere behind a rifle and peering through a scope. It was a chilling thought.

It changed nothing. I still had a job to do.

I felt sure Sean was being held around here somewhere and I had to find him before Fisk decided to cut his losses and put a bullet in his head.

THIRTY-FIVE

I moved back along the track, as swift and silent as I could, keeping to the cover of the bushes and checking the surroundings as I went. Subconsciously, I felt time ticking away.

I cut across the track and past the low abandoned building I'd noted earlier.

I could hear the generator a little more clearly now, coming from behind the warehouse. From the lack of any cables running to the warehouse I guessed the place was having to run off its own power. There may have been the big pylon behind me but that was no good without any take off to a sub-station. It was the electrical equivalent of a motorway bridge over a village without any turnpike.

I ran along the length of the abandoned building, a fast, low movement straight to the far corner, stopping with my back against the crumbling concrete.

The gap between where I was standing and the rear corner of the faded blue building on the side of the warehouse was about twenty yards. For half of the distance, I would be in view of the two guys I'd spotted, but only if they turned to check what was behind them and they would only do that if I made enough noise to catch their attention.

I moved quickly, prioritizing stealth over speed and reached the corner seconds later. I kept the MP5 machine gun at the ready hoping I wouldn't need to use it. If I had to pull the trigger it would alert everyone in the area to my presence and that would not be a good thing.

I held position, my shoulder against the flaking blue paint, listening for any movement. I could hear the dull sound of the generator but nothing else.

The door on the near side of the building could well have been a great way into the building, but with it in plain sight of the two guys around there it was out of bounds. At least for now.

Around the corner was a stretch of mixed asphalt and concrete wide enough to get two trucks side by side. Across it were more structures running parallel to the rear of the warehouse. They were now mere skeletal frames of buildings and only the furthest had any roof remaining. I guessed from their design they may have been used for boat building in the past, but that had probably been around the same time the old pick-up had been dumped.

High up on the back of the warehouse was a single security lamp that cast a pallid yellow glow over the area. Stacks of metal racking and broken wooden pallets had been discarded against the concrete wall, and about half the way along I could see a small block-built structure no bigger than a tool shed jutting out.

From the newness of the masonry it had to be a recent addition, perhaps built no more than a year ago. Its metal roof joined the main building at a shallow angle with just enough of a slope for rain to run off. A rusty metal pipe rose halfway up the wall, capped with a ninety-degree elbow directing exhaust gases away from the building.

This was where the generator was.

I moved out, picking my way along carefully next to the broken asphalt roadway running between the buildings, noting fresh tire tracks in the dirt. That was no great surprise.

I saw a shadow moving along the building in my direction and ducked out of sight, crouching behind a pile of old pallets. Through the gaps I saw someone appear into view around the generator block.

It would have been quite easy to think he was just a token security guard, some retired rent-a-cop who couldn't give a damn about a load of old buildings, but the dark jacket and dusty canvas jeans tucked into work boots was the sloppiest security uniform I'd ever seen. The unmistakable cut-down shape of the AKS-74U Russian assault rifle he carried was the clincher.

The casual way he was walking and the attention he paid to the phone told me he wasn't really expecting to find anyone. I could have shot him there and then. An easy single shot, and if I'd still had the silenced Glock I might have tried it. But I needed as quiet a take-down as possible.

I placed the MP5 gently on the ground, reached down and pulled out Santos's knife, the sticky tape taking a few leg hairs with it. I was way back in the shadows, well out of sight. I let him walk past me, still intent on texting.

As the knife clicked open he turned, his hand dropping towards the AKSU's grip and trigger. He was too slow and it cost him. I erupted from the shadows, bringing the knife down hard with all my strength behind it. The short, tough blade punched through his forehead above the right eye with a soft crunch. He dropped so quickly and heavily it almost took the knife out of my hand as he fell.

It wasn't quite as noiseless a takedown I'd been after, but it could have been far worse, and I counted my blessings. If he'd been more alert or patrolling properly with his hand already on his gun, I would have had no choice but to use the MP5.

The knife was embedded deep. It resisted being extracted from his forehead but I tugged it out, wiped the stained blade on his jacket and closed it back up, this time slipping it into my pocket. I dragged his dead body into the deep shadow between the pallets and checked his pockets. He had a crumpled pack of cigarettes, a lighter, a few loose dollars and a two-way radio. I switched his phone off and then checked the radio. It was a straightforward device and simple to use. But it had no earpiece connected, it just had the inbuilt speaker. Its use in me being able to listen in on the group's movements were outweighed by the fact it would give away my position.

I switched it off and discarded it by his body, next to his gun.

I made quick progress getting to the stocky generator building. I felt it was unlikely another guard would be patrolling so closely after the guy I'd just taken down.

As I got closer, the steady thudding rattle of the generator overpowered all other noises. It wasn't that loud, the small building muted its running, but as the rest of the area was so quiet it sounded like being next to a locomotive.

The metal door of the generator shed had a chunky padlock and bolt. I figured it would be possible to snap it open, there were enough pieces of metal bar around that could have done the job, but I wasn't interested in going in. Aside from the noise it would be too dark to make out anything useful, even with the flashlight on the MP5.

I carried on past the blocky shed and found the raised fuel tank used to feed the generator. It was difficult to see properly in the half shadows, so I had to click on the MP5's flashlight to trace it. A lot of the line was metal, either steel or copper, but where it turned a corner between the warehouse wall and the shed a rubber connection had been used to join the pipes.

Santos's knife proved its worth again. With a little bit of effort it cut through the tough rubber. Fuel immediately began dribbling out. I figured the generator would have enough reserve to keep running for another few minutes before cutting out, and by that time I'd be nowhere near.

There was far less junk discarded along this section of the wall after the generator, and I could see a shadowy doorway set into the concrete blocks a little further ahead.

I could also see light spilling out from the far side of the warehouse, which tied in with what I'd seen earlier from the boat. The lighting was way better around there, and I figured that would be the main way in to the building.

I carried on cautiously, leaving the noise of the generator and the growing stink of diesel behind as I made my way towards the shadows of the doorway.

I was nearly there when two sharp rifle shots cracked out

through the night and I fell to the ground.

THIRTY-SIX

The shots came from behind me somewhere in the mid-distance and I'd hit the dirt instinctively.

It wasn't the sound of a small hunting rifle, someone shooting at rabbits in the dark. It was something more powerful. Something military grade.

I hadn't been shot and there had been no sound of anything near to me being hit but it was damn disconcerting. I got to my feet, wounded arm throbbing again, and hurried to the shadows of the doorway.

There were two wide concrete steps with a metal door at the top of them. The black paint was peeling off, showing it had been red at one point in its life. I went up the steps and tried the door. It wouldn't budge. It was either locked or rusted closed. I wasn't getting in that way.

I went back down the steps and carried on to the corner of the warehouse, pausing before the corner.

There were another two rifle shots, still mid-distance, then the constant blare of a distant car horn.

It didn't take much for me to work out what was going on. During the call I'd made to the emergency services when on the boat I'd advised them to avoid using sirens and lights. A stealthy approach so as not to spook Fisk and his goons. I guessed it had to be the first police response teams and reckoned that Fisk had stationed Dawson and probably Jenner to cover the approach road.

I grimaced. From the lack of return fire, I imagined that Dawson had stopped them in their tracks.

On the plus side, if he was covering that area I would be safe from his sniper fire where I was. At least for now.

It was a big assumption.

The sound of the horn stopped. Other than the chugging of the generator behind me the night was quiet again.

I peered around the corner.

I could see pretty well, thanks to the lamps mounted high up on the wall. There were six in total but only three were still working. The hazy glow they gave out was plenty to see by and was way better than the single lamp at the rear of the building. It also meant that I'd be exposed against the pale walls and stand out like a bloodstain on a bed sheet if anyone was looking at this side of the warehouse. However there were no signs of any CCTV cameras, either on the walls or mounted on any poles in the area.

A couple of yards from where I was at the corner of the building were a pair of large roller shutter doors, each big enough for a truck. Just beyond them was another sturdy metal door, presumably for staff access. They were all shut.

On the far side of that last door a single-story lean-to structure had been built onto the warehouse, very similar to the blue building on the other side. At some point in its life this one had been painted pink, which was now flaking off, making the place look like it had a bad skin condition. It had windows but there were no lights on inside.

The place looked empty, but I knew it wasn't.

There were three vehicles parked on the concrete.

Nearest to me was a dark Chevrolet Impala sedan, its nose some yards away from the second roller door and parked at an angle. It gave the impression that the driver had been in one hell of a hurry. Beyond that, against the peeling pink building, was a silver SUV, and tucked in after that was a blue van.

Seeing the vehicles gave me a rough idea of the number of people I could be up against. The minimum was three, one driver in each, but I knew it would be more than that, that was for sure.

The Impala could easily hold five with another five from the

SUV. Then there was the van. Assuming a normal side-by-side seating position in the back, and without being packed in like sardines, that meant there could be another ten plus three up front.

Twenty-three armed men. Plus Fisk.

But that was a maximum.

I'd taken out three guys on the boat, plus the one I'd just killed with the knife. That took it down to nineteen.

I knew about the two I'd seen around the other side of the building lying in wait, and it was reasonable to guess that Dawson and Jenner as a team would be covering the entry road together.

So there could be fifteen men inside the warehouse.

I doubted there would be – it was based on the calculated maximum – but I wouldn't have been surprised if I was up against eight.

It was not a comforting thought.

Plus I still needed to find a way to actually get into the warehouse without raising an alarm or getting involved in a massive gunfight. Having a couple of my old Ranger buddies with me right then would have been very welcome. It still wouldn't have been easy, but it would have tipped the odds of success well in our favor.

The crack of another distant rifle shot shook me out of my thoughts and inaction. I could hear distant police sirens. There was no stealth required now.

I moved low and fast to the Impala, crouching by it and checking out the area from the new vantage point.

It was a good move. From there I could see further along the front of the pink lean-to and spotted two figures standing in front of the van. Even though they were partially in shadow I could see from their body language that they were having an agitated discussion. I could also see the telltale angular shapes of their AKSU rifles.

I made it to the side of the warehouse, out of direct sight of them, eased past the shuttered doors and along the wall to the metal door. All it had was a big exterior pull handle and an escutcheon plate that looked like it took a key to a mortise lock. I slowly pulled the handle, testing the door. There was no movement. It was shut so solidly I reckoned there were probably deadbolts inside. I wasn't getting in through there and I was running low on options.

I moved to the corner of the pink lean-to. I was no more than twenty yards away from the talking men and could hear their voices, speaking low and urgently. I couldn't make out what they were saying, they might have been speaking English with an Eastern European accent or maybe talking in Armenian. Either way I got the impression they were nervous and close to bugging out.

It was a shame they hadn't decided to do that a few minutes before I arrived. I switched the MP5 to single shot.

I came round the corner with the gun leveled, found my first target and fired. The first guy dropped and before his mate could react, I fired again.

The gunshots cracked through the darkness, the sound echoing around the area. It didn't matter. Dawson's shots had already set a precedent. I doubted anyone inside the building would be paying much attention to any shots from outside.

I ran in a crouch along the flaking pink wall keeping below the window line and over to the two men. They were dead. I'd scored headshots on them both and it was not a pretty sight. Ignoring the mess, I quickly went through their pockets. Apart from the usual cigarettes and change they both had the same two-way radios, neither with any earpieces, and one of them had a car key with 'Ford' on it. I looked at the two vehicles near to me. The SUV was a Chevrolet Yukon. The van had FORD across its front grille. I pocketed the key figuring it was worth having the option of driving away once I'd found Sean, rather than us being on foot.

I heard the distant boom of a shotgun and the crack of pistol shots.

The radios crackled and a voice blared from the tinny speakers. I switched one off and turned the volume down on the other but kept listening.

The voice was speaking the same language as the two dead guys which I had to guess was Armenian. The only word I understood was my name. He'd definitely said 'Riley'.

There was a crunch of static and a different voice responded with a couple of short sentences which the first speaker acknowledged sounding satisfied.

"*Team B*," the voice was speaking English now though with a definite accent. "*Status.*"

"*Approach secured. Situation growing but holding station for now. Out.*" I reckoned that was either Dawson or Jenner.

The voice spoke in Armenian again then waited. The message was repeated followed by another pause.

I'd heard all I needed to and switched the radio off.

Whether the voice on the other end of the radio had been trying to contact the guard I'd killed with the knife or the two in front of me didn't matter. There would be someone coming my way soon and there was no point hanging around outside.

There was a door into the pink building just after the van. That was my way in. I flicked the fire selector on the MP5 back to three-round-burst then gently pulled the door. It creaked open and I crept inside, gun held ready.

I guessed at one point it had been a reception area judging by the few scattered chairs and chest-high counter ahead of me.

Two figures were standing behind the counter, both smiling at me and saying nothing.

THIRTY-SEVEN

I almost shot them before realizing it was the remains of a life-size poster stuck to the wall behind the counter.

The end of the counter had been flipped up to allow access through to a door that led into a darkened corridor beyond. I went closer, ignoring the smell of rotting paper and damp wood, and let my eyes adjust to the gloom.

I also listened. I thought I could hear voices from somewhere further inside. It was hard to be sure. There was still the distant whoop of police sirens but those weren't getting any closer.

I carried on in.

The corridor at the back of the reception ran along the length of the pink building with doors on both sides. One of the doors to an outer office was open and ambient light from the outside lamps filtered through. If the door hadn't been open it would have been pitch black along there.

The first door, directly opposite reception, was already open. The room beyond was small and windowless. An office at one point in its life, judging from the broken desk and empty metal shell of a filing cabinet.

I figured Sean wouldn't be held in any of these outer rooms. They had to have him in one of the inner rooms, or more likely somewhere in the main warehouse itself.

I was about to continue when I heard the creak of a door opening and a glow of light appeared part way down the corridor. From the heavy footsteps and voices, it sounded like two men were coming my way.

I backed into the dark of the abandoned windowless office and listened as they approached. From the language a couple more Armenians.

Unless they deliberately looked into the room where I was they wouldn't see me, and I was pretty sure they were headed outside. The downside of that was that they would immediately see their dead friends and come straight back in, guns ready and on high alert.

If it had been just one guy I might have tried using the knife again, but I could feel the growing numbness in my arm and knew it would not have been the most effective option.

The first man came past, turning into reception, and his mate followed. I didn't want them too near and let them get a few paces away. The lead guy was reaching for the door handle when I opened fire and shot his friend. At such close range I couldn't miss.

The three shots blew a ragged hole in the back of his head, and he toppled forward. I was already moving, repositioning for a shot at the guy in the doorway. He turned, reaching for his gun and got my next three shot burst to his chest, knocking him off balance.

But he wasn't dead and now he had a gun in his hand.

It wasn't one of the AK carbines I'd seen the others with; this was just a pistol. A straightforward Colt .45 automatic. Nowhere near as cumbersome as the AKSU, yet still capable of serious damage and it was pointing in my direction.

I kept moving, fast and sideways behind the counter, adjusting my aim, realizing he must be wearing a ballistic vest. I squeezed the trigger just as he fired.

His Colt .45 boomed, and shards of wood flew from the countertop. I felt something hit my face and tasted blood.

Only one of my shots had been on target but that was all that was needed. The guy was dead, a neat hole in the side of his forehead.

He had fallen back against the door and his body propped it ajar. The crack of sporadic gunfire drifted in from outside, followed by a dull thump that sounded like an explosion. The sirens were no closer, but I could hear the unmistakable sound of a helicopter nearby.

I spat blood and checked my face. A shard of countertop wood had speared through my upper lip, the tip embedding in the gum beyond. It hurt like hell but at least the bullet itself had missed me.

I pulled the wooden sliver out and immediately felt wetness as the blood began to flow freely. I had to spit to stop the coppery taste filling my mouth, which only seemed to make it worse. It was the sort of wound that wasn't life threatening but one that took the edge off your concentration. One that meant you made mistakes and might end up dead.

I focused on swapping the magazine in the MP5, clicking the fresh one in place. I couldn't be sure how many rounds I had left in the old one but knew it wouldn't be many.

Another spit. More blood. I resisted exploring the hole in my gum with my tongue, which took some willpower.

I had to get moving. Fisk would be getting more edgy and nervous every second, and that increased the chances of him doing something stupid: like putting a bullet in Sean.

I hurried along the dark corridor and turned left where I'd seen the shaft of light emerging. At the end of the short passage there was a door with an upper glass panel revealing a lit area beyond. I paused and spat blood again, leaving a dark stain on the pale floor.

Looking through the glass I finally saw into the main warehouse. The area was large and open, with only a couple of broken packing crates and a stack of pallets on the far side of the dusty concrete floor. Hanging lights dangled from the roof giving just enough illumination to see the area.

Over to the right of my position, and against the rear of the warehouse, was a long office building built upon a raised concrete plinth, presumably to protect it from any stray forklift. Steps with metal handrails were set at either end of the plinth with a solid metal rail fixed along its length.

The office had been constructed from those thin prefabricated panels used for office walls that you see in most modern high rise corporate buildings.

Light streamed from the windows. That had to be where Sean was being held.

The overhead bulbs dimmed slightly and came back up again. The generator was getting low on fuel. It wouldn't be long before it cut out entirely and that would suit me fine.

Then a face appeared at one of the office windows.

Larry Fisk stared across the warehouse looking directly at me.

THIRTY-EIGHT

I didn't move; movement would give me away. I relied on the shadows to hide me and the fact that Fisk's vision would be affected by the lights within the office and less likely to spot me lurking in the darkness.

The lights flickered, dimmed, and remained low. The generator was running dry.

Fisk moved away from the window. He hadn't seen me, but I knew time was running out as fast as the diesel in the generator.

The first problem was getting to that office across thirty yards of clear warehouse floor with no cover. When the lights finally went out that would help me as far as not being seen but the flip side of that was that I wouldn't be able to see either. I'd have to use the flashlight on the MP5 and that would make me an easy target. I also needed to be able to see who I was shooting and avoid hitting Sean. Assuming he was in there.

I decided to make the move and get in position while the lights were still on. I switched the MP5 to single shot. I had one magazine. Thirty rounds. I needed to be precise. I also had the Glock. Another twelve shots. After that it was down to the knife. I reckoned it would be enough.

I placed my hand on the door handle and got ready to slip out, to make the dash, when the prefab office door opened. I shrank back into the shadows.

Fisk came out holding his phone like some kind of talisman or holy relic and slowly waving it around. Poor signal I guessed.

He walked along the plinth in front of the office still looking at his phone, then turned and leant on the metal rail, his back towards me.

I could have ended him there and then. A shot through the glass in the door. At thirty yards he wouldn't have a chance.

But I didn't.

There was no way he'd have left Sean alone and unguarded. There would be someone else in there, ready to pull the trigger on the hostage. Shooting Fisk only increased the chances of Sean dying. I had to secure my nephew first – then I could kill Fisk. Slowly.

Since my first estimate of the number of men that could be in the warehouse, I'd managed to reduce the headcount by four. The worst case meant there were eleven still around somewhere, but I knew that was way too high. A more realistic guess would be four, but even that felt high.

Two men would be enough for one hostage. The others, if there were others, would be stationed elsewhere – especially with the growing situation outside.

Fisk finally put the phone to his ear.

I risked opening the door, doing it slow and careful. I wanted to hear what he was saying. In the background I could still hear the helicopter and the occasional gunshot.

"Tell me!" shouted Fisk, listening to what was being said, frustration showing in his movements. I wondered who was on the other end of the line. Marshall perhaps? The lights dimmed further.

"What! Perez took her?"

I smiled to myself. It sounded like Claire might be safe.

"And Cresswell?" he was asking about Richard, Claire's husband, Sean's stepfather and the man dealing with the money that was at the core of the whole situation.

I saw Fisk's hand clench into a fist as he received news he obviously didn't like. He spun around and thumped the metal rail making it thrum with the impact.

I froze. The door was only part open, and I was crouched

behind it, but I was sure he'd notice it.

"Goddamn it!" Fisk snarled. "Send me your codes and get the hell out. I'll take it from here."

Assuming there had been enough truth in what he'd told me earlier about matching account numbers to access codes and Marshall having half of them, then it had to be her on the other end of the line.

He paused, listening again and looking up at the dimmed lights. His face reddened with barely suppressed rage. "No– Don't you–"

Fisk stared at his phone and the terminated call. His yell of "FUCK!" echoed throughout the building.

Then the lights went out.

THIRTY-NINE

I moved, shoving through the part open door and running across the flat expanse towards the concrete plinth and the office beyond. There was nothing in the way and nothing to trip me up. I'd estimated the distance to the steps and knew how far I had to go.

Fisk was using the screen on his phone like a torch and had spun to see where the pounding of my boots on the concrete was coming from. It was just enough for him to see my bloodied face emerging from the darkness. He yelled something unintelligible and turned to run.

I was at the steps and moving fast, taking them two at a time, at the same time switching on the MP5's flashlight.

Back in the day we had been taught that the most dangerous part of any room entry is going in through the door. That is where any hostile force expects you to enter. That is why special forces tend to go in through the windows if they can. There is the element of surprise and less chance of getting shot in the bottleneck of the doorway. But sometimes you have no choice. The doorway is the quickest and only way in.

Not in my case.

Using all the speed and weight I had, I adjusted course and crashed through the flimsy prefabricated wall and into the dark office beyond.

The impact drove a jolt of agony through my upper arm, and whatever advantage of surprise I had gained was immediately wiped out by me stumbling over the debris and barreling into someone standing in my way.

We both fell, the flashlight beam dancing crazily as we hit the floor. I felt the crack of bone as my shoulder and body weight landed on the guy's ribcage and he gave a sharp yelp of pain.

In the snatched glimpses of the beam I saw another man across the room next to a figure in a chair.

The guy beneath me tried to move. I felt him shifting position as best he could, trying to reach his gun. I twisted, bringing the MP5 around to point down, dug it into the side of his torso and pulled the trigger. A point-blank shot. The loud crack of the shot matched the jerk of his body.

I rolled off him, swinging the machine gun around towards the man beside the figure in the chair, but I wasn't quick enough.

The man fired first. It was quieter than I expected with very little muzzle flash. I felt nothing hit or whizz past me. In that brief moment all I was aware from the MP5's flashlight was that someone was pointing a gun in my direction.

But with the light on them I knew that my gun was pointing at them and not the seated figure.

I squeezed the trigger and the MP5 barked once, the report shockingly loud compared with the silenced pistol of the gunman. A moment later I was on my feet. My arm and face may have hurt like hell, but my legs were fine.

I moved and fired. Single shots, aimed from the shoulder, all well above the figure in the chair, all delivered quickly, all on the standing gunman. I stopped when he dropped. Five shots. Under two seconds start to finish.

I tasted blood and my chin was sticky. My upper lip and gum were bleeding freely again. The pain in my right arm told me the lip could wait. I needed to keep going while I could still hold a gun. I felt a growing wetness trickling down the back of my arm and worried that might not be on my feet for too much longer.

A quick check with the torch told me the gunman was dead. Eyes open, seeing nothing and sprawled backwards in a position that only the dead are comfortable with.

I scanned back to the guy on the floor. He'd not moved. The single shot to the kidneys had finished him well enough.

There had been no sign of Fisk. From what I knew of him he would have run, self-preservation being his number one priority. Right then that suited me.

I picked my way over to the still figure in the chair and knelt down, my heart hammering fast and just not from the recent exertion. The figure had a black bag over their head, their hands secured with bulky cable ties, and they had no shoes. They sat still, unmoving and for a second I thought I'd been too late or too slow or just too damn old.

Then they took a shuddering breath.

I loosened the hood and gently pulled it off.

Sean blinked, temporarily blinded by the tactical light. I noticed he had a black eye and his bottom lip was split.

"Uncle Dean?" he croaked trying to focus on me. His injuries were superficial and I'd had plenty worse in the past, but this was my nephew we were talking about. I felt a powerful need to hug him, but guys like me don't do that. I also felt the need to hurt those that had done this to him or allowed it to happen.

Fisk would not enjoy his time with me, that was for sure.

"Easy son," I reassured him. "Let's get these ties off and get the hell out of here."

Sean relaxed back in the chair. A few seconds work with the knife and his hands were free. I helped him get to his feet. He moved like parts of his chest and stomach were tender.

"Did they beat you?" I already knew the answer. Sean just nodded.

I looked down at Sean's stockinged feet and thought of Killick.

"What size shoes do you take?"

"Ten," said Sean. Same as me.

I left him, went over to the nearest dead guy and checked his feet. The boots were scuffed and looked a little big, but they would do. It was better than Sean cutting his feet on any broken glass. I wrenched them off and took them back to Sean.

"Thanks, Uncle D." He sat back in the chair and tugged them on.

I clicked off the tactical light once he was done.

"Give it a few seconds for your eyes to adjust," I told him. I put my arm around his shoulders and felt him nod.

"Is mom okay?" he asked.

"Yeah," I smiled though he couldn't see it. "Your mom's played a big part in getting you back."

We took another half minute and I listened carefully but all I could hear was our own breathing, the sounds of sirens outside and a faint buzzing in my ears.

We were good to go.

The entry hole I'd made into the room was too ragged and awkward for us to go through, so we moved to the door. Standing to one side I opened it carefully. The warehouse was not as entirely dark as I expected. Without any artificial lighting I could now see there were skylights in the roof and a number of windows high up at the top of the walls that were letting the faint light from outside filter in.

The whole place was still filled with shadows. I gave it another fifteen seconds but detected no movement, although in all honesty there could have been an entire squad of Green Berets out there and I wouldn't have known.

I doubted Fisk's Armenian friends would be as disciplined or willing to stay around as any US special forces given what was happening outside.

My gun arm was doing that weird thing where it hurt and was throbbing but had also managed to go partially numb. The worst of both worlds.

I removed my arm from around Sean.

"You okay to follow me?" I asked.

"Yeah, I can see enough."

"If any shooting starts you hit the deck, okay?"

"Okay." I made out his nod even in the semi-darkness.

Together we crept along the concrete plinth and down the

steps to the warehouse floor. There was still no movement from anywhere around us, so I decided to switch on the tactical light again. There was something I wanted to check.

I wanted to know which way Fisk had gone. I crouched and swept the beam across the floor. There was a definite trackway to the door I'd come through but there was something more. Scuffed footprints in the dust, faint but still visible, branching away at an angle towards the roller shutters. I followed the trail with Sean behind me and reached the inside of the metal door next to the roller shutters. It was the side of the warehouse where the vehicles were parked. I checked the metal door. The deadbolts had been slid back and it was unlocked.

I motioned Sean to stay back and switched off the flashlight. Then I opened the door, keeping well out of any firing line should anyone be waiting outside.

There were no shots.

I went outside.

After the darkness of the warehouse the night outside felt brighter, even though the security lamps were now off. The sound of the helicopter was much louder too.

The Chevrolet Imapla was still there, as was the Ford van, but the silver Yukon SUV had gone.

"Shit!" I hissed.

Fisk had got away.

FORTY

"What's up?" Sean whispered.

"He's gone," I said, shaking my head. "Fisk's gone."

"Cement factory," said Sean. "That's where he's gone. I heard them talking about it."

I must have looked puzzled because Sean continued.

"It's right here, just next to this place! We can catch him!"

I was torn about what to do.

I was also hurting and could tell Sean was too.

I'd done what I'd set out to do which was rescue my nephew. The responsible thing now was to sit tight and let the authorities sort things out.

"Uncle Dean!"

I looked at Sean. "What?"

"You gonna let him get away?"

Right then he reminded me so much of his father. His proper father.

I dug out the keys to the van.

"You can drive," I said, passing the keys to him.

*

I was right; the kid *could* drive.

He took the old Ford van around the rear of the warehouse and powered onto the access road before slewing hard left onto a dirt and cinder track.

"Safety belt," he said, noticing I was sat there unrestrained.

I grabbed the belt and clipped it in place.

"You know what you're doing?" I asked above the roar of the van's engine.

"A buddy and I come here drifting," he shouted as if that explained everything, his eyes fixed on the track ahead. I had an idea what he meant. Basically it was skidding cars around for fun, but it was usually tight little Japanese rear drive machines rather than an old Ford van.

We took the first bend, sliding far less than I expected, and picked up speed down a straight section, kicking up a plume of dust in the van's wake.

I let him concentrate, thinking that Claire would never forgive me if Sean got us killed immediately after rescuing him.

The old Ford's high beams speared into the darkness, picking out the twisting route as the van thundered along the packed dirt road, the body and suspension rattling and engine snarling as Sean coaxed all the speed he could out of it. Then he was on the brakes, the van dipping before he flung us sideways, got back on the throttle and steered into the slide. Stones and gravel clattered against metal as we hurtled onto a small side track away from the dirt road. I clutched the MP5 to myself, making sure I had the safety on, hoping that Sean knew what he was doing. I'm not a good passenger at the best of times but this was testing my nerves to the limit.

And then I saw the barrier directly ahead.

Three blue barrels with orange plastic fencing strung between them. There was no track visible beyond, just darkness as the ground dropped away into nothing. It was a dead end.

Sean kept on going.

"Erm…" was all I had time to say before the Ford pitched forward as Sean hit the brakes hard and the tires bit into the dirt. It was too late. There was no way we could stop in time.

But that wasn't Sean's plan.

The van smacked into the center barrel and tore through the plastic fencing as the front wheels locked and the nose tipped over the edge. I was glad that Sean had reminded me about the safety belt otherwise I'd have been through the screen.

The whole van pitched forwards. Then Sean was on the throttle again, rear tires spraying gravel as the old Ford flew down the steep slope.

The worrying thing about a dip of this size was that there had to be an equivalent bank on the other side. The slope bottomed out, pressing us into our seats. Sean kept the throttle pinned and engine roaring, using all the van's momentum to propel it up the steep bank on the other side.

I glanced over at my nephew and saw his concentration, teeth gritted hard in what looked like a grin and eyes bright as he gripped the wheel.

The van scrambled up the bank, launching over the top of the crest into the air before landing heavily, suspension banging and the whole vehicle swaying from side to side. As Sean sawed at the wheel keeping it on track my head smacked against the door frame.

He got the big Ford under control and in the van's main beams we saw the rear of Fisk's Chevrolet Yukon.

FORTY-ONE

Fisk had been driving without lights, presumably not to attract any attention. That meant he'd had to drive slow.

That all changed now.

I saw the track ahead light up as he whacked the Yukon's lamps on, and the SUV took off like it had been prodded with a sharpened stick.

Sean had his lips drawn back as he focused on keeping the van on track and in pursuit. We would be hard pressed to catch and overtake the big Chevrolet, but I was pretty sure we wouldn't lose it now. My nephew was proving himself a damn skilled wheelman.

The SUV jinked left, narrowly missing a parked bulldozer, and then swung hard right onto a dusty concrete roadway. Sean followed, the old van sliding wide around the corner and fishtailing as it straightened up.

These were access and utility roads designed to be taken at fifteen miles per hour, not fifty. Sean was doing well considering what he was driving.

Fisk had gained a few more yards and was pulling away. It wasn't surprising. His Chevrolet Yukon might have been heavier, but it had a big V8 engine and four wheel drive whereas our Ford van only had a six cylinder and rear wheel drive with precious little weight over the rear axle.

There was also the fact that the SUV had been built to cope with this sort of rough terrain and the van was far more at home on smooth blacktop.

We could still see the rear of the Chevrolet lit up in the van's high beam. Fisk wasn't getting away. I wound down the side window, leaned out with the MP5 as far as the safety belt would allow and fired a trio of three round bursts from the bucking van. The rear screen of the Chevrolet shattered and a taillight blew out, but it continued pulling away.

Then the brake lights lit up. Fisk rapidly shed speed and the nose of our van dipped as Sean also braked. I lost my firing angle and ducked back inside.

The SUV took a hard left between a set of site buildings and disappeared from view. Sean followed, the old Ford running wide and clipping one of the buildings. Metal crunched as the fender crumpled and the headlight shattered but we were still going.

"Sorry!" he said.

"Not my van," I told him. As long as we didn't get killed in the process, he could bust it up all he liked.

We saw the taillight of the Chevrolet turning left into the darkness. Sean was hard on the gas then back on the brakes, driving as fast as he could trying to make up the distance.

The van lurched around the corner and we saw the single taillight of the SUV some distance ahead. Fisk was heading directly towards the river.

"This is a dead end!" yelled Sean above the howl of the van's engine. Had Fisk taken a wrong turn, or did he have a plan of what he was doing? Through the open side window I could hear a helicopter getting closer. There was a flash from the single brake light remaining on the SUV then we lost it in the darkness.

A second later our Ford's remaining headlamp picked out the rear end of a huge tracked excavator. It was what the SUV had disappeared behind.

Sean slowed the van and took the turn wide. As the headlamp swept around the concrete and packed dirt area, we saw the Chevrolet SUV rolling onwards. I readied the MP5 but then paused.

The big Yukon was rolling slowly towards the edge of the area and the dark glint of the river beyond. Something wasn't right.

"Stop here," I told Sean. He brought the van to a halt, tires crunching on the dirt surface. Above the sound of the engine I heard the chopper pass low overhead.

"You get out of here," I said, opening my door.

The interior light came on and a series of gunshots split the night as bullets punched through the thin metal of the van.

FORTY-TWO

I tumbled out, hitting the hard dirt awkwardly. A jolt of agony shot up my spine and I felt a hot pain below my ribs and knew I'd taken another bullet.

"Uncle Dean!" shouted Sean, scrambling across the seats.

"Go!" I yelled hoarsely. "Get out!"

I expected to hear more shots but then realized it wouldn't be like that. I wouldn't hear the shot that killed me.

Lying on my back I saw Sean's face appear over the edge of the passenger seat.

"Get out of here!" I growled at him.

He shook his head, the same stubborn set to his features I'd seen in Claire, then his face disappeared from view.

The van started to move. Sean spun it around in a tight arc, placing it between where I lay and the direction the shots had come from.

I tried sitting up. It hurt but I managed it. I'd been hit in the lower torso and the side of my already ruined shirt was sticky with blood.

Sean was out of the van, kneeling next to me and supporting my back. I managed to reach the Glock stuck into the back of my trousers and pulled it out, handing it to him. I'd landed on it when falling out of the van and it had hurt almost as much as being shot.

"Help me up," I asked Sean. He looked unsure. "Come on. Do it," I said.

"Hadn't we best wait for the EMTs?" His concern was touching but now was not the time for sentiment.

I held out my hand. "Come on. Time's wasting."

Sean sighed and took my hand, helping me up.

The Chevrolet SUV was buried nose first in a row of bushes some fifty yards away, but that wasn't the direction the shots had come from. I looked around.

I could hear the sound of approaching sirens even though I couldn't see any lights yet.

The helicopter returned and a floodlight stabbed down at us. It didn't help and I shielded my eyes from its glare. A moment later the light swung away towards the river and I saw the edge of a low wooden boathouse.

"Stay here," I said to Sean.

He looked at me with concern. He didn't have to say anything. I gave him a brief smile, a nod and then turned and jogged towards the boathouse.

I say jogged, it was probably more of a stumbling fast walk, but I was hurt and running on adrenaline and determination alone. Maybe if I'd been thinking straight I'd have stayed there with my nephew and let the authorities sort it all out from there. Maybe that would have been the sensible thing to do.

But somewhere deep inside I knew had a mission to complete. I was too damn near to getting Fisk and bringing him to justice, or killing him in the process, to give up now.

In the chopper's light I could see that a wide flat jetty protruded straight out into the river, presumably where barges or cargo boats could be loaded with stone or gravel or similar. The wooden boathouse was off at ninety degrees to this butting up next to its own concrete pathway.

As I got there the chopper moved away. By then I was sure it had to be a police one, although exactly what their intentions were, I couldn't make out.

I let my eyes adjust, deciding to keep the MP5's flashlight off for the time being. After a few seconds I found the boathouse door. The lock had been smashed off and the door was ajar.

I went in quickly, getting out of the doorway and away from

being framed by any light from outside.

It was dark in there, the only light coming from the reflection off the river, but as the whole side of the boathouse was open it wasn't too bad. I could make out a long wooden walkway that ran along the entire length of the place.

Then I saw the movement of a flashlight towards the far end, its beam playing over the interior of a dark R.I.B. I brought the MP5 up, held ready, and trod carefully along the walkway towards the light. It had to be Fisk.

I was halfway there when I heard the engine cough into life.

I squeezed the trigger, loosing off a three-round burst. The R.I.B.'s engine rose to a howl and the dark shape of the boat roared away out of the boathouse.

I swore long and hard. I'd lost him. Again.

But had I? I switched the MP5 flashlight on and scanned the area. There were five remaining boats along the jetty, some better than others, and there was a metal cabinet against the far wall near the door. I stumbled over to it, found it was already unlocked, and looked inside.

It was sparsely populated. There were only three keys on the hooks inside. I took them all, ran to the boat that had caught my eye and jumped on board, the fresh bullet wound reminding me of its presence as I landed.

There was no guarantee that even if I could find the right key that the boat would have any fuel. At first glance it looked like a wreck. The hull had primer patches, there were no grab rails or brightwork, there wasn't even a windshield.

It was the pair of fresh Yamaha engines that had appealed to me.

The second key fitted and turned. A dashboard light came on and I hit the only button that could have been the starter.

Nothing happened.

I pressed it again, and this time the big outboard motors belched into life. I threw off the mooring rope then rammed the throttle forward.

The engines stumbled and coughed then rose to a powerful roar as the boat shot out from under the roof of the boatyard, with me clinging on to the wheel for all I was worth.

FORTY-THREE

Fisk had a good forty seconds' lead on me but, whereas he had an R.I.B. with a single engine, I was in a streamlined speedboat with more than twice the power.

Neither of us were running with lights on our boats. Illegal and dangerous but right now that didn't matter. I could see the foaming wake from his boat on the river without much problem and I was going to get the bastard.

I veered the speedboat over to the left of his position, keeping my right side free to use the MP5. I took a moment to switch the submachine gun to fully automatic, figuring that would be more useful now. In doing that I almost lost control. The boat wobbled in the water, the note of the engines warbling back and forth as the propellers tried to find clean water to bite into.

I heard the helicopter behind me and the floodlight came on, adjusting position on the water, finding my speeding boat. No help to me at all. Then it moved forward along the path of the wake from the R.I.B. and pinpointed Fisk for me. That was much better.

I could see I was gaining fast despite the lack of windshield making my eyes water in the cold night air.

Fisk's R.I.B. veered left, losing the light for a second as he cut directly across the river. I followed, wondering what the hell he was doing.

Then I knew.

A large freighter was coming up the river directly towards us and it appeared like Fisk was going to ram it. It was suicide. I eased the throttles back further. He was caught.

The R.I.B. continued turning, picking up speed. It was madness. He would get hit by the freighter for sure. The helicopter circled overhead, doing its best to track his movements. I held position, fighting a growing feeling of nausea and the increasing buzzing in my ears. I shook my head to clear it, and kept watching.

I had guessed wrong. He was going to make it. Maybe not by much but his desperate move was about to pay off.

There was no way I'd be able to get in front of the big ship now, I had to pass behind it, giving Fisk his lead back.

I turned the wheel and opened up the engines, aiming for a point beyond the rear of the freighter and across its turbulent wake. The speedboat bounced over the churned water jarring my body and making me grunt in pain. I clung to the wheel with white knuckles and kept the boat going into the smooth water beyond. Fisk's R.I.B. was well over a freighter's length away from me now. I steered towards him and opened the throttles as far as they would go. The engine note of the twin Yamahas rose to a howl and the sharp prow lifted as my boat scythed across the water towards him.

I needed to get close enough to use the MP5. A burst to his boat's engine would put an end to his escape. If a stray bullet hit his leg, then so be it. I wouldn't be shedding any tears.

My tatty but powerful speedboat tore across the water, steadily closing the gap. The helicopter's beam remained tracking Fisk. There was no way out. He needed to give up.

We were travelling downstream on the Columbia River, away from the main flow and into a narrower side channel that ran between the shore and a large long island. We were also close to passing under a wide road bridge.

I was in range for the MP5, but the bucking of the boat on the water meant I needed to be much closer to stand any chance of making my shots count. The helicopter began pulling up, gaining height to clear the bridge, and the beam of the floodlight strayed from Fisk for a second.

But I still had him.

I was to the right of the wake from Fisk's boat and gaining fast, the twin engines behind me powering hard through the smoother water, drawing closer to him every second.

I raised the muzzle of the MP5, keeping one hand on the wheel. It wouldn't quite be firing from the hip but it was close. I'd be using best judgment rather than aiming properly, but it would do.

And if a bullet didn't stop him, I'd ram the bastard.

I steadied myself as best I could and put pressure on the MP5's trigger, just as the right-hand engine coughed sending a twitch along the boat. I snatched a glance down at the gauges on the dashboard. It was only now I noticed that none of them were working and that I had no idea of how much fuel there was in the tank.

As if answering that question both engines gave out a full-on sputter and the boat faltered, speed dropping. There was nothing I could do, and I was out of time.

I steadied the speedboat as best I could, re-aimed the MP5 at Fisk's R.I.B., squeezed the trigger and emptied the magazine. It had only been half full and was gone in barely over a second. Fifteen 9mm bullets at fifty yards.

It made no difference. I hit nothing. Not Fisk, not his boat, not even a barn door.

The engines behind me gave a final coughing belch then cut out leaving me dead in the water, drifting in the dark of the night.

FORTY-FOUR

I slumped in the seat, watching Fisk's boat pull away.

I felt drained. Just like the speedboat my tank was empty. I'd nothing more to give.

The gentle rocking of the drifting boat might have been relaxing for some people, but it just made my nausea return. I felt like I was going to pass out but couldn't take my eyes off the fleeing R.I.B.

The light from the chopper stayed with it for a few more seconds then the boat disappeared into the shadowy darkness under the bridge.

It was a cloudless night and there were a few stars in the sky, moving gently above me. It was all so dark. I could hardly see anything.

I was on my back, lying in the boat, not knowing how I got there from the seat. It was cold. It really felt like autumn now.

I felt my side. My shirt was soaking wet and sticky. I wiped my hand on my pants and lay there trying not to pass out.

I'd been stupid to race after Fisk after being shot. All the exertion of trying to be a hero had done no good at all and now I was slowly bleeding out in a small unlit boat, drifting at the mercy of the current in a large river. The chances of being found were not good.

But at least I'd found Sean, and Claire was probably okay.

I closed my eyes and felt a buzzing faintness closing in. I wanted to sleep, I was so tired, but closing my eyes just made me feel sick.

Fisk was still out there. I had to find him.

My hands found the empty MP5. It could still be useful.

I pressed the button for the tactical flashlight and hoped for the best.

FORTY-FIVE

The hands wouldn't leave me alone.

Finally I was comfy and didn't feel nauseous, but they kept moving and tugging at me. I kept my eyes closed hoping they would go away but they didn't. I felt something happening to my side, where I'd been shot, then there was more movement.

I woke up enough to hear voices talking swiftly and efficiently and opened one eye.

"He's awake," said someone.

I decided to shut my eye again and drifted off into a semi-unconscious state. Let whoever was there get on with whatever they needed to do.

After that, all I could recall were snatches of images and random words from various figures around me.

Sean above me, telling me to hold on.

A middle-aged Asian EMT with a serious face and an easy smile telling me to relax.

Sirens.

More movement.

Strip lights passing above me as I was wheeled along a corridor. People in hospital scrubs exchanging rapid medical terms with each other.

Then darkness for a while.

*

When I next woke up, I felt like I had a brain made of fluff and lint.

I was lying on a hospital bed in a private room, all alone except for a cluster of silent machines monitoring whatever life signs they were meant to. The room was dimly lit and the window blinds closed. I had no idea what time it was, though in my mind I still thought it was night.

Even though my mind was fuzzy a torrent of questions started flooding through it. Were Sean and Claire okay? Had Fisk been caught? That was a big glowing beacon of a question. Then what had happened to Linda Marshall? I wondered how Dan Perez's wife was, then about Dan himself. The thoughts jumbled and collided as I tried to sort things out in my head.

I had been dressed in one of those unflattering hospital gowns that don't cover your ass and my arm had been dressed and bound. It felt sore and was as stiff as hell, but I could move it without too much pain, providing I did it slowly.

I took stock of my other injuries.

My lip felt odd, but I couldn't detect any stitches. I guessed they had used superglue, or the medical equivalent, to stick that part of me back together.

Unsurprisingly, the side of my stomach hurt. At the time I couldn't recall if it had been a through-and-through shot or if the bullet had stayed in me. It didn't matter now. A dull ache below the ribs let me know it was waiting for the pain killers to fade before treating me to some serious discomfort. For now it was tolerable, even with an annoying itch beneath the dressings. But I was alive and could live with an itch.

My dry mouth was another matter.

I tried to sit myself up and failed. It hadn't been much of an attempt. More thought than any actual action.

I used my good arm to carefully shuffle up into a half sitting position, wincing as the stomach muscles around the bullet wound protested. I took my time and was careful but was sweating by the end of it.

A jug of water and an empty glass had been placed on the

bedside table to my left, my uninjured side. Someone had applied some common sense. I didn't bother with the glass; I drank the water straight from the jug. It was warm and could have been fresher, but I didn't mind.

You might have been expecting my concerned family to tumble into the room at that point, a tearful and emotional reunion, a serious but friendly cop to intervene and tell us all some good news, but this isn't the movies or a cheap TV mini-series.

I found the nurse call button and used it. A homely, middle-aged woman opened the door within thirty seconds, smiled and came over to the bedside. Her name tag said 'Jill'. She helped me get into a more comfortable sitting position and asked how I was feeling.

"Better," I told her before asking what time it was. Apparently it was mid-morning, a full day and a half after I'd been admitted. That was a shocker.

I asked about Sean and Claire, and although Jill didn't know she said she would find out. She was a good nurse, didn't fuss and seemed to genuinely have my best interests at heart. I found her easy to like.

It was only after she had refreshed my water that she asked if I felt ready to speak with some police officers that had been eagerly waiting for me to wake up.

They can't have been that eager I thought, as there had been no uniform guard either inside the room or, as far as I could tell, stationed outside the door. I gave her the go ahead to send them in.

Three minutes later I was staring at Linda Marshall's face.

FORTY-SIX

The five inch by seven inch glossy photo was not flattering. You want to look like a supermodel, go to a professional studio, not a bored cop with a cheap digital compact tasked with creating ID badges.

"Yeah, that's Marshall," I told the two Feds. I'd only seen her the once, but it was enough.

The older guy was sat in a chair next to the bed. He had a rumpled suit like he'd slept in it, tired eyes and a quiet manner. He'd introduced himself as John Hudson, no 'Special Agent', the ID he showed me told me he was FBI. It looked real enough and I'd no reason to doubt him.

His partner was a couple of decades younger, slick, and would have loved the opportunity of saying 'Special Agent' if he'd had the chance. All I got from him was the name Smith. Judging by the sharpness of the creases in his suit and the haircut he was probably a fan of The Matrix. I wondered where his glasses were.

"She says you shot her in the butt," said Hudson.

I frowned. "I bet she says a lot of things about me."

Hudson smiled. Smith didn't.

"You're not her favorite person, it has to be said, but she is cooperating with us, and we'd like you to do the same." Hudson's accent had hints of the Southern states in it, maybe Virginia. It made him sound relaxed. He placed another photograph on the bed in front of me. "How about this guy? You know him."

Peter Killick's smarmy pockmarked face stared back up at me. The picture made him look slightly boss-eyed.

"Killick," I said. "He tried to shoot me."

"Did you shoot him?" asked Smith.

"No. I disarmed him and let him go." There was no lie there.

"Know where he is now?" said Hudson.

I shook my head. Smith's nostrils flared. He didn't believe me, but I didn't care. I guessed Killick had taken a long vacation somewhere far away, or he was lying bootless and dead in the desert and hadn't been found yet. I preferred the thought of the second option.

"Are you sure about that?" Hudson didn't believe me either.

"Yes. I have no idea where he is." I kept eye contact with Hudson. Across the room I heard Smith's annoyed huff.

It was my turn to get exasperated.

"Look guys, I've been awake for less than two hours and no one has told me if my sister and nephew are okay. Before going through any more of this I'd like to know." I looked between Hudson and Smith. "So are they?"

Hudson sat back in the chair and looked me in the eye.

"You want a coffee?" he asked.

The question stumped me for a second. I wasn't sure if the doctors were allowing it, but I felt like I needed one. I nodded. "Sure."

Hudson turned to Smith. "Chris, do the honors will you. Get a receipt."

Agent Smith's lips were a tight line. He glared at me.

"Bit of cream, bit of sugar," I smiled at him.

He turned on his heel and left the room.

"I guess you'll pay for that later," I murmured. Hudson laughed softly.

"He's a good guy. He'll be a great agent in a few years." He returned to looking at me. "Okay, officially off the record but not that it should matter. Your sister Claire is physically fine – her world's been shook up, but I guess you knew that already. Sean took a beating but nothing worse than a rough bar fight and he'll be fine too. Reckon he's less shook up than his mom, but I guess that's youngsters for you. With me so far?"

I nodded.

"We have been unable to locate your brother-in-law, Richard, as yet. That's all I can say on that score. You'll get to know more later no doubt."

I started to open my mouth, but Hudson held up his hand to indicate he hadn't finished.

"Your next question is going to be about Captain, or should I say ex-Captain, Larry Fisk," he paused when he saw the look that crossed my face. "Yeah, thought so," he added. "Well, Portland's finest didn't get him so he's out there in the wind, probably on a flight to Cuba or somewhere we can't extradite him from."

"Fuck," was all I said.

"Sorry Riley, not my problem." At least he was being level with me.

Hudson picked up the photos of Marshall and Killick, returned them to his folder, and dealt another four photos onto the bed like they were cards. Santos, Lane and two other guys I guessed were Dawson and Jenner. All dark uniforms, all looking serious. Hudson was also looking serious and looking straight at me.

"You seen any of these guys before?"

The door opened and Smith came in with two coffees. He handed them to Hudson who in turn handed one to me. I guessed Smith wasn't thirsty.

I took a sip from the cardboard cup. It was hot but I was very ready for it.

I was about to speak when he raised a hand. "Look Mr. Riley, I know you've been through a lot so please think very carefully and consider the fact that CSI have been very thorough."

Agent Smith sighed loudly and rolled his eyes. Hudson ignored him.

"So tell me about these guys?" He gestured to the pictures of the four SWAT team members that were arrayed in front of me.

I pointed at the picture of Lane. "I shot him in self-defense."

"Go on."

245

Santos next. "Not shot but also killed in self-defense."

Hudson raised an eyebrow. I guessed he'd seen the crime scene photos.

My finger rested on the third picture. "Never saw this guy," I pointed at the fourth, "or him."

I took another sip of the hot coffee. Considering it was from a machine it was pretty good.

Hudson gathered the pictures back up and returned them to his buff folder before taking out more pages of glossy paper, each with multiple photographs on them.

These were not pictures of cops. They were all dead guys and I had killed them.

"Do you recognize any of these men?" said Hudson.

I had to be careful what I said, depending on how Hudson and Smith were going to play it. By the letter of the law, I had committed multiple murders and it wasn't in the line of duty. I wasn't a cop anymore; I was a civilian.

I considered what to say as Hudson and Smith looked on.

"Who are they?" I asked.

"Does it matter?" said Hudson.

I picked up the top sheet and looked at the pictures. The first four images were of the guy I'd shot in my house, a wide angle and then details.

"Looks like one of my rooms," I said.

"And the guy?" said Hudson.

I paused. They hadn't cautioned me, and I wasn't under arrest. At least not yet.

"I'm wondering if I should have a lawyer present before we go on." Smith and Hudson exchanged a look.

Smith leant against the wall and crossed his arms. Hudson sat back in the chair and regarded me levelly.

"Mr. Riley, there's enough evidence to tie you to at least half a dozen homicides as well as the assault of police officers in their line of duty, let alone a number of other minor offences. It would be very easy to build a case that would see you in jail for the rest of your natural life."

Hudson let the facts sink in before adding, "If we wanted to, and it was in the public interest."

"So what are you saying?" I asked.

"We've pieced together some of what went on from a few sources. What you appeared to have done was justified. Maybe not entirely legally but we understand your motivation and actions. From our background checks you have an exemplary record from your time in the Rangers, were respected as a police officer, and have a reputation as a decent kind of guy."

That last bit was nice to know. I wondered if they had spoken to Dolores. I'd made a mental note to get her a big bunch of flowers and some expensive chocolates for distracting the cops staking out my house.

Hudson continued. "What we want from you is to get the complete picture; we still have a number of gaps to fill in."

"Am I being charged with anything?"

"No. We just want your help." Hudson gestured to the photo sheets lying on the bed. "All of those men are known to have had criminal associations, some internationally. As far as we're concerned the world is a better place without them, and if you were the one to kill them then we have an answer and can close that case."

Agent Smith had been quiet while his older partner had done all the talking but now he spoke.

"What you should have done was come to us. We could have helped." He genuinely believed what he said, and maybe on one level he was right.

"We just want to get as complete a picture as we can," Hudson repeated, "and currently have no intent to charge you with anything. Besides, you are being interviewed in your hospital bed, on pain medication and without any lawyer present. Nothing you say to us now would stand up in court."

I stared at Hudson for a long moment and he held my gaze. Even when I'd been on the force this would have been true. I wasn't under caution, and I believed him.

I took a breath and looked over to where Smith was standing.

"You might want to get a chair, this may take a while," I said.

We went over details from the very start to the point at which I passed out on the speedboat. I told them plenty, if not every single detail.

The whole process took well over an hour and I felt far more tired at the end of it than I expected, considering I'd spent the time sat in bed. Hudson and Smith thanked me, and even Smith seemed genuine, so I guess I'd made the right impression.

Nurse Jill came in directly afterwards, checking on me and gently telling me off about the coffee. My side felt stiff and painful, and my wounded arm itched underneath the dressing. I said nothing but maybe she could tell anyway.

She checked a chart, gave me some painkillers, then helped me lie back down telling me to get some rest.

The tablets helped plenty. I don't even remember falling asleep.

*

"Wake up." Something or somebody shook me. It wasn't gentle. I fought my way out of sleep but evidently I wasn't waking up quickly enough. Something hit me on my wounded arm and the jolt of agony did the rest. I bit back a grunt of pain as my eyes opened.

Someone was standing next to my bed looking down at me.

"Hello Riley," said Fisk.

FORTY-SEVEN

On the other side of the bed was a blond-haired guy holding a silenced pistol. I recognized him from Hudson's photos. It was Dawson. He'd been the one to hit my arm, probably using the hard metal of the gun.

I looked back at Fisk.

"Miss me?" he said.

My mouth was dry. I managed to find enough saliva to swallow. It must have made me look nervous because a slow smile grew across Fisk's face.

"I thought I'd pay a final farewell visit, us being old pals and all."

He nodded to Dawson, who went to stand by the door. I wondered why there hadn't been a cop outside. Then I realized that such protective custody only really happens in the movies and the Feds had no compelling reason to feel I was either going to do a runner or that I was in any danger.

The blinds had been drawn on the small window between my room and the corridor beyond. So had the ones on the outside window, even though we were several stories up. I had no idea of what time it was and felt totally disoriented.

Dawson was wearing a doctor's white coat and Fisk still wore a suit, a freshly pressed light grey affair. Apart from the gun in Dawson's hand they looked like a doctor and specialist consultant.

"Nothing to say?" Fisk asked.

I pointed at my mouth then at the full glass of water. I pulled myself up into a sitting position, ignoring the pain in my side.

The water was a stretch away. I reached for it, fingers not quite brushing the glass. Fisk let me struggle for it, watching as my fingers finally touched the lip of the glass, hooked a fingertip over and slowly pulled it closer until I could get hold of it properly. I took a swig while he watched me. The water tasted warm and metallic, but it would do. Besides, it all bought me time and that was something I desperately needed.

I shifted position, making the effort look more awkward than it actually was, using the chance to loosen the bedsheets around my legs as best I could.

"I expect you know why I'm here," said Fisk looking down at me as I slowly sipped the water. I was relieved that my fuzzy head had cleared quickly, and I was able to think again. Maybe that was thanks to the adrenaline. Fear will do that, and there was no doubt I was afraid. It was a bad situation and one I couldn't see any easy way out of.

Fisk's eyes were fixed on mine. There was a cold and furious madness there that I'd never seen before. He continued speaking, not really caring if I was listening. "But before you say goodbye, I want to let you know I'll take care of Claire and Sean after you've gone."

"Go on. I know you want to tell me. Get on with it," I sighed. Getting him to carry on talking gave me more time. Time for me to think. Time for there to be a distraction from the door. Time for the cavalry to arrive. I wanted as many extra seconds as I could manage.

I struggled into a sitting position, further loosening the sheets around the far edge of the bed as I shuffled and moved.

Fisk reached into his pocket and pulled out a syringe. He smiled and held it up so I could see. Maybe this was some kind of revenge for me sticking him with all that Ketalar.

"What's in there?" I asked.

"Cocaine," he beamed. "A big dose for my old buddy. You'll suffer a huge stroke or embolism or something like that. The most likely thing is that you'll die in agony, but if you do manage to survive, you'll be a vegetable. Unable to walk or talk, and locked inside a body that can't control when it shits or pisses itself. You've no idea how good that will make me feel while catching glorious sunshine on the beach and sipping chilled mojitos."

An image of a lizard sprang to mind, and I sniggered. Fisk truly was a reptile of a man.

"What?" he snapped. My short laugh had annoyed him.

"Go skin cancer!" I smiled nastily. Not that it would get a chance. If I was going to die, I might as well try to take him with me.

If I could find a way.

Fisk's eyes hardened and for a moment I thought he was about to stab the syringe into me there and then. A moment passed then he relaxed and took a breath.

"Nah, I tan easy."

I ignored him, turning my attention to Dawson standing by the door.

"Hey Dawson, good to see you. Where's Jenner?" I asked, trying a different tack. "I know where Lane and Santos are, but I'd like to get all four of you. Complete the set."

Dawson tensed, saying nothing.

From that, I guessed his buddy Jenner hadn't made it.

"Shame," I said. "Someone else beat me to it."

"Ignore him," Fisk said to Dawson.

"Yeah, just think of the money." I knew that would touch a nerve too. "Wherever that is," I added, taking another small sip of water while slipping my free hand underneath the sheets.

Dawson shifted position, holding his anger in check. Fisk looked at me, eyes filled with venomous hatred as he spoke.

"Hey Riley, I haven't told you about Sean and Claire yet. About all the fun times we have planned for them."

Fisk told me. In detail. Taking a malignant pleasure from it.

The things a mother should never see her son subjected to. The acts a son should never see performed on his screaming mother. Fisk had it choreographed like a sadistic play culminating in the final acts that left one of them dead and the other both physically mutilated and mentally scarred. As Fisk talked, I caught the look of anticipation on Dawson's face, thinking about his involvement, and I decided the world would be a better place without him.

Fisk finished by telling me that I shouldn't worry because I'd be either dead or as good as by then.

"The heroic old US Ranger, dying in agony as he shits himself in his hospital bed. Quite pitiful," Fisk sneered.

"Vindictive bastard, aren't you?" I snarled back.

Fisk smiled and readied the syringe.

FORTY-EIGHT

I tossed the remaining water from my glass over Fisk's crotch.

"What the fuck!" he began, stepping back.

I hurled the empty glass at Dawson. He reacted instinctively, twisting as it smacked into his chest. But the glass didn't break, not even when it hit the floor.

I was too busy to notice. I threw the bedsheets off my legs and towards Fisk, catching a lucky break as they snagged on the syringe enough to make him fumble and drop it.

The main thing was my legs were free and I could move. I launched myself out of the bed towards Dawson, barreling into the corrupt SWAT cop with my good shoulder and slamming him into the door before he could react. A jolt of pain stabbed through my side as I felt stitches there burst open.

There was no finesse in my approach, just simple savage brawling at close quarters. I grabbed his wrist, forcing the gun aside just as the silenced pistol fired, a bullet thudding into the floor. Dawson had grasped my bad arm, locking us in a violent dance as we pivoted up against the door, and he drove his knee up into my side.

If it had been in the side I'd been shot in then he might have ended the fight within seconds. As it was, his strike didn't faze me. I guess the painkillers were helping deaden any hurt and my raging adrenaline was compensating for any slowing of reactions.

I twisted his wrist, trying to bash his gun hand against the door, but he was younger and stronger than me and resisted. His knee smacked up into my side, and then again harder. We were in a deadlock, and I couldn't keep this up for much longer.

I could hear Fisk scrabbling around behind me.

I had to get Dawson between me and Fisk otherwise that syringe would stick in me at any moment and then it would all be over.

I had Dawson's gun pinned. I couldn't move it, let alone direct it towards Fisk, but I could feel the clip release under my finger. I pressed it and the magazine dropped out onto the floor. There would still be a round in the chamber though, and that single shot would still kill me just as easily as a full clip.

Fisk was coming for me. I could only catch a hint of movement from the corner of my eye, but it was enough to know I'd got a problem.

"Hold him!" yelled Fisk.

I dropped, bending at the knees as I fell and holding onto Dawson as best I could. He wasn't expecting me to fall like that, or so heavily, or to rely on such a messy approximation of a judo throw.

Dawson tumbled over me, crashing heavily across the end of the bed and into Fisk's way. The gun went off as he fell, the bullet punching through the outside window and rattling the blinds.

I reckoned the stitches for the bullet wound in my side had torn and felt like I'd had a hot poker stuck in there. No doubt I was bleeding again but now was not the time to check.

The door was behind me. I should have turned and opened it and run. That would have been the sensible thing to do. But the idea didn't even occur to me. I was in full-on fight-or-die survival mode.

I saw Dawson as the biggest problem despite not having any bullets in his gun. He was already trying to struggle to his feet, using the side of the bed for support but he wasn't up yet.

I rushed forward, lashing out with a foot like I was trying to take a penalty from the fifteen-yard line and make it clear the stadium. I caught him in the face. A shaft of agony lanced through my foot, and I knew I broken bones in there. There was a dull, wet clack from Dawson's face as his teeth smacked together and he fell away from the bed across on the floor spraying blood across the tiles.

Fisk was on me now and I felt the prick of a needle as the syringe stabbed into my arm.

"Die, you fucker!" he spat, pressing the plunger.

I smacked him away with the back of my hand, catching the side of his face. It was a weak blow but enough to make him let go of the syringe. I snatched it out of my arm and threw it across the room, wondering how much of the cocaine he'd managed to stick in me and many seconds I had left.

Dawson was crawling across the floor, blood dripping from his mouth, but Fisk was already coming back at me, his kick delivered low and dirty. I barely managed to block it, taking most of the force on my hip as it drove me into the bottom edge of the bed. I went with the flow and tumbled around it, falling to the floor on the side nearest the door.

I got to my feet as quickly as I could, but it wasn't quick enough because Dawson was right there in my face.

Only my training saved me, and then only barely.

His blows came in hard and fast. I blocked, minimizing damage but just prolonging the inevitable, nothing more.

He kicked his knee repeatedly into my side again, this time directly into the bullet wound. I felt wet and sticky there and guessed that a tell-tale blossom of blood told him exactly where to hit. It was a hard series of blows that sent waves of pain through my midriff. Fisk remained standing on the other side of the bed, watching Dawson pummel me into submission.

I abandoned defending myself and grabbed Dawson's head with both hands, drawing him close as if to kiss him. The onslaught stopped as he started to resist, not knowing what I was doing.

But it was too late, I'd got him close enough.

I sank my teeth into his nose.

Dawson tried to pull away but I went with him, biting hard as he screamed. Blood and snot poured over my mouth. He tried hitting my face, frantic to make me let go, but I was too fucking determined and the blows only jarred my head which made his own pain worse. I ground my teeth like I was chewing a bad steak. Flesh and cartilage tore as I shoved Dawson away turning to spit out the chunk of meat that had been his nose. His hands went to his mutilated face, trying to stem the blood that streamed through his fingers. A bubbling moan escaped him as he staggered around the room.

I turned to find Fisk pointing a gun at me. He'd had enough time to collect the silenced Glock and reinsert the clip.

"Enough!" he commanded.

There was nothing else I could do. I held still.

I wondered when someone from outside the room would come and investigate what all the noise was about, and it worried me it might cost their life.

In engaging with Dawson, I'd ended up across the room and was closer to the outside window than the door. A stupid mistake that had me trapped.

Dawson stumbled across the floor moaning, gore streaming down his face as he searched the blood-spattered floor for his severed nose.

"Really gonna look like I died in my sleep now," I growled at Fisk, trying to remain focused.

"Like I fucking care anymore," he replied, leveling the gun. There was shake to his hands.

"I've got the account numbers from Richard," I bluffed, slowly moving closer to him, avoiding the whimpering form of Dawson. "How much are they worth?"

"Liar!" snarled Fisk.

"I'll write them down. Let you have them. How about that? Surely that's got to be worth more than killing me off." I'd managed to get next to the end of the bed and Fisk was now by the door. "How much are we talking, Larry? How many millions?"

That was when the door handle behind Fisk rattled.

FORTY-NINE

"What's going on in there?" said a man's voice from the corridor, the handle rattling frantically as the door bumped in the frame.

The distance between us was close enough to try, but wide enough to be unwise.

I had no choice. I lunged forward.

Fisk pulled the trigger.

The shot was close enough to feel the bullet pass me and punch through the window beyond, but I was on him and fighting for the gun. Fisk was desperate, hanging on to it with all his strength, teeth bared. I had anger and skill on my side, but it wasn't enough. I was hurting and weakened. He began to overcome me, and the barrel of the gun slowly moved towards my blood-soaked face.

Someone started kicking at the door.

Fisk took the initiative and headbutted me. I staggered back and Dawson grabbed me from behind. I caught a glimpse of his face, now a horrific mask of gore and mutilated flesh.

"Shit!" said Fisk as the door behind him burst open. He turned and fired and a young man in orderly's overalls fell to the floor. There were screams from outside.

Fisk ran.

Dawson had his arm around my neck forcing me backwards. I went with it, using my weight and staggered with him across the room. He twisted as we moved, and my head slammed against the window.

The glass, already weakened by the bullet holes, finally shattered and I felt cold air rushing past my face. Dawson brought his hand around underneath my jaw and pushed my back hard up against the window frame. I felt myself tipping over.

We were about the same weight but by no means evenly matched. He had over twenty years of youth on his side, younger muscles plus modern SWAT training. Whereas I was just a mean old bastard, full of rage.

I twisted, feeling shards of glass dig into my back, and reached down, grabbing between Dawson's legs. He had a fraction of a second to realize what I was doing before I twisted, hauling up and out, pitching his balance onto and over the window frame. I felt more stitches in my side rip and saw his eyes widen in his ruined face before he toppled backwards and disappeared into the darkness.

I suspected that the four-story drop made enough of a mess that I wouldn't ever need to worry about Dawson again.

I don't remember any screams or sound of impact because I was already staggering towards the door after Fisk as soon as Dawson had gone.

Nurse Jill was screaming as I went out the door.

"Which way?" I croaked, and she pointed towards the stairwell. I jogged that way as fast as I could, blood-stained medical gown flapping around me.

I had no idea what to do if I caught up with Fisk. I was hurting and unarmed, and he had a gun. Some part of me told me to give it up, don't be stupid and get killed.

But I couldn't let him get away.

I heard people shouting and saw Fisk turn a corner some way ahead, his shoes slipping on the smooth polished floors. I ran on, my bare feet finding more grip than the smooth soles of his brogues. I rounded the turn just in time to see the door to the stairwell flapping slowly.

I barged through the door and felt a bullet zip past me. Larry Fisk was standing on the stairwell landing below, his gun tracking me. I hit the floor, diving out of sight.

Right then I had a moment where I thought I wouldn't be able to get back up. The pain in my side was as bad as it had been, my arm was throbbing like it was being pounded with a hammer and I was sure to pass out at any moment. But lying there would allow Fisk to get away and that was not acceptable.

Riley, the wounded old lion, about to meet his end. Well, I'd damn well go down fighting.

I'd heard a door open on the level below so hauled myself to my feet and went after him. I guess I wasn't thinking straight.

I went down a level and peered through the side door. It was all quiet beyond. I turned to go down another level, and that's when the bullet hit me.

The shot hit me in the upper shoulder, spraying the wall behind me with blood. Fisk was on the broad stairway landing below, both hands on his gun. He altered his aim, but I was already moving.

He fired again as I half-ran, half-leapt down the flight of stairs and I felt the stinging burn of the bullet as it grazed a bloody streak across my thigh. I landed heavily, careening hard into Fisk and slamming him against the wall. I heard the sharp crack of his head hitting the brickwork and his grunt of pain as the gun dropped from his grip. I tried to kick it away but only succeeded in sliding it towards the top of the next flight of stairs. Fisk elbowed me out of the way and staggered towards the gun.

I realized I was on my knees. All my wounds were screaming at me to lie down and stop and die. But I almost had him. I got to my feet.

Fisk was almost at the gun but I reached him first, grabbing his hair and yanking him back. His yelp was cut off as I locked my forearm around his neck and squeezed. His hands grasped my arm, and right then I knew this wasn't a fight I could win. I was too weak and all my reserves were spent. I tried grasping for his face with my free hand, searching for his eyes, as we lurched over the top step locked in our deadly embrace and tumbled down the stairs to the landing below.

As we fell I twisted, feeling the tearing of cartilage and hearing the unmistakable crunch of bone that goes with a broken neck.

I released my grip on Fisk's head and rolled off his dying body. I reckoned I'd picked up a couple of broken ribs to add to the collection, but Fisk had cushioned the worst of the fall for me. I saw his eyes blink once then go wide. A moment later he was gone.

Finally it was over.

My own pain decided to take center stage and I closed my eyes unable to stop a groan from escaping. I heard urgent voices and the sound of people rushing as I drifted off into the mercy of unconsciousness.

Finally it was over.

I drifted off into the mercy of unconsciousness.

FIFTY

Seven days later I was discharged from hospital. Patched up and on pain killers but able to walk and clothe and feed myself. Just about.

Whilst I'd been in there, Maria Perez had died. I thought of Dan and the kids and made a deal with myself to do something nice for them when I got out. It wouldn't bring her back, but it would be something. Besides: I owed Dan, in a good way.

Agent Hudson had dropped in to see me, this time without his Matrix wannabe buddy. Apparently there was a lot of fallout from the investigation into Fisk, and Central Precinct was in a mess. Some cops had left the force, a couple had taken early retirement and one had eaten a bullet. Morale was in the gutter.

He mentioned what they needed was an experienced sergeant there, if only for a while. I knew what he was saying but it wasn't anything I wanted to go back to.

I asked how the case was going with the Armenians and the money trail, but he couldn't tell me much as it was still ongoing. I got the impression it wasn't going as well as they liked. There was still no sign of Richard Cresswell.

We talked fishing and families for a bit and then he left. I found a bottle of Jim Beam Devil's Cut bourbon in a gift bag beside the bed and Special Agent John Hudson went up in my estimation.

I don't remember what day it was when Claire collected me in the Chrysler minivan, driving me home through the late September rain. Sean had wanted to come along but had to attend a trauma counseling session that day. I knew Claire had planned it that way when she started talking.

"Richard's still missing," she mentioned it casually, like commenting on the weather. It was something I already knew. I simply nodded as the wipers thudded rhythmically across the windshield and let her continue. "No messages, nothing. The FBI still want to speak with him, but they don't know where he is, or don't want to tell me." Her voice was still steady, but her hands gripped the wheel a little tighter. She was doing a good job keeping a lid on her emotions. "What do you think has happened to him?"

That was the sixty-four thousand dollar question. Or rather the multi-million dollar question.

What could I say? I'd been in a hospital bed for the last week, and at least half that time asleep. With Marshall arrested and Fisk dead that only left the Armenians, and although I reckoned I'd put a dent in their business, organized crime gangs are like cockroaches – there's always more of them than you first thought. I reckoned they had got to Richard, extracted the information they needed, and he was now a body in the river waiting to be discovered. I decided to keep those thoughts to myself and sugarcoat the lies.

"I don't know. He's a clever guy," that was something I'd never doubted. "He'll work out his best option is to speak to the FBI. Anyway, how are you doing?" I asked, changing the subject.

She shrugged. "Better than I thought I'd be. Sean's taking it well, but then he and Richard have never been close."

That was also something I knew. I guess it takes a while to bond with a stepfather, but over the previous ten years Richard had always preferred parenting the easy way, just buying stuff for Sean rather than spending time with him. It was one of the things we had discussions about. Sometimes heated ones. I also had my doubts about how much he really loved Claire.

Claire eased the car forward through the city traffic and took the turn towards my neighborhood, driving in silence for a few minutes.

"We're going to lose the house," she said. This time there was more tension in her voice. "I'd no idea how much he'd borrowed against it."

It took a moment for that to sink in. It was a big place, not a Malibu mansion, but still an impressive chunk of real estate in a good area. I wondered how much Richard had leveraged against it – and why – and thought that maybe he wasn't so clever after all.

"You know you can stay with me," I said without thinking.

Claire shook her head. "It's not that bad. There'll be enough left, you know – after it's sorted out – for a small place. Especially with me working."

"Okay, but the offer's there if you need it."

She pulled onto the driveway behind my Dodge pick-up. It was still tilted to one side on its slashed tires. I couldn't help letting out an annoyed huff of breath.

Claire looked over at me.

"Come on big brother, let's get you inside."

The rain wasn't that bad; we got inside without getting too wet and immediately my mood improved.

Claire had stocked up my refrigerator, freezer and pantry with plenty of food so I wouldn't need to go to the store for a while. The kitchen had been deep cleaned and the whole place had been tidied and smelled fresh. I really appreciated it and let her know, even giving her a gentle hug.

"Let me know what I owe you," I told her. After hearing she was losing the house, I couldn't have her subsidizing my food bill.

"Nothing." She rummaged in her bag and brought out an envelope, holding it out and smiling at me. "I used the money you gave me to get the laptop. There might be enough left to fix your tires."

I couldn't help laughing, even though it hurt.

*

"Wake up shithead!"

Someone slapped me around the face and I struggled towards consciousness, the effects of the painkillers making it a slow process. Too slow. I was slapped again and managed to open my eyes to see a bullet-headed ogre glaring down at me.

"Hello sleeping beauty," his guttural voice had a heavy accent and I could smell stale cigarettes on his foul breath. He yanked the covers off and I shivered as the cold air hit my skin. "Get out," he ordered, stepping back to give me room.

As I blinked in the glare from the overhead light, I saw another figure over on the other side of the bedroom. Not as big as the Ogre nor as ugly, nor as bald. He had hair to style and he'd done so, finishing off with a beard that told me he was a fan of Tony Stark and Iron Man. But what got my attention was the gun he held.

I'd used the Heckler and Koch Mk23 before, back when it was new. It was an impressive piece of kit and, with the silencer and a laser sight fixed underneath the barrel, a mean-looking weapon. Assuming Tony Stark had loaded it with the correct subsonic .45 ammunition he could shoot me a couple of times and anyone passing would just think I'd sneezed.

It took me more time than the Ogre liked to swing my legs out of the bed and sit on the edge, but he just huffed in annoyance rather than slap me again. I was just as slow standing up. Everything stiffens up overnight and my muscles still wanted to be asleep. The Ogre led and I followed, collecting my bath robe on the way, Stark and his assassination pistol bringing up the rear.

My mind was as reluctant to work as my muscles as I tried to figure out what was going on and what the hell I could do about it. I had already guessed these guys were Armenians or working for them in some way. I'd also worked out that if they wanted me dead then a shot from that Mk23 pistol would have seen to that whilst I slept. No need to even wake me up. And if they wanted me to know I was going to die then why make me get out of bed? That could also be done as I lay there staring down the barrel of the silencer waiting for the squeeze of the trigger to end it all.

Did they think I knew something about where Richard was, or even the account numbers and access codes themselves and were going to try and torture it out of me?

Shit.

When we reached the kitchen and I saw the open laptop on the table I knew I was in a bad no-win situation. I couldn't tell them anything because I didn't know anything, not about what they wanted to know. Nor was there any way I could fight my way out of it. I still had to take my time putting my pants on, so getting into hand-to-hand combat with the Ogre, a guy six inches taller and fifty pounds heavier than me, wasn't going to work. That was assuming Tony Stark didn't shoot me first.

"This is a waste of time," I said. "I don't know anything."

"Sit down," said the Ogre, ignoring me and pointing to the chair in front of the laptop.

I glanced at the clock on the wall. It was 3:30am. I wondered how long I'd last and if I'd see the dawn.

"Sit!" repeated the Ogre, his deep-set eyes glinting menacingly.

I sat, expecting the questions to start and be followed by a lot of pain when I couldn't answer them.

But I did not expect to see a face appear on the laptop screen.

"Hello Dean," said Richard Cresswell.

Cresswell talked. I listened. I had no choice.

FIFTY-ONE

Dawn didn't exactly break; it wasn't going to be that sort of day. The dark of night faded, replaced by skies the color of dull steel and I realized I didn't need the lights on in the kitchen anymore.

Sven the Ogre and Tony Stark had left, taking the laptop with them.

However, they had left large glossy photos of Claire and Sean. All taken without them knowing and while they were at work, out and about and at home. The message was clear. We can get to them anytime – remember that. I wasn't likely to forget anytime soon.

I sipped my third coffee, hoping the taste would take away some of the bitterness I felt, but knew even a stack of pancakes swimming in maple syrup wouldn't be able to do that let alone my preferred coffee grind. I drained the mug and threw it into the sink, shattering it, and stomped back upstairs to take a shower.

*

A week later I was feeling better. At least physically.

The staples in the various wounds had been removed and I was able to drive. I'd stopped the painkillers and had even felt up to enjoying a drop of the bourbon Agent John Hudson had got me, while watching old action movies. I still had to take it easy though, as Claire and Sean and anyone I spoke to kept reminding me.

It was early afternoon, and my cell phone rang. I didn't recognize the number and let it ring, leaving the call to go to the answering service. When it finished, I played the message back, feeling the muscles in my jaw harden as I listened to Richard Cresswell's panicked voice.

I knew what I had to do. I grabbed my keys to the Dodge and twenty minutes later I was close to the Columbia River, driving fast towards the old warehouse from where I'd rescued Sean.

I took the turn off the main road too hard and had to catch the slide as the rear tires lost grip on the damp dirt of the service road, the old pick-up fishtailing as I kept the power on. My truck may have had a V8 instead of the old Ford van's six cylinder, but I wasn't nearly as skilled with car control as my nephew, so progress was quick but messy.

The tires screeched as I braked hard on the concrete by the side of the old warehouse, right next to the two roller shutter doors. One of them was open allowing a faint smoky haze to escape from inside. I hurled the pick-up's door open, then remembered I needed to be careful and took my time getting out and making my way to the open door.

My .357 revolver hadn't found its way back to me, and of course all the other guns had been taken as evidence too, so I'd been forced to buy a replacement piece.

Bill Rose, an old Ranger friend had come up with a nice Colt 1911 at a price I couldn't resist, so that was in my hand now. It felt good and I wondered why I'd never had one before. Most folks never argue with a loaded .45.

The inside of the warehouse was too dark for me to see anything, then as my eyes adjusted I could make out the car parked in the center of the floor space. The skylights above let in just enough dim light to see it was a large German sedan, an AMG Mercedes.

Specifically, Richard Cresswell's AMG Mercedes.

I could see the shimmer of heat above the car, the silver of the paintwork on the roof blistered and blackened, and the remaining windows dark with greasy soot.

The driver's window had shattered, and as I got closer I could see the charred figure in the seat. I was too late to be any use saving him. He had been tied there, copper wire around his wrists binding him to the wheel with more wire wrapped around his throat, securing him to the seat as he burned. His head was thrown back, mouth open in a permanent scream of agony, but any pain was beyond him now. All that remained was the stink of incinerated plastic overlaid with the scent of a pork roast.

I took out my cell and dialed as I walked back to the old Dodge.

It only took ten minutes for the first cops to be on the scene. FBI agents Hudson and Smith got there within thirty. I thought that was impressive but maybe they had been staying somewhere local.

"Are you sure it's him?" asked Smith.

I nodded. "His car, correct height, right watch. Literally."

"How do you mean?" It was John Hudson asking the question this time.

"Richard always wore his watch on the right wrist," I explained. "He was left handed." Hudson nodded as Smith looked back at the remains of the car. "Plus there's the message."

I played the message from Richard that I'd let go onto the answering service. He sounded frightened, plainly scared for his life. He must have been borderline desperate to have been calling me for help and to meet up at such a place. I'd got there pretty quick but someone else had found him first.

"Why do you think his teeth were removed?" Smith again, always suspicious.

I shrugged. "Torture?"

John Hudson looked at me. He wasn't buying it, but it was all I could offer. He sighed.

"And they left his watch," Smith still had his eyes on the car and the CSI technicians surrounding it.

I nodded. "A Rolex Submariner."

The two agents were quiet. It was another avenue of their investigation that had been closed to them. Richard Cresswell could have provided a lot of information, but now he was dead.

"There's no need to bring my sister in for this is there?" I didn't want Claire seeing the blackened corpse. There was no need.

Hudson shook his head. "Not if you can formally identify the body."

I nodded. That was a weight off my mind.

"Okay Dean, you may as well go," said John Hudson. I shook both agents' hands, got in my pick-up and left.

I felt like shit.

The last time I'd seen Richard Cresswell over the video feed he'd been wearing his preferred Breitling Navitimer. I'd seen his watch collection and there wasn't a Rolex amongst them. I'd had to lie to Agent Hudson, a guy I'd come to respect, and I was being used with little choice in the matter.

I was getting pushed around again and there wasn't much I could do about it.

At least not yet.

As far as I was concerned, this was far from over.

THE END

Did You Enjoy This Book?

If so, you can make a HUGE difference.

For any author, the single most important way we have of getting our books noticed is a really simple one—and one which you can help with.

Yes, you.

Us indie authors and publishers don't have the financial muscle of the big guys to take out full-page ads in the newspaper or put posters on the subway.

But we do have something much more powerful and effective than that, and it's something that those big publishers would kill to get their hands on.

A committed and loyal bunch of readers.

Honest reviews of our books help bring them to the attention of other readers.

If you've enjoyed this book I would be really grateful if you could spend just a couple of minutes leaving a review (it can be as short as you like) on this book's page on your favorite store and website.

A Note From The Author.

Thank you for taking the time to read this book and I hope you enjoyed it.

It was fun to write, at times challenging, but it was time well spent and I've grown to like Dean Riley more and more as the story unfolded, though I doubt he'd like me much for all the hell I've put him through. Tough luck really as I have more adventures planned for the guy. So much for his early retirement and spending more time in the workshop.

But a book is nothing without its readers, so I thank you again and trust I have provided you some entertainment.

And provided you have liked it I would greatly appreciate any reviews and letting others know you enjoyed it.

Many thanks,
James Marx

About the Author

James Marx is a boring, middle-class, middle-aged writer with very few redeeming features.

Okay he loves animals; folks tell him he is kind and he has some practical skills that mean his wife finds him useful to have around. At least for now.

But he's really quite boring and forgetful. For instance, he regularly forgets that he's held crocodiles in Egypt, sailed a tall ship across the Bay of Islands, walked with wolves, danced on a volcano and almost drove a 4x4 off a Greek mountainside.

James Marx is unlikely to be appearing in the Booker Prize list any time soon - nor in the New York Times best-seller lists.

But if you enjoy his stories then that will do nicely and is worth knowing.

Connect with James Marx:

Facebook: www.facebook.com/jamesmarxwriter
Instagram: www.instagram.com/jamesmarxwriter/
Subscribe to my blog: jamesmarxwriter.wordpress.com/

About Burning Chair

Burning Chair is an independent publishing company based in the UK, but covering readers and authors around the globe. We are passionate about both writing and reading books and, at our core, we just want to get great books out to the world.

Our aim is to offer something exciting; something innovative; something that puts the author and their book first. From first class editing to cutting edge marketing and promotion, we provide the care and attention that makes sure every book fulfils its potential.

We are:
- Different
- Passionate
- Nimble and cutting edge
- Invested in our authors' success

If you're an author and would like to know more about our submissions requirements and receive our free guide to book publishing, visit:

www.burningchairpublishing.com

If you're a reader and are interested in hearing more about our books, being the first to hear about our new releases or great offers, or becoming a beta reader for us, again please visit:

www.burningchairpublishing.com

Other Books by Burning Chair Publishing

The Fall of the House of Thomas Weir, by Andrew Neil Macleod

Point of Contact, by Richard Ayre

The Brodick Cold War Series, by John Fullerton
Spy Game
Spy Dragon

The Curse of Becton Manor, by Patricia Ayling

Near Death, by Richard Wall

Blue Bird, by Trish Finnegan

The Tom Novak series, by Neil Lancaster
Going Dark
Going Rogue
Going Back

10:59, by N R Baker

Love Is Dead(ly), by Gene Kendall

A Life Eternal, by Richard Ayre

Haven Wakes, by Fi Phillips

Beyond, by Georgia Springate

Burning, An Anthology of Short Thrillers, edited by Simon Finnie and Peter Oxley

The Infernal Aether series, by Peter Oxley
The Infernal Aether
A Christmas Aether
The Demon Inside
Beyond the Aether
The Old Lady of the Skies: 1: Plague

The Wedding Speech Manual: The Complete Guide to Preparing, Writing and Performing Your Wedding Speech, by Peter Oxley

www.burningchairpublishing.com

PUSH BACK

Printed in Great Britain
by Amazon